HARVEST OF CAIN

By Jack Nelson-Pallmeyer

EPICA

Harvest of Cain
© 2001 by EPICA
The Ecumenical Program
on Central America and the Caribbean (EPICA)
1470 Irving St. NW, Washington, DC 20010
(202) 332-0292; fax (202) 332-1184
E-mail: epica@igc.org
Web page: www.epica.org

Cover art: Heriberto Valdez
Book and cover design: Carlos Armando García
& Ann Butwell

Library of Congress Cataloging-in-Publication Data

Nelson-Pallmeyer, Jack.
   Harvest of Cain/ by Jack Nelson-Pallmeyer.
      p. cm.
   ISBN 0-918346-27-4
      1. Americans—El Salvador—Fiction. 2. Intelligence
officers—Fiction. 3. Liberation theology—Fiction. 4.
Peasantry—Fiction. 5. Clergy—Fiction. I. Title.

PS3614.E45 H37 2001
813'.54—dc21

                                                    2001023277

To Sara, Hannah, Audrey and Naomi.

ACKNOWLEDGEMENTS

Thanks to Sara Nelson-Pallmeyer, Dave Gagne, Bob Hulteen, Mardi Pearson, Allison Carlson and my students at the University of St. Thomas for their encouragement as I set out on this project, and to my friends at EPICA who made the book possible. Thanks also to Mauricio Alarcón, Siobhán Dugan and Erin Yost for their comments.

Saigon 1972

Peter Jones left the embassy through a side door that allowed him to avoid tear gas and protesters. He walked past bicycles and cyclos, motorcycles and madness on his way to the park where Bui Thi sat on a bench in prayerful silence.

Seeing her calmed him, and the chaos that would soon befall the city receded into the background. He watched her for several minutes. When he finally approached, his heart was beating against his chest so wildly that it defied the gentleness of their embrace.

Walking silently on a pathway leading away from the busy street, they stepped aside to let a motor bike pass. As the bike got closer, a young man looked up at Bui Thi, smiled, took a gun from beneath his shirt, shot her point-blank in the heart and sped away.

HARVEST OF CAIN

One

❧

Father's Helper

Octavio rubbed sleep from his eyes as his father stood over him like a friendly giant hiding in the darkness. He slipped on his pants and stepped carefully over his brothers as his father handed him a cup filled with coffee and sugar. He drank it, took a tortilla and quietly walked out the door.

Every day for the past month Octavio and his father walked a narrow path leading to a small plot at the edge of forbidden trees. His father's greeting was always the same and always pleased him: *"¿Cómo está mi ayudante?"* These words came with a gentle slap on the back that made Octavio feel safe. He liked being called his father's helper.

Octavio and his father rose early to tend seeds they had planted like artists in a field his father called *la isla de esperanza*—the island of hope. Octavio's father seemed especially happy today. "This is the day," he said confidently. He had said the same thing yesterday and the day before and the day before that, but Octavio knew today would be different.

His premonition was right but not in the way that Octavio hoped.

Father and son wound their way expectantly down the narrow path. As they approached the little island of hope that nestled up to El Patrón's sea of coffee trees, Octavio ran ahead. *"Cuidado,"* his father yelled. "We must not trample a single plant."

HARVEST OF CAIN

One look at Octavio's face and his father knew the long-expected day had come. They gazed triumphantly at the field. Their smile-cracked faces were silent shouts of joy. There were twenty rows of corn with forty seeds in each row. Most had sprouted. Even a small field could help ease the hunger of the family.

"The earth has given birth to new life," his father said. He reached down and touched a plant that stood no more than two inches tall. "The earth gives us life," he said. "Corn is a gift from the gods. We must always be grateful."

Octavio and his father carefully removed weeds that encroached on the new plants. Octavio worked close to the plants with tiny fingers while his father skillfully maneuvered the machete around the edges. Looking at the sun rising, Octavio's father turned to face his son. "Well, *mi ayudante*, I must go. We'll return tomorrow," he said.

Octavio started home on the path on which they had come. His father took another leading to the entrance of the estate of El Patrón. Octavio was excited to tell Mamá about the corn. He started to run and then stopped abruptly. On the path before him stood a dog.

Dogs in Pueblo Duro were unnoticed and unnamed. But even from a distance and with the sun only now burning away the darkness, Octavio could see that something was terribly wrong.

The dog moved its head from side to side as if trying to shake free from an invisible attacker. It showed its teeth and growled menacingly.

Octavio screamed, "*¡Papá, ayúdeme! ¡Socorro! ¡Socorro!*" He reached down, picked up several stones and retreated slowly in the direction of the field. Fear gripped his body, but he didn't run. He knew that would only embolden the dog.

The dog moved slowly in his direction, panting furiously. Octavio could hear its uneven breathing above the noise of his own pounding heart. He moved steadily backward, screaming for

Papá and at the dog, hurling rocks, wiping away tears and fighting fear. He found a sturdy stick a little longer than he was tall, picked it up and continued his slow retreat.

The sound of his father's voice and footsteps on the path filled him with hope. "Move slowly," his father cautioned but the dog lurched toward Octavio before his father reached him. Octavio swung the stick. The dog pulled back.

"Move away," Octavio's father shouted to both boy and dog as he thrust himself between them. The dog retreated, circling as if uncertain how to attack.

Octavio stood safely behind as his father danced with the dog and kept his eyes glued to its menacing head. His father took a step forward and thrust the machete hard. The blade ripped into the ground as the dog jumped back. He shouted again, "*¡Váyase! ¡Váyase!*" and then retreated as the dog darted forward.

The dance continued. Octavio pelted the dog with stones, but its eyes were fixed on Octavio's father. Suddenly, the dog sprang forward with irrational fury. Its jaw caught Octavio's father's leg as the machete found its mark and left the dog writhing and then silent in the blood-soaked earth.

That night his father returned home after many hours of clearing weeds from the base of El Patrón's coffee trees. He ate a tortilla with salt and a little rice and went to bed. The next morning Octavio awakened to a room bathed in sunlight. "*¿Dónde está Papá?*" he asked. "At the plantation," his mother said. "I am to give you a message. The corn seedlings must wait 'til tomorrow."

Several weeks passed. On this particular morning, like so many others, Octavio's father stood over him in the darkness. They took their coffee and tortilla with them as they walked. His father moved slowly and limped slightly. Octavio kept a question in his mind because he knew his father preferred silence when it came to his own pain.

When they arrived at the field, Octavio's concern shifted from father to corn plants. They were several inches taller but the weeds had grown faster still. His father worked slowly, but together they weeded around most of the plants.

That evening Octavio's father stumbled home from El Patrón's. Lucía tried to give him supper. "*No...teng...o hambbree...*" His voice was slurred and his forehead burned like the ashes in the cook fire.

Lucía helped him into the hammock and saw puss oozing from his leg. Octavio fetched their neighbor, Rosa, who examined the wound. She placed an old cattle iron in the cook fire and waited. A few minutes later she pressed the red-hot iron on the open sore as Octavio's father screamed. She then wrapped the wound in herbs and announced that she had done all she could.

Octavio's father lay disoriented and delirious for three days. He ate and drank nothing and recognized no one. Rumors spread throughout Pueblo Duro that he was possessed by a demon. Some said God sent the demon to punish him because he had planted corn too close to El Patrón's coffee trees.

Neighbors came to the house to pray and sing, but the demon remained. Rafael, a family friend, spent days and nights outside. When Lucía invited him in, he would stay only a few minutes and then return to his self-appointed post outside the house.

Octavio placed his mat next to his father's hammock. He was brave to sleep so close to a demon.

He awoke to groans and shouts as his father bumped into the chair by the door and then smashed it to pieces. His father grabbed the machete and stumbled out the door, his eyes crazed, foam and spittle covering his mouth and chest. Octavio knew that the demon possessing the dog had invaded his father. He tried to run to him but his mother restrained him.

A group of women were huddled in a circle in front of the house saying prayers. Octavio's father lurched towards them with his machete, a demented look of death on his face. As the women screamed and fled, Rafael raised his rifle and fired. His aim was true.

The bullet of mercy saved the women and ended his friend's torment, but it compounded the family's grief. Rafael didn't know about demons but he did know that rabies was always fatal in isolated communities without public health facilities. Lucía, her husband, friends and family had spent the last days playing out a perverse version of Russian roulette. They lost. What's more, they knew the bullet had not killed the demon. There was an abundance of demons in Pueblo Duro.

Two

✦

Black Robe

"Black Robe is coming." Octavio spoke with a mixture of fear and excitement. As he ran out the door, his grandmother moved quickly to the stove and added several sticks to the fire above which sat a small pot of beans.

Carmen went to the doorway and looked out. She couldn't see Padre Eduardo, but the steady stream of people scurrying about like red ants converging on a fallen mango convinced her it was true. People were moving in the direction of the field that was used for football and the priest's yearly visit.

As she walked down the path that converged with another shared by near-invisible neighbors, Carmen cast a concerned glance at Octavio's mother. Lucía's tear-soaked face resembled an eroded field after a torrential rain.

"Where were you?" Carmen asked reproachfully. "People talk. You shouldn't be away. Not ever. Especially now." Lucía was still wearing the previous evening's dress and her lips were crimson red. "You're supposed to dress like a widow…" Carmen's voice trailed off as she noticed the bruise on Lucía's face.

Lucía said nothing and looked away. After a moment, she turned and managed a slight smile. "Thank God the padre is here," she said.

"You have the money?" Carmen asked, shuddering to think what her friend must have done to get it.

"Thank God it's almost over," Lucía said more to herself than to Carmen. "It's a miracle. He came today of all days," she said crossing herself.

Her husband's body lay outside the family shack on a piece of wood, washed, covered and surrounded by flowers. Padre Eduardo's arrival meant her husband could be buried after a proper blessing from a priest if, that is, Lucía had the necessary coins. With a proper blessing, her husband's soul could be kept out of hell and perhaps rest in peace.

Lucía looked as if she had kept her husband's soul out of hell by sacrificing her own. Although her husband had just died the most horrible of deaths, Lucía considered herself lucky because his death corresponded to the priest's yearly visit. Death wasn't always so timely. This made receiving the all-important blessing difficult for some and impossible for many.

Some families were tormented by the thought of a loved-one burning in hell while they waited for Padre Eduardo to come. To avoid this anguish, one family carried their daughter's decomposing body in a casket to the regional center at Somotillo. They arrived on Monday, after a two-day journey, and found the church empty. And so they waited. Patiently. Padre Eduardo returned on Saturday. The stench forced him to move the mass and close the church because it was considered a health hazard.

Some said this proved that God works in mysterious ways.

Carmen left Lucía and walked down the path. She noticed Octavio perched high in a tree. Octavio had claimed a limb offering a perfect view of the field and all that would follow. He was sitting with his friend Eusebio.

Octavio didn't know whether Black Robe was God or a devil but he knew he was a magician. Once a year, always the last Sunday in January when the coffee harvest was in and Carmen and the others had a few *colones* in their pockets, Padre Eduardo came to Pueblo Duro and did magic.

Octavio and Eusebio knew Black Robe was a magician because the people paid him to shout at them and burn magic sticks that made their noses hurt if they got too close.

Black Robe carried a book that no one else could touch, and he spoke words that sounded familiar but which no one but Black Robe understood. He knew if Black Robe had arrived sooner and if the family had had the necessary coins, then the demon would have left and his father would still be alive.

The book was magic. What Octavio didn't know was how the magic worked. Maybe if you held the book then you had power to ward off evil spirits or send people to hell. Perhaps the book contained magic words. Or maybe the words became magic when spoken by a magician.

Eusebio, seven and a full year older than Octavio, had his own ideas about the book. "Last year my family went to Somotillo," he said, "we saw Black Robe. His church is bigger than El Patrón's mansion. Do you know where they kept the book?"

Octavio tried to imagine anything bigger than El Patrón's mansion and looked at his friend expectantly.

"In a big glass case near the front of the church. A big LOCKED case. Only Black Robe touched the book. If anyone but Black Robe touches the book they die," he said with authority.

Octavio's eyes widened as he listened to his friend's words. "You sure?"

"*Seguro*," Eusebio responded. "Black Robe took the book from the case and when he was done, he put it back, locked it and took the key. No one but Black Robe touched it. I tell you, touch the book and you die!"

Octavio wondered why his grandmother warned him about snakes and about swimming in El Patrón's pond but never said anything about the book. He wasn't sure about his friend's knowledge of magicians or the book, but since Eusebio was older Octavio wasn't taking any chances.

The book was scary even if you didn't touch it because of hell. Black Robe spoke so much about hell that Octavio and Eusebio thought that the magic book must be all about hell. The magic in the book could land you in or keep you out of hell, depending of course on the magician.

The boys didn't understand much of what Black Robe said when he yelled at the people. God loved them but hated most of what they did, Octavio thought.

Black Robe yelled about communists agitating, stealing babies or killing them or something. God didn't like many things, Octavio concluded, like *guaro* or getting drunk or workers causing trouble, but most of all Octavio knew God hated communists. Octavio didn't know about communists but he knew there were a lot of them burning in hell.

And sitting right next to them all covered in flames were those who hadn't received the proper blessing. There was a blessing when you were born, a blessing when you died, a blessing when you had water thrown on you and another if you got married or even if you didn't. There was a blessing for when you did something really bad like steal oranges from El Patrón's orchards, swim in his pond or kill someone. That was called sinning.

People needed blessings for almost everything and they had so many unmet blessings over the course of a year that Octavio thought Black Robe would have to stay in Pueblo Duro forever if he hadn't worked so fast. Either way he'd be rich because it cost money to stay out of hell.

Octavio didn't know much about hell either. He knew it was a place where God sent bad people after they died and that it was hot. So hot as to burn you up only you never really burned up and so there was no end to the pain. The thought of sitting in the fires of hell and never getting out sent a shiver down Octavio's spine.

No, best not touch the book, best watch out for communists, best listen to Black Robe, best be blessed and pay for it somehow and best do what you had to do to stay out of hell, Octavio thought to himself.

Octavio looked at the people blanketing the field where a rickety wooden platform sat pathetically, like a broken vase on a table. Black Robe had finished yelling about communists and *guaro*, avoiding trouble, the need for blessings and the threat of hell.

Following the sermon, he gave the people a tiny wafer and said magic words. The people dipped the wafer in a cup of blood that because of the magic tasted like wine. Then Black Robe drank the rest of the blood and said more magic words.

When he finished yelling at the people to keep them out of hell, he put the book away. This made Octavio feel a little safer.

Then the people lined up to receive blessings. The people with money came first. They told Black Robe what they'd done, and he decided which magic they needed. After they dropped the right number of coins into the black box sitting next to him, Black Robe bowed his head, closed his eyes, held his hand over their heads and uttered the magic words that could keep them or a loved one out of hell, at least until next year.

Octavio looked at Eusebio and spoke about the other thing that was bothering him: "Why does Black Robe make them eat bodies and drink blood?" he asked.

Eusebio shrugged. "Same reason we got water poured all over us. Keep us out of hell," he said.

"I don't mind the water," Octavio said, "but there's no way I'm going to drink blood," he said defiantly.

"Even if it keeps you out of hell?" Eusebio responded thinking of the flames.

Just as Octavio's chin was sinking further into his chest he noticed his mother approaching Black Robe. She was moving forward in the line with those who had money. This made Octavio proud. He was glad his father would stay out of hell. His father liked *guaro* some and even got drunk sometimes, but Black Robe's magic would keep him safe. Black Robe would tell God that his father didn't have to burn with communists. His father was safe.

Octavio didn't know that the cost of keeping his father out of hell was three *colones* and his mother's soul. And he couldn't imagine what would happen when the demons turned against the magician.

Three

Red Pajamas: Chile 1973

Peter Jones looked as undignified as the mission he was about to accomplish. He ran up two flights of stairs with a box under one arm and perspiration dripping from his forehead like a leaky faucet. His life seemed destined for a train wreck with the question of survivors hanging precariously in the balance.

Peter's inner life was dry and turbulent like a desert storm, another casualty of distorted truth where deceptive memories serve as blind guides. It was an occupational hazard in the Agency that lies became truths, and opposites were true or false depending on the circumstances. For Peter, deception was something more. He unconsciously feared and avoided a pristine view of his life that might feed an impulse of self-discovery.

Preoccupied with angry reporters waiting downstairs, Peter carelessly pushed open the door at the top of the stairwell. Startled soldiers turned frightened eyes and automatic weapons on him with a determination that offered a preview of what he would find within. Fear rekindled a hopeless memory of death's sudden sting and then dissipated like a morning fog.

The soldiers stepped aside with the uncomfortable deference of junior partners as Peter entered the bloodstained office and surveyed the untidy scene.

Large windows overlooking the plaza were shattered. A gaping hole, where wall and roof intersected, let in sunshine that spotlighted bomb-twisted concrete and steel formations resembling the sculptures of eccentric, modern artists. Sporadic gunfire filled the streets, helicopters hovered and tanks pointed ominously in his direction.

Peter cast a quick glance at the body and took a deep breath. He closed his eyes, searched and found his refuge of severed emotions. It was a place Peter first discovered in a bottle, in Vietnam, after another political murder. He eventually buried bottle and feelings together in a ritual of unenlightened despair.

The demons safely shelved, Peter picked up his walkie-talkie. "I need five minutes to arrange the room. Who's handling the press?" he asked.

"Vargas," the muffled voice responded.

"And another five with Vargas. Send him up."

Peter walked towards the dead man fearing the work of an overzealous killer. Allende's body slumped over the blood-soaked desk. What remained of his head rested in a pool of blood. Pinochet had ordered a murder with the appearance of suicide. With no danger of an independent autopsy, the head wound could pass as self-inflicted. Reporters could see the body in its original position.

Colonel Vargas entered the room.

"Photo. Nothing more," Peter said efficiently. He handed Vargas a piece of paper and motioned to the desk. "Read it there. A few pictures and clear the place out. No questions."

It was then that Peter noticed the dead man speaking. Allende had arranged his desk to make a final statement that neither the Chilean generals nor their U.S.-backers wanted to convey.

His head rested on a bloodied copy of the Chilean constitution. Next to him sat a copper pot and a phone directory for Santiago. The reference points were all transparent to Peter Jones. Chile had a longer history of democracy than the United States, and Allende's constitutional desk prop was meant as a reminder.

The desk also pointed to Anaconda and ITT which helped orchestrate the coup following nationalization of copper and telecommunications industries.

Peter put the directory into a drawer and closed it. He walked over and set the pot harmlessly on a nearby bookshelf. He returned to the desk, lifted Allende's head, removed the constitution, crumpled it and placed it in a plastic bag. He took a revolver with one spent cartridge and placed it in Allende's right hand. He littered the room with pornographic pictures, Cuban cigars, red pajamas, a copy of *Mein Kampf* and drug paraphernalia.

"Ready," Peter said through the walkie-talkie.

He took the plastic bag and proceeded to a side door. He opened it cautiously, acknowledged the soldiers, paused and glanced back at Vargas. "Good-luck." His voice trailed into the hallway.

Reporters flooded the room. "I have an announcement before reading a brief statement," Colonel Vargas said confidently. "Do not touch the body or anything else in the room. You are free to take pictures. The room will be sealed off in five minutes."

He then read the Agency's prepared text. "Our great country, brought to the brink of disaster by a communist government, has been rescued by the patriotic armed forces. Our intent was to try Salvador Allende as a traitor to Chilean democracy. Mr. Allende, however, took his own life by discharging a bullet to his head. Thank you."

On the way to the airport Peter heard a radio broadcast interrupted by a special bulletin: "This morning, Salvador Allende, president of the Chilean Republic, committed suicide." The following day, pictures of Allende's office, with all its scandalous images, graced the covers of newspapers worldwide. No one asked why Allende kept a pair of red pajamas in his office.

Four

❦

Indigestion

For the poor of El Salvador, religion was a wounding comforter. It gave birth to a simple faith that, like a deformed child, was a mixed blessing destined to surprise and disappoint.

On the one hand, everything could be attributed to God's will—death and disease, wealth and poverty, crop loss and landlessness. Misery's causes remained hidden beneath the divine mystery of unasked questions. On the other hand, life was so miserable that survival itself was a miracle attributed to God.

Religion had many advocates inside and outside of the church. Not least among them was Padre Eduardo, a priest who came to an unfortunate end.

The son of a powerful landowner, Eduardo was a rather typical priest. He served the area in and around Somotillo, a regional center marked by wealth, marred by poverty and swimming in coffee. Rural communities spread out from Somotillo like broken spokes on a wheel.

Typical among them was Pueblo Duro, a rural backwater of tiny huts and fields without a town or school and only a little hope. In Pueblo Duro, desperate lives and rocky plots intersected with a few rich and powerful men whose plantations produced coffee, the red gold that spawned ample quantities of money, prestige, arrogance and power.

Padre Eduardo visited rural communities like Pueblo Duro

once a year. He collected fees for baptisms, marriages, funerals and forgiveness. The Catholic Church in and around Somotillo blessed the landowners with good news. Eduardo in turn reveled in the many earthly rewards that came from ignoring the spiritual food of Jesus in favor of the actual banquets of the rich.

He feasted on their food, delighted in their company and grew intoxicated with their liquor and power. That his overburdened heart stopped pumping at his father's mansion during a feast celebrating the year's plentiful coffee harvest was more than a little ironic.

During his fourth visit to the buffet table, Eduardo's face grew flush and his body stiffened. Holding a shrimp to his lips with one hand and a platter in the other, he fell face-first onto the buffet table into a shrimp salad. He died with a mayonnaise-soaked smile on his face.

Eduardo's death left poor people in the area around Somotillo a little confused but with a few more coins in their pockets. His successor, on the other hand, caused more than a little indigestion for those in higher circles.

That things were likely to change with the coming of a new priest was apparent when Padre Ricardo arrived in Pueblo Duro carrying a soccer ball.

Ricardo was a thin, well-educated man with dark hair and eyes, short legs, long arms, small bones and tiny ears that seemed glued to the side of his head. Like Eduardo, he was born into a large landowning family. Similarities ended there.

Padre Ricardo walked the dirt roads and pathways that were the invisible arteries of the impoverished community of Pueblo Duro. Like an artist on foot he painted a mental portrait one family, one house, one field at a time.

Homes pieced together with scraps of wood, cardboard and tin dotted the landscape. Red beans and coffee simmered on wood fires as mothers and daughters shaped tortillas with skilled hands.

Outside, children, chickens and an occasional pig scurried about. There were scraps of wood awaiting the next fire, water barrels and surprisingly clean clothes, hanging on barbed-wire fences or scraggly bushes.

Each residence sat at the edge of a small, jutted field that was tended by men and boys and inhabited by an abundance of rocks and weeds. Bean and corn plants fought valiantly against the encroachment of the coffee bushes that established physical and mental boundaries.

Octavio and Eusebio were confused because Padre Ricardo didn't wear a black robe. They didn't know what to call the new magician, and they were still trying to figure out why the previous magician couldn't save himself. Octavio thought maybe the demons were too strong for any magician to control. Eusebio figured Black Robe had gotten careless and mixed up a word or a phrase in one of his magic spells which led to his end. Both boys wondered what had become of the magic book now that Black Robe was dead.

The two boys followed the new priest with eager concern. Eusebio sometimes walked with Ricardo as the new priest explored the arteries of Pueblo Duro, but Octavio was afraid and kept his distance.

Ricardo, priestly collar around his neck and soccer ball in hand, entered each home with quiet enthusiasm. His deeply intense face gave way easily and often to cavernous grins that showcased his white teeth and made his ears even harder to see.

"*Cómo está?*—How are you?" he asked, simply. Or "*¿Cómo amaneció?*—How did the sun rise for you?" After exchanging smiles, and a brief word, he moved on. The people, unaccustomed to seeing a priest in Pueblo Duro, didn't know how to behave in his presence, a problem compounded by Padre Ricardo's passion for soccer.

The soccer tournament was Pueblo Duro's equivalent to the

World Cup. Each Sunday afternoon for the past ten weeks *Equipo Jóvenes* and *Equipo Viejos* had battled for bragging rights in the community. The Youngsters had defeated The Old-timers in five of the previous games, and their victory today would put the issue to rest.

Sunday was a quiet day, so with nothing much to do, a large crowd—much larger than the one that had attended Mass at the same site—gathered for the game. Vendors hawked *tortillas*, beer, mangoes, soda and gum. Men wagered *colones* on their preferred team although in the beginning almost no one was willing to bet on The Old-timers because their best player was sick and his replacement was an awkward looking priest.

The game began but came to a near standstill as Ricardo gained control of the ball near the middle of the field. Members of The Youngsters froze and looked at each other apprehensively. Padre Ricardo, focused on the ball and, determined to make a good impression, moved down field and deftly kicked a goal.

Nobody attempted to stop his shot because they didn't want to mess with a magician who had the power to put them in hell. The crowd watched this spectacle and suddenly all bets were off. No one would put money on The Youngsters.

Padre Ricardo stopped the game and gathered the teams in the center of the field. "I am a priest," he said, "and a man. I love soccer but you must treat me like any other player. Let's enjoy the game. Besides," he said smiling, "I will score almost as easily even if you try to stop me." Ricardo's goal was not counted, and the game began anew.

Ricardo was a determined but undisciplined player. He ran willy-nilly across the field demonstrating great endurance. His long, gangly arms and short legs were less than ideal but his enthusiasm partially compensated for his physical deficiencies.

The first half ended with The Youngsters leading one to nothing. The score would have been worse had it not been for the fact that Ricardo, despite awkwardness, was a good player. Time after time a member of The Youngsters would ready himself for a clear shot only to have a sliding Ricardo get enough of his foot on the ball or get in the way sufficiently so as to thwart the effort.

Towards the middle of the first half, Ricardo's repeated dives and timely blocks led members of The Youngsters from fear to frustration. Ricardo often found himself in the middle of players competing for possession of the ball.

The players—at first those from The Youngsters and later his own teammates—flailed wildly in the midst of a crowd but hit Ricardo's shins with surprising regularity. Had The Youngsters concentrated more on the ball and less on Ricardo's shins they would undoubtedly have had more than one goal.

The crowd was unsure what to make of a soccer playing priest who chased a round ball on a makeshift field with his arms twisting in the wind one moment, only to hang low to the ground the next so as to nearly cause him to stumble. Like a broken windmill, Ricardo flailed about out of control and out of character. This delighted the children but confounded many adults.

People in Pueblo Duro had never seen a priest sweat so profusely or run so fast. Scandalized by such un-priestly conduct some people spread rumors. Padre Ricardo, they said, had missed an easy goal and uttered a profanity. Or at least one formed on his lips.

The second half went much like the first. Ricardo ran about like a crazed animal only this time he tried to avoid battling for possession of the ball in the midst of crowds.

With a few minutes remaining and The Youngsters clinging to a one goal lead, Ricardo got control of the ball near the center of the field. He raced down the left sideline, stopped abruptly, shifted towards the center and kicked a perfect pass to Marcos who kicked the ball twenty feet over the net. The crowd howled with laughter but the fiasco got the attention of The Youngsters.

Ricardo had nearly tied the score.

The subsequent throw-in pass went to Sancho. Sancho was a powerful player, a young man who had a slight limp courtesy of a National Guard bullet received at a student protest at the University in San Salvador. He kicked the ball about ten feet ahead, flattened Ricardo with a crushing body block, reclaimed the ball and proceeded down field with unerring determination.

His teammate Carlos then pretended to trip over Ricardo and sat on the poor priest who could do nothing but watch as Sancho kicked a goal making it two to nothing, which is how the game ended.

Ricardo limped off the field and sat down feeling the pain of his bloody shins. He looked up to see a beautiful young woman smiling. "Welcome to Pueblo Duro," she said. "You have absorbed the weight of many blows belonging to your predecessor." That said she turned and walked away. Ricardo grimaced as he stood and kicked the ball to Eusebio who seemed to have lost all fear of the new magician.

"Who is that?" Padre Ricardo asked.

"El Patrón's daughter," Eusebio replied.

The next Sunday, Eusebio carried the Bible to Padre Ricardo who read the Gospel at the community's Mass. Octavio watched skeptically from his prized spot in the tree.

Throughout the following months people who hadn't played soccer ever or in years joined the Sunday afternoon games. Padre Ricardo was always invited. Opportunity is a great tempter and many felt they had ample reason to kick a priest.

———

Ricardo's unorthodoxy wasn't limited to his passion for soccer. When visiting local households he ground corn and washed clothes. He attempted to shape tortillas, a natural art form among the local women. He finished one, put it down, and pretended not to notice when they gathered it up and reshaped it.

He also worked alongside workers in the fields. The conversations that accompanied such activities were brief, in part because Padre Ricardo was a quiet man, and in part because rumors abounded that a communist priest had come to disrupt the community.

Juan, a seasonal coffee picker battling weeds in the small corn patch he rented from Padre Eduardo's father, Julio Díaz, received daily visits. Words were as rare as a cool breeze but Padre Ricardo made the most of them by asking provocative questions.

As sweat poured down his face, Padre Ricardo wiped his arm across his eyes. "Juan?" he said.

"Yes, Padre."

"I would like to ask you something," he said.

"Yes, Padre."

"Why don't the children go to school?"

There was a long pause as Juan moved uncomfortably back and forth fidgeting with his machete. He looked at the ground as if the soil offered clues that might help solve a profound mystery. "There is no school," he responded.

"Ah, yes," Padre Ricardo said. "There is no school."

This conversation was followed by another hour of work and more silence.

"Juan?"

"Yes, Padre."

"The weeds are winning. I will stop by again tomorrow," Padre Ricardo said.

"Good-bye, Padre."

The next day was the same. More weeds and sweat. Another question. "Juan?"

"Yes, Padre."

"Your children do not go to school because there is no school?" he said.

"Yes, Padre." Juan wondered about a priest who had difficulty understanding something so obvious.

"Why is there no school?" Padre Ricardo asked.

This too seemed clear. "*Somos pobres,*" he said.

Padre Ricardo nodded. "Yes. We are poor."

The next day the work and conversation continued. "Good morning, Juan."

"Buenos días, Padre."

"If we could eat rocks and weeds," Padre Ricardo said as he reached down to rescue a corn plant, "there would be no hunger in Pueblo Duro."

"Padre?" For the first time Juan initiated the conversation.

"Yes, Juan."

"I have been thinking."

"Thinking is good," Padre Ricardo said.

"About the school," he said.

"Yes."

"We don't have a school because...well...because of the books. Schools have books...you know...and our children can't read," Juan said. "Giving us a school would be like giving a fish a bird's nest for a home."

"I see," Padre Ricardo said. After hoeing carefully around some emerging corn plants he responded further. "But children learn how to read and to use books in school."

"Yes, Padre."

These short interchanges interrupted long hours of work marked by silence as sweat from their common labor watered the weeds and corn. The following day Juan seemed eager to talk.

"Padre? Your question."

"About the school?"

"Yes, Padre. I think...it is God's will that we don't...don't have a school," Juan said.

Padre Ricardo carried an armful of weeds to the edge of the field. "God's will?" he asked.

"Padre Eduardo told us that," Juan said crossing himself.

"What else did Padre Eduardo say?"

"We are special," Juan said. "God blessed us. God...made us poor."

"And why did God bless you so?" Padre Ricardo said with a slight smile creasing his lips. His voice was sincere, like an unrehearsed confession.

"*Somos malcreados*," Juan responded. "We drink...we are...we are stupid. Like oxen. Our drunkenness shows we are unworthy to be rich," Juan said.

The next day almost before the weeding began Juan was ready for more conversation.

"Padre?"

"Yes, Juan."

"I have been thinking," Juan said.

"About the school?" Padre Ricardo asked.

Juan's weathered face softened into a toothless grin. "No, Padre. *Preguntas. Demasiadas*. You ask many questions. About poverty."

"What answer have you come to?" Padre Ricardo asked.

Juan paused and tried to dislodge one of a thousand rocks that inhabited his field like unwanted guests. "God made us poor for the same reason He made these rocks...so we will appreciate heaven. Heaven must be a beautiful place. We suffer here a little, but our joy with God is forever."

Padre Ricardo tracked these ideas, not to divine inspiration, but to the theology of Padre Eduardo. He looked at Juan who was about sixty years old with few teeth, a field full of rocks and almost nothing to show for a lifetime of hard work. He was thinking sixty years of poverty and misery must be an eternity but he remained silent.

"Padre Eduardo said nothing can separate us from God's love. Except communism."

"Padre Eduardo said this?"

"Many times," Juan said. "And General Calderón."

General Adolfo Calderón was the most ruthless military leader in the province. It was of more than a little interest to Padre Ricardo that the General said this. "When did Calderón speak to you?" Padre Ricardo asked.

"Yesterday. The *campesinos* who work for El Patrón were called to a meeting. El Patrón and the General are forming a new group. To fight the communists. We were more than a hundred. They gave us beer," he added. "General Calderón said God loves us and we will all be safe unless...unless communism comes. But if communism comes that is the death of God."

Padre Ricardo looked at the rocks and the corn and then glanced at the coffee trees surrounding Juan's field. "Do you know any communists?" he asked

"Sí, Padre." Juan dipped a cup into his bucket. *"Pero solamente uno.* Only you," he said as he poured the water over Ricardo's head offering temporary relief from the sun's oppressive heat. As the water mixed with sweat and trickled down his face Padre Ricardo looked up at Juan who spoke matter-of-factly. "He says you are a communist and you are very dangerous."

Padre Ricardo looked weary. His mind drifted to a dark space far away. He bent down and helped Juan push a boulder to the edge of the field.

Five

❧

The Tempter

Julio Díaz spoke of the untimely death of his son but spent little time grieving. Only those who knew him well understood his meaning. Eduardo's death was untimely, not only because he was a young man, but because it occurred at a critical juncture in El Salvador's history when the Church was changing. Eduardo was a son, a priest and an ally. Padre Ricardo was a Jesuit. This cast suspicion like an eerie shadow on a stormy night.

Julio's great-great grandparents had come from Spain and had prospered by growing indigo for export until synthetic dyes were invented in Europe.

A crisis gripped the family until rich Salvadorans discovered that coffee thrived in the hill country. The highlands, once abandoned to the poor who grew beans and corn for subsistence, were taken from the *campesinos* through a combination of debt and deceit, forced labor and taxes, and in some cases outright violence.

Julio knew three kinds of people. Allies shared his vision for El Salvador. Reluctant allies wanted changes that Julio considered unacceptable but they could be made to see things his way. Others with principled commitments understood only the language of violence.

A meeting between Julio and Padre Ricardo was inevitable. Neither would have chosen a relationship but their destinies were linked like thunder and lightening during a violent storm. As Padre Ricardo walked on a pathway headed towards Juan's cornfield he was intercepted by a gun-wielding man on horseback.

Padre Ricardo directed his vision towards the man's eyes and away from the gun. The man shrugged his shoulders and spoke with only a turn of his head, pointing with his lips in the direction of his saddle. Padre Ricardo mounted the horse and sat behind him.

If Julio wanted to know more about his son's replacement the opposite was also true. Padre Ricardo had heard much about Julio Díaz, whom the *campesinos* referred to as El Patrón. His name was ever present in the vocabulary of the people. Would El Patrón give them a loan? How were they to make their payment to El Patrón. El Patrón might offer work picking coffee. El Patrón had medicine. Padre Ricardo wondered whether the visit was a good will gesture, a sizing up or a warning.

Julio Díaz walked to the window in his study overlooking the entrance to his estate. He watched Padre Ricardo approach the house with short, deliberate steps, his eyes focused on the driveway and away from the alluring garden.

Ricardo walked directly to the front door, past a new Jeep parked conspicuously in his path. He entered Julio's office with the assurance of someone who was comfortable in different worlds.

"Padre Ricardo," Julio said, his hand extended. "My name is Julio Díaz. The *campesinos* call me El Patrón," he added.

Julio Díaz was a proud, bitter man, with soft skin and an uneasy smile. His hands were as smooth as his clean-shaven face on which his angled nose appeared slightly off-center, like a poorly placed picture. His handsome fingers were laden with gold. He wore a cotton leisure suit and a hand-woven tie on which red coffee beans cascaded gently into a half-filled canasta.

"So I have heard," Padre Ricardo said. "It is a pleasure to meet you, Señor Díaz. I am sorry about your son," he added.

"Only God knows the day of our coming," Julio said crossing himself. He was taking measure of the man who stood before him. "Would you like something?" he added pointing to the liquor cabinet.

"Coffee," Padre Ricardo said looking at a pot warming on a hot plate near the edge of Julio's desk. He reached out to retrieve a cup but was restrained by Julio's glance.

Julio reached down and pushed a button on his desk. A servant appeared instantly, approached the desk, poured the coffee and departed. Padre Ricardo took a sip from the cup. The richness of the blend surprised and pleased him.

"You like the coffee," Julio said with pride.

Padre Ricardo took another sip and smiled. "I haven't tasted coffee like this since my days as a student in Europe," he said. "It is ironic that a Salvadoran must travel to Europe or the United States to drink good Salvadoran coffee."

"Our best blends are for export, but we keep enough for our own use," Julio said. "I believe priests should drink only Salvador's finest. I will see to it before you leave," he added. "You know," Julio said, "I wanted to be a priest."

"What prevented you?" Padre Ricardo asked.

"My father. And the demands of business. I decided that one of my sons would be a priest," he said. "I consider myself a student of theology," he added. "Perhaps you don't approve."

"On the contrary," Padre Ricardo said. "Theology is simply a fancy word for people making sense out of their lives, God and the world. All of us are theologians," he added.

Julio looked skeptical. "Theology in the wrong hands can be dangerous."

"You are troubled by Vatican II?" Padre Ricardo asked.

Julio weighed his words carefully. "Yes, and by Medellín, by the so-called theology of liberation. I believe the Church must find its way in the world," he added, "but liberation theology is nothing but Marxist propaganda. It threatens both our country and the Church."

Padre Ricardo flashed back to when, as a young seminarian, he observed some of the deliberations of Vatican II. It was an exciting time. Pope John XXIII convened a meeting of bishops from around the world in Rome in 1962 to reassess the role of the Catholic Church. The meeting lasted three years. It ushered the Church belatedly into the twentieth century.

More important, for priests like Padre Ricardo, and more threatening to people like Julio Díaz, was the gathering of Latin American bishops several years later in Medellín, Colombia. Bishops there were influenced by priests and nuns who worked in poor communities. They declared Latin American societies sinful. Inequalities of wealth and land ownership were said to be examples of institutionalized violence resulting in hunger and misery. The bishops declared that the Church's task was to work with the poor and to call the rich to conversion in an effort to free their societies from the bondage of sinful social structures.

Standing in the estate of one of Salvador's wealthiest families, Padre Ricardo understood in a new way the contempt that rich Salvadorans had for liberation theology. It was no wonder conservative priests, business leaders and large landowners like Julio cursed Medellín. Its emphasis on social justice pointed fingers in their direction like a crowd looking for a scapegoat.

Padre Ricardo looked at Julio Díaz with a measure of sympathy that surprised him. He had not expected a theological discussion.

"A central question of Vatican II," Padre Ricardo said, "was how to make God and the Church relevant to a modern world of technology and progress. The bishops at Medellín saw that our world, our Latin America, our El Salvador are full of misery."

Julio's face remained stoic but the veins in his forehead betrayed anger. "And it preached class conflict and not the Gospel as the way to redemption," he said, his voice rising.

"Repentance, conversion and forgiveness offer hope for redemption," Ricardo responded. "But they are relevant to life here and now." Both men were silent for a long time. Julio didn't like letting others, particularly adversaries, inside his mind but he was unable to remain silent.

"If you are talking about redemption from poverty then we must be free to create wealth. This talk of God taking sides with the poor hurts everyone. Inciting the poor against the rich violates the harmony of relationships ordained by God."

Padre Ricardo looked out the window onto the orange grove. "It is God's will that you live as you do while the poor die in their shacks?" he said pointedly.

"God has given us special privileges. Along with special responsibilities," Julio added.

"And the poor?" Padre Ricardo persisted.

"God takes care of the poor," Julio said. "Their so-called misery is of no consequence. They are happy. Their poverty only serves to heighten the glory of the next life." Padre Ricardo listened carefully.

"We are the agents of salvation," Julio continued. "We do what must be done to arrest the cancer that threatens to deny God on whom salvation depends. That cancer is communism."

"Who is the 'we' you are referring to?" Padre Ricardo asked. The question went unanswered.

"What troubles me," Julio continued, "is that there are those within the Church who pollute the minds of the poor and rob them of God. They are destroying the Church in the name of God."

"I don't understand," Padre Ricardo said.

Julio emptied his glass of whiskey with a long swallow, refilled it, and turned to face Padre Ricardo. "I think you do." He regretted having said too much and listened too little. It made assessment of his adversary difficult.

Julio hesitated and then reached into a drawer in his desk and removed a small envelope. "Follow me."

The two men proceeded to the driveway. Julio spoke briefly to a servant who returned and put a case of coffee in the Jeep. "For you," Julio said. "Consider them goodwill offerings. We hope that our differences, whatever they may be, will be resolved in friendship."

Julio tossed the keys to Padre Ricardo who caught them instinctively with a snatch of his left hand. "There are many keys, many levers of power," Julio added. "Many doors can be opened."

"It is a generous offer," Padre Ricardo said touching the smooth surface of the Jeep's door. "It must have cost plenty."

Julio appreciated people who counted costs. The rich aroma of coffee and the distinctive smell of the new Jeep's interior filled the air.

"Too much," Padre Ricardo said. He tossed the keys to Julio and walked out the driveway onto a pathway that led through Juan's field to the community.

Six

Cynthia

Cynthia Randolph was the victim of a recurring nightmare that taunted her during times of insecurity or self-doubt. A small girl, a playground, ripped flesh on asphalt, the smell of iodine, her father's newspaper, her father. Images battled each other in the distorted vision of a childhood memory.

She awoke this morning in a cold sweat, jumped from her bed, showered, and proceeded directly to the office. Peter Jones awaited her.

"Robert isn't pleased," she said cradling a cup of coffee.

"Is he ever?" Peter asked.

"He says Nixon's a moron..."

"How insightful," Peter interrupted.

There were times Cynthia found his sarcasm refreshing. Biting honesty had its place. On other occasions it annoyed her, like a fingernail dragged slowly across a blackboard. She was indifferent to this morning's intrusion.

"He says Nixon's a moron," she returned to her thought, "Ford is worse, and Carter's election means the communists will control El Salvador and probably be marching into Washington by 1980."

"Classic Robert," Peter responded.

Robert Barnes was chief political officer at the embassy, a

title meant to obscure his position as the CIA's top official in El Salvador. The son of a former aide to Joseph McCarthy, he was not the only intelligence officer concerned over the election of Jimmy Carter, but clearly one of the most paranoid.

Carter's determination to quietly clean house was a matter of concern to many career agents. Robert Barnes, who showered with his gun, considered it a personal attack. Robert hated communism, and loved to hate it so much, that he found it where it didn't exist, inflated its dangers where it existed in small doses, attacked it with the entire weight of his being whenever he encountered it, and hated those who couldn't recognize its dangers whether or not they existed.

"Robert wants to line up Church and Pike and personally pull the trigger," she said.

"They paint an unflattering picture," Peter noted in what he knew was an understatement. Senator Church and Congressman Pike had detailed the Agency's ties to dictators, assassins, murderers, drug runners, torturers and thieves. Pike's report was so stinging that it was buried by members of Congress who didn't mind being lied to and who hated the airing of dirty laundry in public places.

"What do you think?" Cynthia asked. "About Carter I mean?"

Peter seemed unconcerned. "He'll retire a few agents, but he won't prosecute anybody. Our work is the same with or without Carter. No president will allow a communist takeover in Central America. One party talks about human rights and the other about communist aggression. They act pretty much the same."

Peter looked at Cynthia, who was sitting on her desk. She had brown eyes, a small nose and short, curly hair. She looked skeptical. And beautiful. He caught himself staring and realized it had been a long time since he had felt such an attraction. He started to sweat and the room felt suddenly small.

He walked over and filled his cup. Reentering a safer space, he continued. "The beauty of our system," he said, "is that our work is predictable." Peter seemed impressed with what he was about to say. "Republicans and Democrats are for sale to the same bidders. Republicans are conservative. Democrats? We call them liberal but we judge them by their conservatism," he said. "The two parties quibble over who controls the economy but foreign policy belongs to the generals. And to us."

Peter droned on about Watergate weakening the presidency, Vietnam discrediting the military and how few policy makers in Washington wanted to cripple the CIA. Pike's report would never be released.

"Ex-CIA officials don't run bake sales," he said. "If Carter goes too far he won't finish his term. If he finishes one he'll never serve another. I'd bet the store on that." Peter paused to catch his breath. "Robert will outlast Carter."

Cynthia understood his argument but Peter couldn't tell if her nod was a sign of approval.

She was the daughter of a career army officer who taught counterinsurgency courses at the U.S. Army School of the Americas in Panama. Her first assignment was in the Dominican Republic. She transferred to Panama where she worked with a young colonel, Manuel Noriega, who provided valuable information on Castro in exchange for a free hand in the illegal drug trade.

She was a step below Peter in the CIA hierarchy in El Salvador. They had worked together closely throughout the past several years on an Agency probe of radical movements within the churches throughout Latin America.

"According to Robert, no one in Washington thinks Central America is important," Cynthia said. She looked to make sure Peter was the only person within earshot. "He'll be glad to see Stevens go."

Miles Stevens, Jr., the present U.S. ambassador, told Congress that El Salvador was of little importance to the United States.

It had no oil, no gold, no silver. No minerals of any kind. El Salvador's people were so poor they couldn't afford to buy U.S. products, and its government labeled anyone who disagreed with its repressive policies a communist. Robert Barnes didn't quibble with the details, but he was outraged by the ambassador's inability to see larger stakes.

"Any word on his replacement?" Peter asked.

"Dennis Nolte. Robert says anyone will be an improvement," Cynthia said. Cynthia looked serious. "He's placing a lot of weight on our report. Am I invited?" she added. Her expression stiffened. She had touched a sore point between them.

"You know that's not my decision," he said.

Cynthia had contributed mightily to the report but her superiors denied her the right to present it or hear its details discussed. Its classification insured she would never be authorized to see it. She resented her exclusion.

"You know Robert's compulsion for secrecy," Peter said. "He won't even show it to Stevens," he reminded her.

"That's not the point and you know it," she said angrily. "Besides, there's more at stake than Stevens."

"What do you mean?" Peter asked.

"A good agent would know. Don't you think? An agent worthy of attending such a meeting," she added. A playful tone had temporarily replaced the anger. Peter looked at her pleadingly.

"Warren is flying in from Panama this afternoon," she said. Peter looked stunned. General Michael Warren was second in command at the U.S. Southern Command Headquarters.

"You sure he's not here for something else?" Peter asked. She nodded. "Who invited Warren?" he asked.

"Robert and Warren go back a long way," Cynthia said.

"Robert spoke about him when we were in Saigon but I never met him," Peter said. "I just heard stories about weapons being shipped illegally out of Vietnam before Saigon fell. They were stockpiled somewhere in the event Washington couldn't get its act together elsewhere."

"They're real tight. They blame the media and Congress for losing Vietnam and denting their careers. Warren's a real crusader, active in the World Anti-Communist Alliance. I think they're funded by the Moonies," she added. Peter looked nervous.

"Warren's tough," Cynthia said. "He and my father have worked together for years. They're worried about Nicaragua and Carter's talk about human rights," she continued. "My dad says Warren's approaching our report like food for a hungry dog."

"Is Literacy International up and running?" Peter asked.

Cynthia nodded. She and Peter had set up a front organization to serve as a cover for their activities. Through a maze of deceptive paper trails Literacy International was formed. It came complete with a mission statement, board of directors, offices and staff in three countries, and a track record of commendable service dating back to 1967. Within the last several months articles had appeared in the United States, European and Latin American Press offering glowing reports of Literacy International's important work.

"I hope Warren isn't disappointed," Peter said. "He doesn't sound like someone you want to disappoint."

Seven

The Report

Peter stood outside Robert's office staring at the clock. He had 30 minutes. His tasks in the Agency, and painful past, generally overwhelmed his impulse for reflection. He chased away a question about his friendship with Robert before it fully rooted itself in his consciousness but found himself, nonetheless, taking stock of the long road that led him here.

At the university Peter was among the best and the brightest. A devout Catholic, articulate and idealistic, the trajectory of his life was towards respectability and affluence. This seemed natural enough until President Kennedy spoke at his college graduation.

Kennedy promised fulfillment through service to others, a message that resonated with Peter's roots in the Church. Kennedy made the Peace Corps, the Alliance for Progress and the CIA seem like instruments of moral purpose.

Peter weighed his options and was ready to choose the Peace Corps over a Maryknoll missioner program when he unexpectedly received a request to meet a U.S. government official to discuss other employment possibilities. He accepted a position with the CIA and underwent training as a field agent.

Peter saw his work as a vocation, a calling. He was going to help his country change the world. Make it better. Freer. More democratic.

His first assignment in Vietnam turned out badly. Peter pushed papers on the edge of a tragedy he never fully understood while Robert Barnes and others gave, took and lost hearts and souls during one of the bloodiest wars in U.S. history. The political theater of their arrogant dreams was played out on the stage of an endless war where victims with names became body counts and winners and losers learned the art of moral deception.

Peter lost his heart and soul at the same theater on a smaller stage. He met Bui Thi outside the University of Saigon where Buddhist monks were demonstrating for an end to the war. She had joined with the monks to tell the U.S. to go home and to ask the Viet Cong and their communist sympathizers to embrace non-violent resistance. It was a message rejected by the key belligerent.

Bui Thi had escaped the poverty of the countryside, attended school and earned a professorship in history at the University of Saigon. They struck up a friendship that grew into love. It held them together as U.S. policy and the country came apart.

It took only one bullet for Peter to lose the war, one fatal shot to kill the idealism that once fed his heart and soul. After Bui Thi's murder he was befriended by cheap whiskey and Robert Barnes who investigated her death and concluded she had been assassinated by members of a communist cell group convinced she was channeling information to the embassy.

Peter was transferred to Chile where he helped undo Salvador Allende's presidency while rescuing ITT and Anaconda copper from communism, or what the Agency called the excesses of democracy.

Bui Thi's senseless murder catapulted Peter's dislike of communism into something more. His despair needed a mission and when Peter found one, he refilled his depleted soul with something other than a bottle.

In Chile, despite the successful coup, Peter and a few others in the Agency remained troubled. Subversive churches and community groups had encouraged workers and peasants to organize. The resulting organizations and alliances had contributed mightily to Allende's electoral victory. The post-coup repression in Chile undermined most of these groups. However, the disturbing convergence between faith and radical politics was a regional phenomenon.

His star rising in the Agency, Peter convinced his superiors that liberation theology and changes within the churches posed significant new challenges to U.S. foreign policy.

Peter left Allende's office to board a plane to El Salvador. This tiny country was considered a backwater, a place of little strategic importance to the United States. It was far enough removed from areas more central so that Peter could remain inconspicuous, but it was close enough to the religious upheaval impacting the whole region so he could find out what was going on. His specific assignment was to assess and counter threats to U.S. national security interests posed by the subversive groups inspired by liberation theology.

Over the past three years, Peter had traveled to every country in the region. He had used so many fictitious names that he'd nearly forgotten who he was. He spent six months in Brazil where Christian base communities made up of poor Christians committed to social change numbered in the hundreds of thousands. He studied at the Center for Religious Formation in Lima, Peru, with Gustavo Gutiérrez, considered the founder of liberation theology and its leading spokesperson. He visited communities on the southern tip of Lake Nicaragua where Carlos Mejía Godoy wrote revolutionary songs about faith, God and struggle. Peter conducted hundreds of interviews, read scores of books, uncovered dozens of songs and writings that tapped a spirit he could feel in others but could not fully understand. What he had seen and heard both unnerved Peter and served as the basis for the report he was about to present.

Peter hesitated, took a deep breath and knocked on the door.

He entered the office where Robert Barnes and General Warren waited. He felt more troubled than confident, unsure as to the source of his anxiety.

Warren was an imposing figure who seemed to fill the whole room as he stood. The three men sat down. A portrait of President Ford hung on the wall behind Robert's desk. In the corner of the room sat a large U.S. and smaller blue and white Salvadoran flag.

Peter unlocked his briefcase and placed a copy of his report in front of the two men. He held a third copy in his hands. On the cover was stamped: TOP SECRET. CODE RED. SECURITY CLEARANCE G REQUIRED. The title page read: THE CHURCH AND COMMUNIST SUBVERSION IN LATIN AMERICA. It had a subtitle: LIBERATION THEOLOGY'S CHALLENGE TO U.S. FOREIGN POLICY. The report was 323 pages long.

Peter lacked a G clearance and was denied access to any document so coded. He saw this one only because he had written it. Robert would decide based on today's meeting whether to maintain, upgrade or downgrade the clearance level required for access. Peter assumed his report would be broken down into several documents with different clearance requirements. This was the last time he would be authorized to see it.

Peter was briefing his superiors about a subject that in some strange way clouded his vision. It was as if he were wearing sunglasses in a dimly lit room somewhere deep within the cellar of his own soul. He was to offer an honest assessment of the changing role of the Church in Latin America and its implications for U.S. foreign policy. He could recommend the assassination of the Pope and no one would criticize him. There was to be absolutely no censorship. His paper presented analysis and policy options. No censorship was at the heart of freedom and yet freedom had itself meant so many different things to Peter Jones that he was no longer sure it had any meaning at all.

Page one of the document was the Executive Summary. It described Cynthia and Peter's findings in a few paragraphs. The subsequent nineteen pages were divided into six sections and offered a more detailed summary. The remainder of the document offered technical discussions of key themes.

The six main sections were as follows:

SECTION 1: THE HISTORICAL ROLE OF THE
    CHURCHES.
SECTION 2: TRADITIONAL THEOLOGY.
SECTION 3: TENETS AND METHODOLOGY OF
    LIBERATION THEOLOGY.
SECTION 4: LIBERATION THEOLOGY AND
    MARXISM.
SECTION 5: ASSESSING THE DANGERS:
    INADEQUATE RESPONSES.
SECTION 6: COUNTERING THE SUBVERSIVE
    CHURCH: POLICY INITIATIVES, STRATEGY
    AND TACTICS

General Warren cradled the report in his massive hands. He scanned it enthusiastically as Peter read aloud several paragraphs from the Executive Summary:

The changes sweeping the Church in Latin America defy easy description. It is clear, however, that they have major political implications. Liberation theology is foundational to these changes.

It is simplistic to equate liberation theology with communism or to dismiss it as a tool of Marxists. This error is common to many U.S. and in-country leaders who find it convenient to postulate a thesis without ambiguities. The forces driving changes in the region are more complex. Liberation theology relies heavily on a Marxist social analysis, including class conflict. However, it is a distinctive yet complementary social force.

If it is a mistake to equate liberation theology with Marxism, then it is equally dangerous to underestimate the potential strength of movements whose participants are motivated by Jesus. Collectively they have the capacity to disrupt present political and economic arrangements. Those participating in subversive movements may never have heard of Marx but find inspiration in a distorted, radical understanding of Jesus.

Liberation theology, therefore, not Marxism, is the principal challenge confronting U.S. foreign policy as we seek to maintain long-standing interests in our backyard. Stated another way, liberation theology and the subversive churches are the principal enemies of the United States and our traditional allies throughout Latin America. Waging war against these enemies will present U.S. policy makers with new moral as well as political challenges.

General Warren's initial reaction was favorable. Peter looked at Robert whose glance indicated he should proceed. "Historically, the Church has aligned itself with the economically powerful," he said. "The theological underpinnings of this phenomenon clarify why liberation theology is a serious challenge to our foreign policy."

Peter described colonialism's harsh impact on the poor. It triggered strong resistance prompting the rich and powerful to respond with violence and repression. The Bible, however, was equally important to the rich, he said, because injustice and inequality were propped up theologically.

When Robert asked for clarification, Peter explained how

the colonial system that allowed foreign powers and their allies to take gold and land, enslave people and shift production to export crops was sanctioned by God. "Traditional theology," he explained, "says poverty is God's will; riches a sign of God's blessing; obedience to proper authorities, required. And it promises a heavenly reward. The physical death that results from injustice and slavery is theologically downplayed by stressing the importance of saving souls and a heavenly afterlife and by making a clear distinction between body and soul. One's soul can be saved through obedience to the authorities killing you."

The absurdity of such an arrangement seemed perfectly natural in the context of Peter's appraisal. "The key point for U.S. foreign policy," Peter continued, "is that in countries where economic power and incomes are highly unequal, traditional theology helps maintain order. The success of this theology lessens the need for repressive violence."

Peter summarized liberation theology's basic tenets including the dignity of the poor, the importance of recognizing social sin in addition to personal sins, and Jesus' conflict with powerful economic and religious groups. He noted that liberation theology saw Jesus' crucifixion as a consequence of his life and faith, the resurrection as God's vindication of his ministry and Jesus as an example for Christians to follow. Liberation theologians criticized capitalism and were open to some form of socialism. Many saw the United States as a modern day Roman Empire. Demands for land and other social reforms were building where liberation theology was the strongest.

General Warren looked concerned. "If I understand correctly, then traditional theology sanctions the use of force against enemies of the State," he said. "Does liberation theology encourage violence against the State?"

"Its teachings on violence are complex," Peter responded. "The poor are seen as victims of institutionalized violence."

"What does that mean?" Warren asked.

"Liberation theologians speak about a spiral of violence," Peter noted. "The first violence is economic injustice that kills the poor through hunger and disease. The second violence is rebellion. The third violence is the lethal response of military and paramilitary institutions of the State that according to this perspective repress popular movements. For the spiral to be broken, liberation theology insists that the Church work for justice and de-legitimize State violence used against the poor.

"Most liberation theologians," he added, "do not openly call for violent revolution, but they do not rule it out as an option. They would say the decision for or against violence depends on the responses of the powerful to what are considered the legitimate demands of the poor."

Warren looked skeptical. Peter was not a preacher but his delivery was emphatic. Perhaps too much so. He struggled to regain his composure.

"The important thing," Peter continued, "is that liberation theology differs dramatically from its traditional counterpart. It is not the same as Marxism but it is problematic because it withdraws theological legitimacy from the existing, unequal social order."

The silence that followed made Peter uncomfortable. He could not read their faces, could not tell if they were ready to kill the messenger or merely disturbed by the message he carried. He glanced again and saw the wrinkles on General Warren's forehead tighten like a twisted rope. The veins in his neck stuck out like purple rivers flowing from a hidden reservoir of hate. Warren's body strained under the weight of unexpressed rage that only partially disguised his impatience with Peter's discussion.

Unable to imagine an alternative, Peter went ahead with an explanation of how both the method and content of liberation theology were dangerous.

"Liberation theology encourages poor people to understand and trust their own experiences. I saw Freire's method first hand," Peter said, oblivious to the fact that he was the only person in the room who knew who Freire was. "It is detailed in the report. The method involves small groups who reflect on the causes of poverty, then on scripture and then decide on appropriate actions. The cycle repeats itself in an ongoing process of transformation. The method educates, inspires and motivates the poor. It will not be easy to contain, derail, divert or halt this process."

Robert picked up on General Warren's annoyance. As helpful as Peter's summary might be, both men were in a race to the bottom line. It was already clear that no one in Washington had a clue about these new dangers or what to do about them.

Robert urged Peter to move on. Peter started reading from the final section: "The U.S. failure in Vietnam..."

He realized his mistake as quickly and clearly as a lightning bolt emblazons the sky on a dark night. Most military leaders and embassy personnel in Central America, including Warren and Barnes, were tormented by Vietnam. They were here to redeem themselves. They didn't appreciate anyone assessing their so-called failure, especially someone who had pushed paper as a junior CIA official while they risked their lives.

Eight

Failure and Fair Play

Robert expressed his displeasure by dropping Peter's first name. "Go ahead, Jones," he said.

Peter continued reading:

The U.S. failure in Vietnam must be confronted honestly if we are to avoid similar mistakes and a similar outcome in Central America where security threats are most pronounced.

Firepower could not win the war in Indochina. Nor can it do so here. The battleground will be economic, psychological and political with the military role best described as nontraditional. U.S. soldiers must provide important training but avoid a combat role that would once again fuel U.S. domestic opposition.

Race is an important consideration. As long as we avoid significant casualties among white U.S. forces, we should be able to manage appropriate levels of repression without significant political fallout.

Segments of the Church influenced by liberation theology are a potent enemy inimical to U.S. economic interests. Ironically, many of the reforms sought by this new enemy resonate with values upheld by our own revolution and Constitution. Our dilemma as a superpower is that we cannot always embrace our ideals.

In El Salvador and elsewhere in Central America our rhetoric must mask the substance of policies that are fundamentally aimed at maintaining a stable investment climate. We must try to give the appearance of reforms, so we will need to help our allies oversee elections, rather than steal them. We will need to push through cosmetic land reforms both to pacify U.S. domestic opponents and to influence local politics.

Even token reforms will be opposed vehemently by many wealthy Salvadorans. They will be our conflictive allies. They know from the past that we will not abandon them no matter what they do. They may force us to stretch our moral boundaries.

The alternative to decisive action is to let El Salvador and Nicaragua fall like dominoes. On the surface, changes in either country are of little consequence. These countries have few if any vital resources. The problem is that successful change efforts here may inspire others elsewhere.

Liberation theology is our principal enemy because it inspires hope in people and groups that we don't control. If we are unwilling to allow subversive groups to triumph, to implement changes we deem unacceptable and to inspire changes elsewhere where our vital strategic interests *are* at stake, then our only alternative is to forge an uncomfortable alliance with the political right. We must do so even as we seek to create a political center that we can control largely through the use of economic carrots and sticks.

Given the important role liberation theology plays in many social change movements, such an alliance will mean U.S. involvement in a war against the subversive churches. To the degree that liberation theology succeeds in withdrawing the veneer of legitimacy to an unequal society and in inspiring the hope of the poor majority, it guarantees that greater violence will be used against its proponents.

We will need to work with our allies to manage terror effectively in relation to the political moment. The stronger the subversive movements, the greater the violence directed against them. The Church cannot but be one of the principal targets of the violence. Justifying repression against the Church will require perception management unprecedented in our recent experience.

If liberation theology is an enemy to be challenged and if we are committed to winning the war, then our hands will be stained with blood. The alternative is an unacceptable loss of control in a region considered vital to U.S. national security.

General Warren looked at Peter Jones like a lion ready to pounce. "I'm confused," he said. His voice was sarcastic. Intimidating. "If I understand you then liberation theology is our most important *enemy*." He paused to let the full weight of his yet unstated point sink in. "And yet your report speaks of *challenging* liberation theology. We don't challenge enemies. We *defeat* them, if necessary we vanquish them. Am I clear?" he asked.

The General's icy stare sent a chill down Peter's spine. Afraid to look directly into his eyes, Peter cast a glance in his direction. What he saw was a man who looked both pleased and troubled.

Warren wanted specifics and Peter obliged him. He explained that El Salvador and Nicaragua were flash points where radical theology and radical politics were converging with unforeseen consequences. They were unpredictable testing grounds requiring immediate action.

General Warren looked to be a rubber band stretched tighter by every word. He seemed ready to snap as Peter spoke faster and faster with the unconscious hope that the speed of his words would somehow protect him from Warren's growing impatience.

"The report notes the importance of publicly projecting liberation theology as a tool of Marxism and as an enemy of both the Church and the State," Peter said. "It urges establishment of diplomatic ties with the Vatican, or until such time as this becomes possible, using U.S. influence to warn the Pope about the dangers of liberation theology.

The report states," he continued, "that the Pope and the Church hierarchy have their own reasons for undermining subversive Church movements and recommends crippling the base communities by transferring priests and appointing conservative bishops. It also lays out plans to support fundamentalist groups and sects that are theologically conservative, staunchly anticommunist and unwavering supporters of U.S. foreign policy.

"The report describes the charismatic worship and theology of these groups; how they thrive in the midst of poverty and insecurity; how they help poor people escape the miseries of daily life; how whatever changes they encourage are personal and not political in nature; how people currently drawn to liberation theology will turn to fundamentalist groups as the hierarchy clamps down and as repression intensifies."

Peter took a deep breath and launched another barrage of recommendations that he thought would please Warren but which seemed to fuel the General's ire like water poured on an electric fire.

"The report says we should strengthen alliances with military and business leaders in El Salvador and throughout the region despite occasional tactical differences. It urges increased U.S. military and police training to help manage the levels of violence needed to maintain or reestablish control. The report," he continued, "details the death squads and their relationship to the security forces. It suggests their usefulness as well as possible difficulties on the horizon."

Peter had nearly run out of breath. "Cynthia Randolph and I," he said shifting his voice from the more detached to the personal, "have successfully infiltrated the subversive church movements in El Salvador. Our front organization is set."

Peter was troubled by a feeling he could not quite name. He was like a reluctant prizefighter whose gaze fixed upon the bloodied face of his opponent imprisons the knockout punch that promises victory.

Although it was Peter who spoke, it seemed as if it was no longer his voice that he heard. The report seemed to have taken on a life and an identity of its own. Peter wasn't clear whether he had somehow lost a power struggle or had become so at one with the report that there was no longer any distance between him and it.

Before he could measure the reasons for his discomfort Warren abruptly ended the meeting.

"It's a compelling report," Warren said. "You can go." Warren looked at Peter's copy of the report. "Leave it on the table."

"Well done, Peter," Robert added.

Peter left the room like a bumbling actor yanked prior to the final scene. Robert Barnes took a deep breath, sighed and looked at General Warren who broke the brief silence.

"Do you remember the Hoover Report?" Warren asked.

"Vaguely," Robert said.

"It was a secret paper produced by the White House in '54 with the assistance of former President Hoover," Warren said. "It was a rallying cry for the United States to wage a worldwide war against communism. Without the Hoover Report the CIA would gather intelligence but be limited in terms of covert operations," he said.

General Warren looked directly at Barnes. "Because of the Hoover Report you boys are free to do whatever it takes to defend national security." Robert lifted his eyebrows in recognition.

General Warren continued: "It said that there are no rules to follow in our war against communism, no room for idealized notions of what constitutes acceptable norms of conduct. Survival is the key issue and notions of fair play go out the window. It called on us to subvert, sabotage and destroy our enemies by more clever, sophisticated and effective methods than they use against us."

Warren paused for effect. "This report," he said holding Peter's copy in front of him, "is the best thing I've seen since the Hoover Report. I don't understand liberation theology. Hell, I could read this fifty times and may not fully understand it. The fact is I don't need to read it to know liberation theology is dangerous. It's a war all right, and in a war we do what we have to do."

Robert, who had to deal with Ambassador Stevens looked troubled. "How do we proceed?" he asked.

Warren didn't hesitate. "Restrict access further with an H code. I'll contact Bush. The document in its present form will be available to him as CIA director, to you as station chief and to the President. That locks out Nolte. Frankly, it's important we keep it from Carter. Put together a watered down version and put an F classification on it. Show that version to Carter and Nolte. Keep it simple when you brief Stevens. It's my understanding that you'll be staying." Robert nodded.

"Our job may be complicated by a new administration," Warren continued, "but it's clear what must be done. Carter may or may not come around but the problems with the churches will outlast him. One more thing," General Warren said. "Let Jones and Randolph use their front organization to infiltrate. They can be useful but keep them out of the loop. We learned in 'Nam not to take chances. Jones ever ask you about his lost love?"

"No Sir," Robert replied.

———

Outside the ambassador's office Cynthia handed Peter a glass of iced tea. "How did we do?" she asked. "You look like a ghost."

Peter sighed. "I'll tell you one thing. General Warren is..."

"Hey Jones, Randolph?" Peter and Cynthia turned toward a man standing outside an office down the hall. Peter was grateful for the interruption. "Either of you been avoiding the copy log? Barnes is going to be ticked off. There's more than 300 unauthorized copies again this month. Check your records."

"My records are always in order," Peter snapped.

Cynthia shrugged. "Mine too."

Nine

Carmen

Dark clouds descended over the land giving the appearance of early nightfall. Carmen looked disparagingly at the sky and at her makeshift roof made of corrugated tin, wood and cardboard. It was not a question of keeping the rain out but of positioning the chairs she'd borrowed from neighbors in such a way as to shield her guests from the inevitable leaks.

Carmen had little space within which to maneuver. Her house was a one room shack with a dirt floor. At nightfall she hung hammocks and rolled out straw pads transforming the room into a chaotic dormitory. It was El Salvador's version of a hide-a-bed, one of Pueblo Duro's endless slumber parties.

Carmen stood inside near the wood fire where she had spent an endless stream of days and years. As smoke circled slowly along her leaky roof, Carmen shaped tortillas, laid them on the rounded skillet and, with the speed of a cobra, reached down and flipped them. Miraculously, neither tortillas nor expert hands were singed.

Tortillas are the edible plates of the poor.

On good days, Carmen would smother them with beans and rice: breakfast, lunch and dinner. On feast days add a piece of fish or chicken. On normal days subtract a meal and choose: tortillas and beans or tortillas and rice. On bad days there were no choices beyond tortillas and salt, and bad days were becoming the norm in Pueblo Duro.

Carmen's weathered face, small, bent-over frame and calloused hands made her look older than forty-three. Her eyes were gray survivors of smoke. They were enveloped by wrinkles, but deep within them something youthful and vibrant seemed ready to break forth.

Carmen marked her age in relation to a 1932 massacre, *La Matanza*. A group of about 300 families dominated both the countryside and the country. Life for the landless majority grew desperate as the worldwide depression and subsequent fall in coffee prices made a difficult situation intolerable. The military stepped in to prevent a reformist candidate from taking office.

In response to another year of stolen elections and stolen hope, a revolutionary leader, Farabundo Martí, readied a peasant uprising. Days before its inception, Martí was betrayed, captured and executed. The Salvadoran military went on a bloody rampage. It swept through the countryside murdering more than 30,000 people, including Carmen's parents, brothers and sisters.

Carmen was found beneath the mutilated bodies of her family. She had no recollection of her specific tragedy but *La Matanza* was a reminder to all Salvadorans of freedom's boundaries. It was seared into their collective soul. Carmen reckoned she was two or three at the time of the massacre. So today, in 1973, she was "about forty-three."

Carmen left the fire and walked to the door. She surveyed the dark clouds, took another glance at her roof and returned to the problem of the chairs.

"*Dios Mío*," she uttered unconsciously. Carmen and her common-law husband Marcos depended on the land for survival. El Patrón's land. Julio Díaz allowed Carmen's family to build a house and grow corn and beans on a small plot in exchange for one-third of their harvest. He offered seasonal work picking coffee for about fifty cents a day, provided credit to purchase seeds and fertilizers for an additional share of their harvest and helped during emergencies. For a higher price still.

61

The system was a god-send...for El Patrón. Illness stalked Carmen's house like an unwanted vulture. Three of her children died due to lack of medicines. She stood by helplessly as Lucía's husband died from the bite of a rabid dog and as Lucía prostituted herself to keep him out of hell. Much of the time, her family was hungry, in debt or both.

Carmen's situation was shared by most Salvadorans, including her neighbors who had similar arrangements with El Patrón and other landlords and similar histories of impoverishment.

"You look as nervous as a new puppy," Doña María said as she entered Carmen's house carrying her family's only chairs. Doña María was Carmen's neighbor, a midwife and something of a local gossip. "It is true, no, that the padre asked that the meeting be here?" she asked.

Carmen had no idea why a priest wanted to meet in her house. It was, however, unthinkable to question it. It was as natural for her to do what a priest asked as it was to wake up in the morning. Respect for a priest was a matter of custom. It reflected regard for the Church and the office of the priest not necessarily the person himself.

Carmen's actual experience with priests and with the Church was limited. Padre Eduardo had come to Pueblo Duro so infrequently that the devoutly religious Carmen often trekked to Somotillo to attend mass. It was a fifteen-mile, four-hour journey on foot and by bus. She cajoled Marcos into accompanying her on special religious holidays. For Marcos the trip was always an infuriating ordeal.

Until recently, the service was in Latin and Padre Eduardo never looked at the people as he said mass facing the front of the church.

"Why should I go to church?" Marcos protested. "The priest won't look at me. He speaks a language I don't understand. And he reads from a Bible that he locks in a case and won't let me see."

"Because God wills it," she would say. "It is a sin not to go to church."

Marcos exaggerated, but only slightly. Following Vatican II the mass was in Spanish and although few priests really looked at the people, they did face them. There were even a few priests who encouraged lay people to read the Bible.

There were times Marcos preferred the Latin that he did not understand to the Spanish that he did. He found little inspiration in hearing his poverty was God's will and his obedience to Church and government authorities required, and little comfort in the promise that the streets of heaven are paved with gold. He also felt strangely uncomfortable with the statue of a bloodied Jesus nailed to a cross which hung on the wall behind the altar.

"This is God's son?" he said to himself, "And he's going to help me?"

It was not Carmen's religiosity that troubled Marcos. He, like everyone, believed in God. But her attachment to the Church was something else. For Marcos the Church was another center of power for the rich.

There was a story well-known in the community of Pueblo Duro about the naming of El Patrón's sons. On the day of birth, El Patrón crossed himself, held the baby above his head and announced both surname and title. He declared his first son, "Mario: The Landlord"; his second, "Miguel: The Colonel"; his third, "Humberto: The Businessman"; and his fourth, "Eduardo: The Priest."

Before they left the womb El Patrón had chosen a role for each son calculated to expand the influence, prestige and honor of the Díaz family by filling a nitch within each of the four pillars of Salvadoran society.

El Patron chose the priesthood for Eduardo because the Church in El Salvador was an institution of power and an instrument of the powerful. The Church which blessed the conquest remained closely tied to those with money and guns. Rich Salvadorans routinely offered bishops and priests gifts such as cars, homes and jewelry. Beyond these material benefits, ties to the wealthy provided the clergy with social standing, invitations to parties and access to circles of power.

The Church for its part blessed the military dictatorships and steered clear of controversial social issues. One could say that in El Salvador the Church was seduced by the powerful, except little seduction was necessary. Padre Ricardo said the main hope for the Church was that Jesus forgave prostitutes.

Marcos may have disliked El Patrón and his powerful sons, but he got along with them because he could think of no other possibility. He was more open about his abhorrence of the Church, but Carmen dismissed his protests and nobody else showed an interest.

A prostituted church with a Latin mass and a pay-per-service priest like Eduardo did not inspire loyalty in Carmen or the others. It didn't have to. The very existence of a church, a priest, statues of the virgin and popular religious festivals kept a cultural attachment to the Church alive. Loyalty implies a conscious choice for or against something, but Carmen and most other Salvadorans did not choose to be religious. They simply were religious.

If a neighbor said it was likely to rain or the corn crop would be good this year Carmen would respond, "*Si Dios quiere*—If God wills it." When one of her children died for lack of a ten cent vaccination or if a rain storm washed away corn seedlings Carmen explained, "*Dios así lo quiso*—It was God's will."

When Padre Ricardo asked Carmen to attend and host a meeting of her neighbors she agreed without hesitation. She knew little about the meeting or the priest who requested it. She would have said yes to Padre Eduardo if he had made a similar request.

Had she thought about it, and she hadn't, Carmen would have noted significant differences between the new priest and the old.

Padre Ricardo didn't charge for baptisms, weddings or funerals and perhaps even more stunning, he actually lived in Pueblo Duro.

At the present moment Carmen looked puzzled.

"What's wrong?" Doña María asked.

"What should I do?" Carmen replied, shaking her finger at the holes in her roof. "If I put chairs in a circle as Padre said, people will be wet as fish."

Doña María looked at Carmen, sympathetically. "What should we do?" she asked.

"Perhaps we should wait until he arrives," Carmen suggested.

After sitting in silence for several minutes the women rose. They placed chairs throughout the small room in a distorted shape that insured that no one would receive an unsolicited shower. The two women looked at the chairs, and at each other, shrugged, sat down and waited.

Ten

The Twelve

Padre Ricardo's smile graced his rain soaked face as he entered Carmen's home. "Good afternoon," he said enthusiastically. It was as if he had entered a fine cathedral. "Everything looks perfect," he added. "Thank you." Carmen looked at the water leaking through her roof. "Everything is fine," he repeated.

"We made coffee and sweet bread," Carmen said.

"Excellent," Padre Ricardo said. "And the others?"

"They will be here shortly." Carmen spoke more confidently than her feelings warranted. She wondered about Marcos.

The others arrived drenched and disoriented. None knew why they were summoned or exactly why they had come. Marcos was the last to arrive. He trudged in looking more defeated than defiant. After greeting each other the uncertain guests sat down looking more than a little uncomfortable.

"Welcome to the Lord's supper," Padre Ricardo said, grinning, as Carmen passed around a loaf of sweet bread. Each person received a small piece that they devoured anxiously. Marcos grimaced knowing a family supper of tortillas and salt awaited.

Carmen and Doña María continued their hospitality. They served a half cup of sugar wetted down with hot coffee. Padre Ricardo drank from a real cup. The rest used tin cans, glass jars, plastic lids and an assortment of other items capable of holding liquid. After serving their guests Carmen and Doña María sat down with the others.

Jesus who walked among outcasts would have felt immediately at home among this group. The oldest was Rafael, 64. Padre Ricardo stumbled upon Rafael during one of his walks through the community. He was sitting with friends by a still drinking *guaro*, an alcoholic beverage distilled from sugar cane. The men went from embarrassment to confusion when Padre Ricardo sat down, listened for hours and shared a drink.

Like many *campesinos*, Rafael had few teeth. More striking was the absence of his right hand. On one visit to the still, the men told Padre Ricardo about *La Matanza*, including how a soldier cut off Rafael's hand with a machete.

"'I could kill you now,' the *guardia* told me," Rafael said. "But it is better for communists to die slowly.'" Rafael's grin was puzzling. Father Ricardo could not tell whether it concealed vengeance or forgiveness.

Land, two hands and a machete are minimal requirements for *campesino* survival, but Rafael was left handed and so good with a machete that landowners continued to hire him to clear around the coffee trees.

To Rafael's right was Margarita, the youngest at age 12. Her long, coal-black hair was braided down her back. Her deep brown eyes betrayed a lack of innocence, as if they had seen enough pain for a lifetime.

To his left sat Elena, 17. Elena was Margarita and Eusebio's older sister. She and Margarita did cleaning and laundry at the largest of El Patrón's coffee estates. Elena spent much of her time avoiding the unwanted advances of El Patrón's son, Mario. At the estate, El Patrón's daughter, Isabel, taught Margarita to read, something Julio Díaz said would only turn to trouble. Isabel, according to Marcos, was the only member of the Díaz family worthy of respect. Her compassion rivaled her family's arrogance.

Seated next to Elena was Sancho, whose nickname at university was Chispa, the spark. He and Elena were friends. Sancho was the oldest of Carmen's children. He had lived with an aunt in San Salvador for more than a decade. There he attended school, including one year at the National University.

Sancho had a deep scar above his right knee. Despite Carmen's appeals, Sancho returned to Pueblo Duro after the recent death of Octavio's father. He had not yet learned, as the others had, to get along in a community dominated by El Patrón. He was for all practical purposes an outsider. He had returned to Pueblo Duro less than two months ago, and he'd already clashed with El Patrón's arrogant—and some would say pathological—son Miguel, who graduated from the military academy and headed the Treasury Police that took its inspiration from *La Matanza*.

Marcos, perhaps identifying unconsciously with the troublemaker, positioned himself next to Sancho. And recognizing a troublemaker, Carmen seated herself next to her husband. She had no idea what the meeting was about, but she knew her husband's large feet often found rest in his mouth, which produced indiscretions with alarming frequency. Padre Eduardo's yearly visits convinced Marcos that he would leave any meeting with a priest a poorer man. He was here because Carmen would make his life miserable if he were not. By way of contrast, Doña María would have caused a riot had she *not* been invited. She waited impatiently for the meeting to begin.

Completing the circle were Juan; his son Carlos, who played the guitar; Rosa, whose knowledge of herbal medicine made her something of a community doctor; and Tomás and Ana López. Tomás and Ana were unique within the group in that they owned a small piece of land on which they grew corn, beans, mangos and avocados. El Patrón openly coveted their land. Carmen winced as Marcos broke the silence.

"Padre," he said as Carmen crossed herself and closed her eyes, "we are..." and then he paused stumbling for words. Carmen crossed herself again. "We are...honored that you are with us."

Carmen's anguished expression gave way to a look of amazement. Her husband had used—miraculously it seemed—an appropriate word, "honored," when addressing a priest. Gaining confidence, and before Carmen could finish her silent prayer of thanksgiving to the Holy Virgin, Marcos continued. "But why have you called us together?" he asked. "Surely we are poor enough already."

Before Carmen could utter a prayer asking the evil spirit inhabiting her husband's tongue to depart, Padre Ricardo spoke approvingly. "Our whole community is more than poor enough. But we are also richer than we think."

Marcos thought a priest who saw riches amidst their poverty would fleece them more thoroughly than Padre Eduardo. Yet, whether by divine wisdom, or fear of Carmen's wrath, or guilt over Padre Ricardo's bloody shins, or respect for the sincerity with which the new priest spoke, Marcos found the strength to listen.

Padre Ricardo reached into his bag. He gave a well-used Bible to each of the twelve. Octavio, who was watching anxiously from the doorway, sprinted away.

"Not all of us can read," Padre Ricardo said, "but there is great power in this book. We will teach each other to read. You are going to be God's voice in the community."

Those sitting around the circle were stunned. Most could not read. This would be the only book in their homes. It was certainly the only gift any of them had *received* from a priest. How to make sense of his words? Power was not found in a book. They knew about power because they didn't have any. They could barely speak for themselves, let alone be God's voice.

"These are your Bibles," Padre Ricardo said. His smile was as deep as a canyon, his voice warm like the afternoon sun. He asked Margarita to read a passage from the New Testament gospel of Luke.

As Margarita found the desired verses, some of the others looked uncomfortable. She waited for those who could read to help the others turn their Bibles right side up and find the proper page. "If you do not yet know how to read," Padre Ricardo said, casting a glance at Juan, "do not be ashamed. This is no sin. What *is* sinful," he continued, "is the society that denies you the opportunity to read."

Padre Ricardo looked at Margarita, who began to read slowly: "And Jesus came to Nazareth, where he had been brought up, and he went to the synagogue as was his custom on the sabbath day."

A few verses later she came to words Jesus spoke to define his ministry:

> The Spirit of the Lord is upon me,
> because God has anointed me to preach good news
> to the poor. God has sent me to proclaim release
> to the captives, and recovery of sight to the blind,
> to set at liberty those who are oppressed,
> to proclaim the Lord's year of jubilee.

As Margarita finished there was a long silence. Mesmerized by words that were unfamiliar and shocking, the twelve struggled to take them in.

Rafael, holding the book firmly, his eyes closed, spoke first. "I want to hear it again," he said, his voice rising. "Read it again, please."

Margarita had seen these faces nearly every day of her life but they looked different somehow. Overflowing with anticipation, her friends seemed out of focus but real. It was as if she were seeing them for the first time. She read the passage again. Slowly. Deliberately. Clearly.

> The Spirit of the Lord is upon me,
> because God has anointed me to preach good news
> to the poor. God has sent me to proclaim release

to the captives, and recovery of sight to the blind,
to set at liberty those who are oppressed,
to proclaim the Lord's year of jubilee.

"These words are in the Bible?" Juan asked.

"Yes," Padre Ricardo responded.

"Are they found in all Bibles?" Juan said.

"Yes."

"Padre, what do these words mean?" Carlos asked.

"A good question," Padre Ricardo responded. "Why did Jesus come?" There was a long silence.

"It says Jesus is good news," Margarita said.

"Good news for whom?" Padre Ricardo asked.

"To the poor," Juan said with amazement.

"What is good news to the poor?" Padre Ricardo said. "What does Jesus say?"

Elena spoke. "The end of oppression," she said. As the others pondered her words carefully, Tomás spoke. "What is jubilee?"

Looking at their faces Padre Ricardo realized no one knew. "The jubilee," he said, "is talked about in the Old Testament book of Exodus. The Exodus," Padre Ricardo continued, "is the story of how God helps free an oppressed people, the Israelites, from slavery in Egypt. It is a very important story for us but it will have to wait until another day. The jubilee is part of this story.

"Land for the Israelites, like for us, meant life. Landlessness meant death or enslavement. The Bible says the land belongs to God. People can use the land responsibly, but they don't own it. Land is to be available to all the people. The jubilee was a year in which the land, God's land, was redistributed among the people. And debts forgiven. A redistribution of land was required every fifty years and a cancellation of debt every seven years in order to break the cycle of poverty."

"Poverty went against God's wishes," Padre Ricardo added. "It was important that a few people not end up with all the land."

"Like here in El Salvador," Sancho said. His response was a statement, not a question.

Padre Ricardo nodded. The humble people that gathered this day in Carmen's home chewed on Jesus' words like a feast prepared especially for them. Rafael sat listening for a long time. He lifted his head, opened his eyes and spoke.

"I will tell you what these words mean to me," Rafael said. "All my life I have heard about God, prayed to God, hoped for God. It would be better to be an atheist than to believe in this God who was a lie. It was their God. Created in their image. I'm sixty-four years old and only today learned that Jesus hates our poverty as much as I do."

Padre Ricardo turned to Carmen who had been silent throughout. "Carmen," he said, warmly, "What do you think about these words of Jesus?"

The streams running down her cheeks rivaled those that entered through her battered roof. "I think," Carmen said, sobbing. "I think..." Overcome with emotion she could not continue. It was the first time anyone had asked her what she thought about anything.

Eleven

Bitter Fruit

If Padre Ricardo had a fan club in Pueblo Duro it was among the children who delighted in the antics of a soccer-playing priest. Eusebio had become Ricardo's shadow. He would make his way to the soccer field and watch the new priest play with abandon. During a break or after the game Padre Ricardo would kick the ball around with Eusebio and the other children. Eusebio was often seen walking side by side with his new friend carrying the soccer ball, and he brought the Bible to the priest each Sunday as the Gospel was read during mass.

One morning as Padre Ricardo passed by Eusebio's house he was surprised that the boy wasn't there to greet him. Eusebio was still sleeping. An hour later his mother sensed something was wrong when Eusebio showed no interest in breakfast. Encouraging Eusebio to eat was like ordering a fish back into the water. A poor appetite was a sign that a cold that wouldn't go away had become something worse.

"*No tengo hambre*—I'm not hungry," he said, weakly. Eusebio's glazed eyes stared blankly at the food before him. He wiped his arm across his face redistributing the ugly substance which oozed from his nose. It was the color of well-used antifreeze and the consistency of watery glue. Eusebio's hair, brown with a few blond patches, reflected poor nutrition rather than fashion in Pueblo Duro. His mother held a screaming baby and before she could prevent him, Eusebio was out the door. That morning he stayed close to home with only enough strength to gather a few sticks for his mother's stove.

Eusebio's appetite did not improve at lunch. He set down his tortilla, picked up his sling shot, and left to pursue his favorite target: mangos which grew in a nearby tree. Ripe mangos, delightfully sweet, soft and juicy, are one of nature's wondrous gifts to the palette. Eusebio's family, directed by the immediacy of hunger, ate them bitter and green.

Outside the house Eusebio coughed. His tiny body convulsed with each spasm in his chest. His mother ran outside, handed the baby to Sancho and carried Eusebio in. He was as hot as a rock baking in the midday sun.

Sancho found Rosa and when they returned Eusebio was lying on a hammock in an area opposite the stove. Rosa spoon fed herbal medicines and tea to him like a rejected lamb. For the moment he seemed comfortable. She walked over to the door where Sancho stood, his face solemn and concerned as he pondered the fate of Elena's brother.

"He needs medicine or he will die," she said, her voice anxious and shrill. Her gaze moved from Sancho, to Eusebio's mother and back again.

Eusebio's body, weakened by malnutrition, was no match for the germs attacking him. A doctor was out of the question. Too distant. Too expensive. Medicine could be had. For a price.

The coughing spells, frequent and intense, sprang from deep within his lungs. They convulsed his body like an epileptic seizure. His body grew weaker and his temperature rose. A simple antibiotic would have prevented and perhaps could still reverse his deterioration. But the family had no money.

Sancho ran to Tomás and Ana's and borrowed their horse. He mounted quickly and took flight. The horse ran furiously and perilously up and down pathways more suited to feet than hooves. He raced past simple houses made of mud as near naked children ran barefoot to the edge of the path laughing and waving. Chickens and pigs scattered while an occasional cow demanded and received the right of way.

As he approached the estate of Julio Díaz, Sancho came to a paved road. The land was beautiful and rich. Acres and acres of coffee bushes graced the hills. The green beans covering the branches were still several months from harvest. Huge trees rose gloriously to the sky providing the shade that the coffee plants coveted. Further on, an orange grove embraced the land like a sunset kissing the ocean. To the left was a small pond. Its glistening waters coaxed local children to defy fences marking off property lines until several were chased away by bullets from the guns of Julio's henchmen. Up the hill a mansion stood framed with pillars of marble. At the entrance to the driveway was a gate and a small structure that looked like a toll booth.

It was flanked by two armed guards.

Sancho often walked Elena and Margarita to El Patrón's estate. But Sancho had never been inside, not even as a coffee picker. The guards, seeing the horse, eyed him suspiciously. One walked to the booth, reached in through the window and picked up the phone. He spoke briefly and returned with instructions for Sancho, who waited nervously. As Sancho made his way up the driveway, a guard in front of the house motioned him past the garage, where a Cherokee with tinted windows sat. He proceeded to the side entrance where he was met by Elena.

Upon seeing her, Sancho felt more acutely the indignity of his mission but he also felt calmer. Even at this moment he was aware of how much he loved her. Elena folded her desperation into his as Sancho explained Eusebio's illness.

She knew El Patrón, what kind of man he was. Speaking and then wishing she hadn't, her voice betrayed the doubt she was feeling.

"Do you think he will help us?" she asked. She continued awkwardly. "Jorge told me to meet a visitor and bring him to El Patrón's study," she said. "He didn't tell me it was you."

Elena walked Sancho from the side entrance down a long hallway which led past the kitchen and the laundry room. As they reached the entry way by the front entrance Elena looked mournfully at Sancho who looked as out of place as a grave digger at a wedding reception. Sancho had never seen a house so large or so elegant.

Once he and his friends had driven through a rich neighborhood in San Salvador where Julio Díaz and other rich Salvadorans have their second or third homes. They hoped to get a glimpse of houses hidden behind walls and fences. It was a costly excursion. A security guard positioned in the towers overseeing the street recorded the car's license plate number. His friend was arrested, kept for a week, tortured and then released.

Sancho was inside such a house. The entry way itself was easily four times bigger than Eusebio's home where he lay close to death. A marble staircase spiraled upstairs leading to eight large bedrooms, three baths and an extra study. On the main floor to his left was a spacious living room.

The walls were covered with paisley wallpaper that seemed tacky and out of place. Caned rocking chairs surrounded a coffee table made of cedar. End tables holding wood-carved lamps shaped like lion's heads flanked a leather sofa that looked uninviting in the sticky heat. A gigantic Persian rug covered much of the marble floor. In the corner an RCA television with a 22-inch screen and stereo system built into a wooden cabinet was pressed against the wall. Loud voices of English actors filled the empty room as subtitles flashed across the screen without meaning.

To Sancho's right was a large formal dining room. An oak table centered the room like a well-placed portrait. It was covered with a silk cloth and could seat twenty-four people, perhaps more if one removed the center panel with its thirty-six candles. Each end of the table had a small button connected to an electric buzzer in the kitchen to summon servants.

Between the living room and formal dining area was an indoor garden, a tropical paradise with an open roof surrounded by walls, which created an awkward yet delightful sensation of being outside and in at the same time. The waxy plants were deep green. Red, purple, white and yellow flowers colored the ground and reached out from bushes and branches offering gifts to bees and hummingbirds that darted about and then paused to feast on their sweet nectar. A mango tree reached tall above the roof of the house as two giant cockatoos, perched atop shafts of bamboo, screeched between bites of *plátano*.

Sancho and Elena's anxiety rose as she guided him through the garden towards Julio's office. She squeezed his hand gently as they stood waiting.

They could see Julio Díaz through glass panes on the door that remained closed in order to ease the burden of the air conditioner. He sat behind a huge oak desk, positioned near a large window offering a perfect view of the orange grove. A round table with four chairs sat elegantly in the middle of the room calling attention to the oversized chandelier that hung from the high ceiling and made the huge room seem even bigger. On the wall opposite the desk was a flowered couch located strategically next to a well-stocked liquor cabinet. The wall was decorated with paintings from artists around the world, including an original Monet. A machete hung as an ornament next to a life-size portrait of Maximiliano Hernández, the leader of *La Matanza*. Wooden book shelves covered the other walls from floor to ceiling.

Julio Díaz was a master choreographer of humiliation. He sat sipping coffee casually from an elegant cup. A tray of sweet rolls was to his right, an expensive pen and pencil set at his left. He looked up, glancing at Sancho and Elena standing nervously in the hallway. Julio sifted through papers, reached down and pushed a button on the intercom. "Jorge?" he said, expectantly.

"Yes, Sir," a garbled voice responded.

"Usher our friends in."

Sancho and Elena entered the near frigid room. As he prepared to leave, Jorge was interrupted by a stern voice. "Give plenty of beef to the dogs and groom them." Julio pointed with his lips to the chairs under the chandelier. "I'll be with you shortly."

He fidgeted with papers for another ten minutes and pressed the intercom button once more. "Tell Mario I need to see him in my study. At his convenience." Another ten minutes passed. Mario arrived and spoke to his father in a quiet voice. Julio nodded as Mario turned slowly, walked to the couch and sat.

Julio summoned Elena to his desk. She looked like a nervous butterfly. Her eyes the color of fertile earth, her brown hair pulled back in a ponytail which she flipped unconsciously over her right shoulder. She wore a simple skirt that fell gracefully to her ankles, well-worn sandals and a white blouse. She was a picture of modesty and simplicity, an attractive seventeen-year-old woman.

Elena was uncomfortable in a room she cleaned regularly but otherwise did not enter. El Patrón ordered Elena to serve coffee and a pastry to Mario who undressed her with his eyes. Elena, unaccustomed to this role, retrieved a cup and saucer from Julio's desk, poured the coffee awkwardly and brought it to Mario.

"Sugar and cream," he said. His voice was cold, his slight smile an invitation to cynicism. Elena returned to the desk, retrieved sugar bowl and cream pitcher and brought them to Mario. She took a cube of sugar and placed it in his cup. He sat motionless. She added another and then another. Mario moved his hand indicating he was satisfied. She added cream cautiously, her eyes shifting constantly between the cup and his loathsome face. Elena brought the cream and sugar back to the silver platter on the desk and returned with the plate of pastries. Mario found several to his liking. Elena returned the tray to Julio's desk, glad this part of her ordeal was over.

Julio motioned to a place on the couch next to Mario. Elena hesitated, walked over and sat down. Mario placed his left hand high up on her thigh. She removed it instinctively. He placed it there again. Firmly. She sat stiff and still.

Having set the stage Julio spoke. "What can we do for you? Tell me why you have come."

Sancho wanted to remove the machete from the wall and hack El Patrón and Mario to pieces. Instead he took a deep breath and thought of Eusebio. "*Buenas tardes.* Good afternoon, Patrón. *Buenas tardes*, Don Mario. Thank you for seeing us." Sancho held his hat by his side. He had lived in the city a long time, demonstrated at the university, stood tall in front of the feared National Guard. Now, choking on his pride, he struggled to conger up the appropriate deference and self-hatred so pleasing to the rich. It had once been as natural as life itself. "You are a good man, Patrón. My family and I wish to thank you for your many kindness," Sancho said.

Julio's demeanor was casual and demeaning. He had been through similar rituals dozens of times. He loved his power and liked that he could exercise it with or without subtlety.

"We need your help, Patrón. Elena's youngest brother is very sick. He needs medicine." There was no response, not even a movement of the lips, and so Sancho continued. "If you could find it in your heart to help us now, we will give you another hundred pounds of corn when the crop is harvested."

The medicine could be had for fifty, Julio was thinking. His actual words surprised Sancho and Elena.

"Sancho," he said, simply. "Of course we will help."

Sancho, who had been shrinking under the weight of the in-dignity of the whole situation, felt suddenly hopeful. Almost grateful. Julio opened a desk drawer filled with medicines and removed several packages.

"You have been away a long time," Julio told Sancho. He fondled the penicillin that offered Eusebio his only hope for life. "Perhaps you have forgotten that the ways of the university are not our ways." He paused, not because he anticipated a response but because he wanted his words to sink in. "We will help you. And we will take your hundred pounds of corn. But there is something you must remember. It is not healthy to associate with a communist priest." Sancho's eyes alternated between the medicine and El Patron's face.

"You needn't wait," Julio said. He put the medicine back in his desk. "Mario will bring the medicine. Elena, stay a moment and pick up the office."

"Perhaps..." Sancho was going to ask if he could take the medicine but realized to do so was a mistake. "Thank you," he said, glancing at Elena and Mario. "*Adios*."

Julio and Mario followed Sancho out the door. Elena sat, close to tears, alone on the couch. As they departed she walked to El Patrón's desk. She opened the drawer, reached in and took out several packages of medicine. She placed them in the pocket of her skirt and closed the drawer. She placed cups from Julio's desk onto a tray and was startled as the door opened. "I thought...I should return to the laundry," she said.

Mario said nothing.

Twelve

❧

Eusebio's Luck

Elena felt sick as she went upstairs to make the beds. It was the longest day of her life. Eusebio lay dying and she had medicine that might save him. Leaving early would call attention to her deed. She had stolen something for the first time. "God forgive me," she said to herself. Over and over.

Elena put the final case on, fluffed the pillow and placed it on the bed. As she turned to leave, Mario walked in and closed the door behind him. His face cracked with a knowing smirk. He walked over and grabbed Elena's arm. With his other hand he reached in and removed the medicine from the pocket of her skirt.

"You can save Eusebio and yourself," he said, returning the medicine to her pocket and looking her violently in the eyes. Before she could scream he covered her mouth with a powerful hand. He threw her harshly on the bed, removed a pillowcase and stuffed it in her mouth, muffling her screams that echoed in her convulsing body. Mario held one hand firmly around her neck as he used his other hand to remove her skirt. Elena's arms flung wildly in protest landing occasional blows to his back.

Mario squeezed her neck harder and tried to ply her legs apart. The strength of his grip around her neck, the weight of his body, the pillow case stifling every effort for air, combined to erode Elena's strength.

Elena made one last desperate effort to remove the pillow case. Her right hand struck a solid blow to Mario's back as her left hand reached her mouth. Mario, unable to penetrate her, grew frustrated. She yanked the pillow case which had lodged near her tonsils, removed it and vomited in Mario's face. He recoiled instinctively.

"I'll kill you," he screamed.

Hearing noises in the hallway he wiped his face, pulled up his pants and started for the door. As Mario faced her, Elena looked away, unable to bear his sinister smile. He walked over, picked up the medicines and left the room.

Sancho knew nothing of Elena's ordeal. He arrived at Elena's home to find Octavio pleading with his friend not to die.

"You said not to touch the book," he admonished Eusebio with tears drenching his face. "You said, 'Touch the book and you die.' You told me the new magician was different but you touched the book and now you are dying." Octavio saw Padre Ricardo coming and raced out the door.

By the time Elena arrived, hope had given way to anger and despair. Mario did not bring the medicine. Eusebio was dead.

Padre Ricardo found no words appropriate for the anguish of the moment. He sat with the boy throughout the day as life left his tormented body. He struggled to garner the courage to approach the boy's mother who sat dazed and despondent in the corner of the room. Unable to read, she held the Bible that Padre Ricardo had given to Elena.

"*Lo siento mucho*, I'm very sorry," he said. His voice was gentle. He did not expect a response.

Eusebio's mother looked him in the eyes. It was a startlingly uncharacteristic act that surprised Padre Ricardo nearly as much as her words.

"I too am sad," she said. "I no longer have my son. But I am glad for him. His suffering is over. He is the lucky one. We would all be better off dead."

Padre Ricardo built a house and buried eleven children during his first three months in Pueblo Duro.

As he walked the hidden pathways that connected the shacks of the poor, he realized that Pueblo Duro was a microcosm of El Salvador. Three-quarters of the children were malnourished. Their distended stomachs, symbols of deprivation rather than gluttony, were distorted images of Padre Eduardo's. Most of the people could not read or write. Most lived in one room shacks. Most lacked access to clean water. Most were landless.

The misery was compounded by the quiet resignation he encountered. Needless death was a way of life in the countryside. The indignities of life were so intertwined with life itself that all sense of dignity and possibility were smothered. Injustice was life itself.

Like the chasm separating the rich man from Lazarus, there was a gap between Padre Ricardo and the *campesinos*. Not as impenetrable perhaps, but it was there, no matter how determined he was to bridge it. Padre Ricardo was planting himself in unfamiliar soil. Despite good intentions, a gulf between the *campesinos* and Ricardo existed as a consequence of social standing and the accident of birth. As much as he sympathized, the poor were poor and he was not. Solidarity was his choice and there was power in the choosing.

Upon arriving in Pueblo Duro, Padre Ricardo approached Tomás and Ana López who allowed him to construct a simple house at the edge of their property. It, like the homes of the *campesinos*, was a simple one room structure. But even here the differences were striking. To the left, as one entered the door, was a large window capturing the morning sun. Beneath it sat a simple chair and table covered with books, papers, an assortment of pens and pencils, and a kerosene lamp. To the right was an unadorned bed frame with a straw mattress. Atop sat a blanket and pillow, visible beneath the netting which countered the relentless attacks, if not the obnoxious humming, of El Salvador's mosquitos. A Bible and transistor radio sat on the night table in the corner.

Padre Ricardo wasn't the only person in Pueblo Duro to have a radio, but his had batteries that worked. His house had a cement floor which, together with his elevated bed, protected him from the scorpions whose bites were often a deadly curse to infants and small children. His roof did not leak. Outside the back door was a small kitchen area, a *pila* for holding water, and a latrine. The *campesinos* with whom he worked didn't have pillows, batteries, mosquito netting, cement floors, secure roofs, beds, books or mattresses. Their houses were not well-ordered, in part because unlike his, they were shared by three generations of people, including children who were often sick and hungry.

The separation was deeper. It was a separation of ideas. Padre Ricardo had studied in Europe. He spoke Spanish, English and German. His was a world of concepts as well as commitments. At times he was deeply lonely. For all the disadvantages of being an outsider there were advantages, too. Just as the smog of a large city is visible more clearly to a visitor than to a resident, so also it was with the injustice in Pueblo Duro.

Padre Ricardo wondered. How did people survive? How did they find strength to go on? How did they sleep with the mosquitos? What beyond force of habit and necessity moved them? What could make the smog visible, bring injustice into the light where it could be seen and felt and resisted? What would it take to awaken life among the walking dead and physically dying?

Padre Ricardo thought he knew the answer. He left the first meeting of the twelve filled with hope. For life to break the spirit of death which enveloped Pueblo Duro something had to re-trigger the anger and hope of the people. Rage was a necessary response to needless hunger, an antidote to despair. A sense of new possibilities could tame the rage and nurture hope. Each *campesino* stockpiled indignities in a hidden warehouse of deferred hopes and unimagined dreams.

They were surrounded by senseless death and senseless choices, forced to consume next year's seed corn to ward off this year's hunger, to choose between food and medicine, between more hunger and the death of a child. They faced the outrage of constant debt and destitution that seemed beyond words or hope.

Padre Ricardo saw rage unexpressed turned inward. It led to resignation, despair, drunkenness, petty rivalries and battered families. Anyone who idealized poverty or the poor had experienced neither. And yet Padre Ricardo sensed the strength and power of the *campesinos* hidden beneath their resignation and despair.

The gospel stories were written in, for and by communities not unlike Pueblo Duro. The liberating word of Jesus was the key to unleashing creative energy that could channel expressed rage into hope.

Padre Ricardo struggled with his role as a priest. How could he be faithful to God and to the people of Pueblo Duro? He respected their resiliency but could not reconcile resignation with the way of Jesus. He wanted to trust the liberating gospel.

Eusebio's death was not in vain. It brought clarity to Padre Ricardo's struggle. It might have been but another tragic introduction to life and death in Pueblo Duro. Except for Eusebio's mother. She pushed Padre Ricardo over a precipice of uncertainty into unchartered waters that could no longer be avoided. He could not be a priest without letting the Gospel speak, regardless of the consequences.

It was clarity with a sting. Padre Ricardo would share the Gospel with the people. But the new life it brought forth within them would be the target of a furious assault. Had he known how furious, he might have turned and walked away. Perhaps Octavio was right after all. Touch the book and you die.

Thirteen

Isabel

Eusebio's death added to Elena's humiliation. She wanted to stay far from El Patrón's. She considered telling her father about being raped by Mario. She decided against it. Telling her father would accomplish nothing, at least nothing positive. She was afraid he would blame her, or worse yet, seek revenge. This she reasoned would bring greater hardship to the family.

At an unconscious level she knew that telling her father would only expose his powerlessness. He would be trapped between outrage and impotence, the violation of his daughter and his mental and economic captivity.

Elena's indignity included the fact that leaving El Patrón's was never really an option. Her meager salary was critical to the family's survival. Her father would beat her if she quit her job for any reason.

And so Elena told no one and returned to work.

For a time, she lived in fear as she worked in the laundry. Thankfully, she saw Mario only from a distance. But her pain consumed her. Determined to keep her secret, she was dying within her silence. She needed to talk, to weep, to scream, to be held.

When Isabel returned from the University of Central America (UCA) she noticed disturbing changes in Elena who, sad and withdrawn, spoke to no one, not even Margarita. Although not exactly friends, Elena and Isabel had been friendly. Isabel treated Elena and the others with respect. Not like servants. She seemed as resentful of her father and brothers as Elena was, and she had even taught Margarita to read.

Elena withdrew more completely into herself. She had entered a space that could not be filled with words. Her sighs were too deep to be heard. Time had stopped in that upstairs bedroom like a broken watch. The room was utterly empty and yet overflowed with pain.

In a time such as this, within spaces where her sighs echoed in the darkness, Elena experienced the mystery of healing. A silent touch bridged the gap separating the daughter of a rich landowner and a violated servant. One day Isabel found Elena in an upstairs room weeping. She entered, closed the door, sat down and held her. Hours passed. When Elena finally spoke, she did so in broken sentences and deep sighs as bits and pieces of the story spilled forth like water from a shattered vase—Eusebio's illness, Sancho's coming, the coffee and pastry, Mario's hand on her thigh, the stolen medicine, the rape.

Isabel listened intently, held her, received her healing tears and encouraged Elena to give voice to her pain.

Elena's friendship led Isabel to the community. Upon hearing about the twelve, she offered to instruct them. In some small way, she hoped her life could be reparation for the abuses of her family. An excellent student at the Jesuit-run University of Central America—the UCA—she was eager to apply her knowledge of literacy training to the needs of the community. One Saturday morning, Isabel went to the soccer field.

"Padre Ricardo," she called out during a lull in the game. Ricardo looked up to see Isabel. She was in her early twenties and wore a T-shirt that said BEATLES and featured fading profiles of George, John, Paul and Ringo. He pulled a sock over his bloody shin, walked over and shook her hand. "I'm Isabel Díaz," she said. Her smile so overwhelmed him that he was speechless.

"Ah yes, El Patrón's daughter. I'm...I'm glad to meet you," he stammered.

Isabel was embarrassed. "I hate that people call him that," she said.

Padre Ricardo smiled. "I'm sorry," he said. "I hate it, too."

"I wonder if we might talk?" she asked sitting down next to a tree by the edge of the soccer field.

"Of course. My shins and my pride have been bruised enough for today."

Isabel despised the initial moments of conversation with people such as Padre Ricardo. Her family's reputation preceded her and cast doubt on her integrity and her intentions. Padre Ricardo's warmth put her at ease.

"Ignacio says you are a good student. Every time I see him he asks if I've spoken to you about our work in the community," Padre Ricardo said. Ignacio Ellacuría, a Jesuit priest who directed the UCA, was one of the most respected educators in Latin America. He believed a university should train students to help solve the nation's most pressing problems.

"He's wonderful," she said. "He and Elena have both encouraged me to talk to you about the community's literacy work. I would like to help."

"Excellent," he said.

They spent the next hour discussing their common interest in Paulo Freire. "Perhaps Freire deserves credit for recognizing the obvious," Padre Ricardo said, clearly energized by an opportunity for an academic interchange. "People who can't read and write aren't stupid." He pointed to Carmen who watched as Marcos made a fool of himself on the soccer field. "Carmen is full of strength and wisdom and yet no one draws her out of her shell. She is a treasure waiting to be discovered."

"Freire's genius," Isabel responded, "is his method. It lets people like Carmen discover themselves in the context of community learning. He was the first," she continued, "to demonstrate that learning to read and write is critical to self-awareness and dignity."

"And," Padre Ricardo interrupted, "to see that literacy is not an end in itself. Literacy training can validate the life experiences of the poor and equip them with tools of social analysis."

They smiled at each other and then repeated at the same time: "In this way the poor can understand and change their life situation." They laughed. Padre Ricardo was older but they had the same teachers.

"You know," Isabel said, a note of seriousness returning to her voice, "the rich in El Salvador consider Freire a communist because he doesn't want the poor to remain passive."

Padre Ricardo sighed. "It's true everywhere," he said. "When we form base communities we are called communists for the same reason. Pretty soon," he continued, "they will not allow the Bible and the gospel into our country. All they will allow will be the covers because there is too much subversive material in its pages."

There was a long silence before Isabel responded.

"I'm afraid people like my father *believe* we are communists. They are not just using rhetoric against the people. They have eaten and digested it. They will kill you and the others if they think it is necessary. They can't see you as human beings."

Padre Ricardo noticed Isabel was trembling. "May I ask you a question?" he said. Padre Ricardo looked at her sympathetically and then continued. "What would you do if you were me?"

She looked at him with eyes that seemed to peer into his soul. "Go on being a priest," she said. "Awaken the people, learn from them and trust God."

"I am changing and they are changing me," he said. Padre Ricardo smiled. "Permit me one more question?" he asked.

Isabel nodded.

"How can you go on living there?"

"I'm at the UCA most of the time" she said. "My father never cared a thing for me. Perhaps it is because he has always treated me with the same contempt he has for the people that I identify with them and not him. It is ironic that my father is helping me learn to fight against him and his El Salvador. I will fight until we create a new country or until I die." She paused, embarrassed by the intensity of her words. "I've told you more than you wished for."

"Not at all," he said.

"The short answer is I won't be staying much longer."

Fourteen

Womb for the Corn

For several months, Isabel and Padre Ricardo gathered nightly with the twelve under a kerosene lamp. Those who couldn't read and write learned how. Those who could continued learning. They all prepared to teach others.

Literacy training and Bible study were pieces of a common tapestry that helped the community discover the power of which Padre Ricardo spoke.

Each night Isabel wrote a word in large letters on an old blackboard that Padre Ricardo had brought from San Salvador. On this night Isabel wrote the word *LECHE* as she spoke. Milk was available to the poor in Pueblo Duro only if accounts were settled, bills paid, a good harvest in and sold, El Patrón satisfied and illnesses put on hold. In other words, *leche* was a familiar word but a stranger to their tables.

"Let's begin with the letter L." Isabel pointed to the board and underlined the word she had chosen. "Repeat after me."

"eLLLLe," they responded.

"Again."

"eLLLLe," they repeated.

Isabel did the same with each of the letters. She then asked her willing pupils to think of words that begin with the L sound. Padre Ricardo wrote the words they spoke on the board: milk, light, vegetables, lemon, ready, lips, pity, pencil, Luke, far, El Patrón and struggle.

LECHE
LUZ
LEGUMBRES
LIMON
LISTO
LABIOS
LASTIMA
LAPIZ
LUCAS
PATRON
LEJOS
LUCHA

Isabel read each word aloud, pointing to the letters as she pronounced them. L should be the first letter in each word, she told them. There was one word that didn't belong. Several people noticed immediately, while others looked carefully up and down the list.

"The third one from the bottom is different," Rafael said. "The third one from the bottom doesn't belong."

"In more ways than one," Sancho said. Some in the group laughed while others waited for an explanation.

"What does it say?" Rafael asked.

"Patrón," Sancho said, struggling to contain himself. "El Patrón doesn't belong."

Isabel laughed too. She was more comfortable here than at home. When she was with the community, sadness left her eyes. As the laughter faded Isabel returned to the first word she had written on the board. They repeated the letters and the word *LECHE* several times.

"Do you have milk for your children or your brothers and sisters?" Isabel asked.

"My younger brothers and sisters almost never drink milk," Margarita said. "But each day at El Patron's I give milk to the dogs. And meat too."

"*Necesitamos más tierra*," Marcos said. "Our children would have milk if we had more land."

"I want you to think for a minute about land," Isabel said. "Then fill in the blank for me. Land is _____. You don't have to limit yourself to one word. Add several words if you like. Land is very beautiful. Or, land is important to all of us. Whatever comes to mind," Isabel said. Padre Ricardo, stood at the board, chalk in hand. He wrote the people's sentences as they spoke them.

"Land is life," Tomás said.

"Land is never secure," Ana added.

"Land is the womb for the corn that nourishes life," Doña María said, poetically.

"Land is rocky," Juan said, casting a smile in the direction of Padre Ricardo.

"The land is El Patrón's," Sancho said.

Carmen spoke with confidence. "Land is God's gift to the people," she said.

"Land is owned by the few but needed by all," Elena added.

"Land, labor and seeds are gifts of love producing food for our children," Carlos said in a voice that was vibrant and musical.

"Land is God's testing ground for humanity," Rafael said as he tapped the stump of his arm.

"Land is a playground for the rich," Margarita stated.

"Land is necessary," Marcos added.

"Land is a source of medicines for the people," Rosa declared.

"Land is where we bury the children of the poor, too young and too often," Isabel said sadly.

The students stared at the list Padre Ricardo transcribed on the board:

LAND IS LIFE.
LAND IS NEVER SECURE.
LAND IS THE WOMB FOR THE CORN THAT
    NOURISHES LIFE.
LAND IS ROCKY.
THE LAND BELONGS TO EL PATRON.
LAND IS GOD'S GIFT TO THE PEOPLE.
LAND IS OWNED BY THE FEW BUT NEEDED BY
    ALL.
LAND, LABOR AND SEED ARE GIFTS OF LOVE
    PRODUCING FOOD FOR OUR CHILDREN.
LAND IS GOD'S TESTING GROUND FOR HUMAN-
    ITY.
LAND IS A PLAYGROUND FOR THE RICH.
LAND IS NECESSARY.
LAND IS A SOURCE OF MEDICINES FOR THE
    PEOPLE.
LAND IS WHERE WE BURY THE CHILDREN OF
    THE POOR, TOO YOUNG AND TOO OFTEN.

Most could not read their own sentences but for the first time they sensed a relationship between speech and the power of their words. Carmen wanted to know what Padre Ricardo had written.

"What each of you said. Exactly. Word for word," he said.

Carmen had always hated letters and words. Words had been a repulsive mystery, each letter a veiled indignity, a reminder of ignorance worthy of the misery engulfing her. She was beginning to see each letter as a gift that peeled away, wrappings that had once entrapped her soul like the outer skin of an onion.

"Show me my words," Carmen said excitedly.

Padre Ricardo pointed to the board and read her words slowly and clearly. "Land is God's gift to the people." She smiled, approvingly.

"And mine?" Doña María asked.

"Land is the womb for the corn that nourishes life," he read. Padre Ricardo read each sentence as they listened intently. Seeing and hearing words they'd spoken gave them a sense of power. The wisdom of their life experience was getting clearer, like a shoreline viewed from a boat as the fog lifts amidst the warmth of the rising sun.

"How would life be different if you had land?" Isabel asked. It was a thought unrealistic enough to most that they had trouble freeing their imaginations from the imprisonment of daily indignities. Eventually, Marcos spoke.

"We wouldn't be hungry," he said.

"We would have corn and beans to last the year," Carmen added.

"We wouldn't be slaves to debt and El Patrón," said Elena.

Tomás, who had land, looked hopeful. "If we all had land," he said, "we could work together, form cooperatives."

"With land we would have dignity," Rafael noted.

"Yes," Padre Ricardo responded. "With land we could live with more dignity. But dignity is possible. Even now." The discussion went on for a long time, first seeds in a field of dreams where a future filled with simple hopes was planted.

Fifteen

Dignified Lives

Following their first meeting at Carmen's house, the twelve had gotten together frequently for Bible study. It was a regular feature of their literacy classes. They opened their Bibles eagerly in search of more understanding of Jesus, jubilee, faith and land. Padre Ricardo looked at the list of sentences on the board.

"There are many stories that help us see how God is with us in our struggle," Padre Ricardo said. "I want to begin with a question. Rafael says that with land we could live with dignity. Do we live dignified lives?" he asked.

Silence greeted his question. He wasn't sure if the question itself was unclear or whether the group was feeling ashamed. He asked it in a different way.

"Does God love you?" he said.

The group still looked troubled, but Padre Ricardo refused to break the uncomfortable silence.

"These are difficult questions." It was Rafael who spoke. Padre Ricardo nodded. "Because," Rafael continued, "it is a dumb horse who admits he is dumb. Honesty can be painful. There is no dignity in watching our children die," he continued, "in our hunger, in our cowardice, in our ignorance. No," Rafael said, "I should not speak for the others but I for one have not lived a dignified life. And the fact that I have lived so long without dignity makes me wonder about God, too. If God loves us then why do we live in misery?"

"A very dignified answer for someone who has lived an undignified life," Padre Ricardo said with a smile.

Carmen spoke. "I believe the God you are teaching us about loves me, loves us," she said. "But this God is different from Padre Eduardo's God. All my life I heard about a God who taught me to hate myself. I am learning that God's love is the source of our dignity. We have dignity because God loves us, but it is up to us to claim our dignity."

"Rafael is right. We live in misery and our dignity isn't respected," Juan said. "But Carmen is also right. God loves us and gives us dignity. If they are both right," he continued, "then we should not blame God for our misery. We should look closer to home, to the sin of society. I don't think God wants us or anyone to live in misery."

"I'm sorry," Tomás said. "I don't understand."

"Maybe I am the one who doesn't understand," Juan said, "but if God loves us then shouldn't our country, our society work in such a way so that dignified living is possible? If we can't live dignified lives because we have no land or schools or medicines, then I think something is wrong. That is what I meant to say."

Sancho took hold of Juan's idea and bolted like a racehorse. "A society that has schools and clinics only for the rich, where land is owned by a few people, where our rights to speak freely are denied, where hunger is a way of life no matter how hard we work, is a sinful society. I think that God judges such a society harshly. It is our duty to change it."

"I have never understood sin in this way. Sin is a personal matter," Tomás said. "Between me and God. I never thought about systems being sinful."

"Does the idea of social sin make sense?" Padre Ricardo asked. Tomás and the others nodded. "The Jesus you have heard about for so many years, Padre Eduardo's Jesus, what is he like?"

"He is a victim," Sancho said. "Passive and hanging on a cross."

"A robot," Carlos added. "Padre Eduardo said God had a plan for Jesus to die. Jesus came into the world in order to die. To fulfill God's purpose," he said.

"What purpose was fulfilled by Jesus' death? Why was Jesus killed?" Padre Ricardo asked.

"Padre Eduardo said Jesus had to die for our sins so we could go to heaven," Elena said.

"But who killed Jesus?" Padre Ricardo asked. "And why?" There was a long silence.

"The Jews?" Tomás said hesitantly. "That is why they are persecuted because they killed God's son."

"But Jesus was a Jew," Padre Ricardo reminded them. "Who among the Jews wanted to kill Jesus and why?" he asked again.

"I never heard about who killed Jesus or why, " Elena said. "It's as though how Jesus lived and who killed him are unimportant."

Padre Ricardo read several passages from Mark's gospel that described Jesus' confrontation with powerful religious and political authorities.

The word gospel, he told them, was originally a military propaganda term of the Roman Empire. The gospel was the good news of Rome's military conquest, of Rome's subjugation of peoples, of Rome's intimidation of groups who dared challenge unjust Roman power and rule. Jesus, he told them, spoke of the gospel of God that challenged Rome's arrogance and authority.

In a similar way, Padre Ricardo explained, Jesus challenged religious leaders who helped Rome oppress the poor. The high priest, he told them, was the most powerful religious official in Palestine and he was appointed by Rome.

It was a coalition of Roman authorities and Jewish religious leaders who conspired together to murder Jesus. "Jesus challenged both Rome's power and the religious authorities," Padre Ricardo said. "He held them responsible for the oppression of the poor. He also encouraged the poor to hope for and work for a different future, to overcome their sense of despair, to believe in the possibility of a different order that Jesus called the kingdom of God."

"It makes sense that if Jesus came as good news to the poor, that the powerful political and religious groups would murder him," Sancho said. Padre Ricardo nodded.

Carmen looked as though a revelation had set her free.

"Now I understand why I only heard that Jesus was born and that he died and why I heard so little about his life," she said. "They killed Jesus because of how he lived. They told me to have faith in Jesus so I could get to heaven. They never told me about the faith of Jesus. Jesus was faithful to God and this led him to work for the poor. And they never said that this is why the authorities killed him."

"If Carmen is right," Padre Ricardo said, "if Jesus was killed because his faith in God led him to work for liberation then what does that mean for us, for our faith and our lives?"

"God wants us to challenge the powerful in El Salvador," Elena said. "And our own sense of despair."

"Who are the powerful in El Salvador?" Padre Ricardo asked.

"El Patrón and other large landowners," Juan said. "And the military," he added.

"I learned at the University that the rich in El Salvador, the landowners, the military, work in conjunction with the United States," Sancho said. "Maybe the United States controls El Salvador the way the Roman Empire dominated Palestine. Here much of the Church blesses whatever the U.S. wants just like the Jewish officials who worked on behalf of the Roman oppressors."

"We are the ones hurt by this," Rafael said. "It's been that way since before *La Matanza*. But," he added, "Jesus invites us to turn away from shame and despair. He gives us courage to work for change. Jesus reminds us that we have more power than we think."

Padre Ricardo looked over at Tomás. He looked doubtful. "What are you thinking?"

"I'm wondering," Tomás said, "what kind of power Jesus had. If the powerful killed even God's son, then what chance do we have? They crucified Jesus. What will they do to us?"

"They may kill us too," Sancho said. "But they are killing us already with hunger."

"What about the resurrection?" Elena asked.

"They killed Jesus. But they couldn't kill him," Margarita said. "Jesus rose from the dead."

"What does it mean to say Jesus rose from the dead?" Padre Ricardo asked.

"Death isn't the last word," Margarita said.

"What is the worst threat the military government holds over us?" Carmen asked. "It is death. The resurrection of Jesus shows that we should not be ruled by fear of death."

"I think something else is important," Rafael said. "The rich landowners say they produce for life. The military says it defends life. The Church says it blesses life. But the whole time they are speaking of life, they join forces to kill the people. I think it was the same in the time of Jesus. In the name of life the powerful crucified God's son. The cross mocks their claims for life. Their willingness to defend their privileges by killing what was good, what was truthful, even God's son, exposed them."

"If the crucifixion exposed the lies and the brutality of the powerful, then the resurrection shows the intention of God. God is a God of life. Jesus' faith, even his death, was not in vain," Margarita said. "When they murdered Jesus they exposed themselves as liars. And Jesus lives."

"Padre Eduardo said the resurrection is our ticket to heaven," Carmen said. "But, the resurrection does more than guarantee us a place with God when we die. It gives meaning to our life and struggle now. I think the resurrected Jesus lives on in our community and in other communities who try to follow the risen Christ."

Padre Ricardo smiled. It was late but there was a passage he wanted to tell them about from Isaiah. He thought of it when Elena said that land is owned by the few but needed by all and when Sancho spoke about sin being rooted in unjust economic structures.

Isaiah, Padre Ricardo explained to the twelve, was a prophet who spoke to the people of Israel at a time when rich landowners were stealing land from the poor. Margarita read from the fifth chapter: "Woe to those who join house to house, who add field to field until there is no more room, and you are made to dwell alone in the midst of the land." Padre Ricardo asked her to read it again. Margarita repeated the verse and then Rafael responded.

"The rich are taking more and more land," he said. "Isn't that what it means to add field to field?"

"Yes," Elena continued, "they have so much, and the people have no place to live. All the houses and fields belong to them. The poor have no place to plant their lives."

Juan thought of his field. "Each of us farms land that isn't our own. Our corn and beans are surrounded by coffee plants."

"When Isaiah says 'woe' he is giving a warning to the rich," Sancho added. "It is God's warning." Padre Ricardo looked at Margarita. She continued with verse nine:

"The Lord of hosts has sworn in my hearing: 'Surely many houses shall be desolate, large and beautiful houses, without inhabitant.'"

"All my life," Carmen said, "I was told God is angry with me. Angry if I don't go to mass. Angry if I don't pray to the Virgin. Angry if I am angry. Angry for all my sins. Angry if I don't pay for a priest's blessing. Never did they tell me it is a sin for the rich to steal our land and our lives, that God is angry about that."

"El Patrón has never heard this passage," Juan said with sadness. "Or he could not treat us so badly."

"He should be afraid," Marcos added, "His houses may be destroyed. Injustice cannot go on forever. Neither the people nor God will tolerate it much longer."

"Isaiah offers a new vision for the people," Padre Ricardo said as he thought of another passage that could not wait. "He not only condemns injustice, he conveys God's promise to the people." Padre Ricardo paraphrased Isaiah's words:

> The people shall build houses and live in them; they shall plant crops and eat their fruits. They shall not build only to have another rob them of a place to live; they shall not plant crops, themselves go hungry and others eat their harvest; for like the days of a tree shall the days of my people be, and my chosen shall long enjoy the work of their hands.

Night after night the twelve learned new letters and new sounds and repeated old ones. The words Isabel placed at the center of the bulletin board—*LECHE, MAIZ, MACHETE, CAFE, FRIJOLES*—brought them back to the issue of land. There were many needs in a community like Pueblo Duro, a need for schools, clinics and food. But the central issue was land.

Tomás was right. Land is life.

The people learned to read and write as letters and sounds became words, sentences and stories. They were equipped to teach others and they learned about a God who until recently was a stranger to them.

Juan left the meeting and walked directly to his field. He took his machete, cut down a row of coffee trees and planted corn.

Sixteen

ৡৣ৾ঌৢৢৣঌ

A Hell of a Statement

Antonio Méndez paced back and forth in Julio's office like a man possessed. "Why send him here?" he screamed as he polished off another shot of imported whiskey. Antonio was one of the largest landowners around Somotillo. He was president of the coffee growers association and served as mayor and local judge. "Why?" he repeated loudly to himself.

"The bishop," Raúl Ortega said, "the bishop said he had to go somewhere." His voice was grim. "He said Padre Ricardo is a young man. Still impressionable." Raúl, who headed the local police, paused weighing the absurdity of these words. "Impressionable. Shit," he continued. "The man's a God-damn Jesuit. They sent us a God-damn, trouble-making Jesuit."

Although both men were in the same room awaiting the arrival of Julio Díaz and General Calderón neither heard what the other was saying. Their fitful monologues became a conversation united in fury and by the utter impossibility of the situation. Replacing a priest was a routine, an almost insignificant event when priests knew their proper place in the order of things.

But things and priests were changing in El Salvador. It was three years since the first meeting in Carmen's home. Pueblo Duro had awakened from a deep sleep. The twelve, as Padre Ricardo predicted, had become a voice of God in the community.

Ironically, Antonio Méndez, Raúl Ortega, Julio Díaz and other rich Salvadorans once supported the Jesuit-run University in San Salvador. The Central American University, or UCA as it was called, was the product of an alliance between the rich and the Catholic Church. Each feared that communism might spread from Cuba like a communicable disease and each abhorred the radicalism of El Salvador's National University.

Once considered a safe place to educate the children of Salvador's elite families, the UCA now stood accused of producing communists and agitators like rabbits. Rich Salvadorans and the hierarchy of the Church blamed the Jesuits. Raúl looked up as if noticing Antonio for the first time.

"A goddamn trouble making Jesuit," Raúl repeated. He stroked his rifle unconsciously as he spoke.

Julio Díaz and General Calderón entered the room looking tired and somber. They were joined by Julio's son, Mario. All agreed the situation was growing more dangerous by the day.

"For the first time in years, I'm afraid," Calderón said. He puffed on an expensive Cuban cigar. The powerful in El Salvador demonized the communists but they coveted their cigars. "We've waited too long to act decisively," he continued. "The question before us is exactly what kind of response makes sense."

Raúl, who was invading Julio's liquor cabinet, looked up. "I think its time to kill a priest," he said. He offered his suggestion as casually as he selected between scotch and rum.

"I'm not sure we need to do more than we're doing now. At least not yet," Antonio responded.

"Our problem," Julio said, weighing his words carefully, "is that nothing has changed but everything has changed." He listened to his own words and nodded thoughtfully. Looking up he repeated, "Nothing has changed. Everything has changed. That is our problem." Calderón looked exasperated. "Look," Julio continued. "Nothing has changed. The land is still ours. Our party rules. Our workers bring in the coffee. The wages we pay aren't worth shit and the unions still can't do anything about it. Nothing has changed." The others listened intently, uplifted by these reasons for optimism.

"On the other hand," Julio continued, "everything has changed. We've got communist priests teaching the people to read and convincing them that they are like gods. Bible groups meet all over the country. And we had to steal the election again in '72. As a result, we now face an armed opposition. Everything has changed."

Stealing another election was a desperate measure with unforeseen consequences. Shortly after the latest electoral fraud, guerrilla groups formed. They said the oligarchy and military blocked all peaceful prospects for change, making armed rebellion necessary. These groups were now organizing, especially in the countryside. Julio looked disturbed as he spoke and the optimism faded from his friends' faces as if they had bitten into a worm-filled apple.

"There are also new political parties," he continued, "and no matter what we've done so far, the people continue organizing."

Calderón finally understood Julio's point. "What troubles me," he said, "is I'm not sure we're still in control. Something dangerous is sweeping the country. It's like the wind. We can't always see it or touch it but it's there. If everything hasn't changed it sure as hell feels like it's changing."

"The crucial difference," Raúl said returning to his earlier suggestion, "is that we can no longer count on the Church. We've got to make a statement." There was a long silence. "Killing a priest would be a hell of a statement."

"We can still count on the hierarchy," Julio cautioned. "Most of the bishops are as concerned as we are about recent events. They distrust priests like Ricardo and they know their own privileges and authority could be undermined if the communists succeed."

"Maybe," Calderón responded. "But Raúl has a point. The communities are fronts for subversive organizations, even the secular ones. Nobody has firm ground to stand on. A stick of dynamite with an unknown fuse has been lit."

"The idea of killing a priest has merit but it could be counterproductive," Julio said. "It might move the hierarchy in a direction neither we nor they want to go."

"I agree with my father. At least for now," Mario said. "But I'm not sure we know how to fight against priests, nuns and *campesinos* who cart around their goddamn Bibles."

"We better figure out how. And soon," Raúl insisted.

Antonio seemed annoyed. "It's not as though we've been sitting around doing nothing," he said. "Ricardo's got a bunch of poor *campesinos* armed with Bibles. Our *campesinos* have guns."

Over the past three years the men seated in Julio Díaz's study countered the organizing efforts of people like Padre Ricardo by forming ORDEN, the Democratic Nationalist Organization. ORDEN was an organization of poor *campesinos* controlled by rich landowners. Juan attended the founding meeting three years ago in which General Calderón handed out beer and gave a rousing speech warning of the dangers of communism.

ORDEN, he promised, would save the country from communism and help people solve problems, build schools and construct clinics.

Nearly all *campesinos* joined ORDEN, at least nominally. If you were a poor, dependent farmer you had to join. ORDEN didn't build schools or clinics but it did offer other rewards. *Campesinos* willing to spy on others were given preference for year-round jobs or chosen first for seasonal employment. They were given rifles and occasional gifts of beer and rum.

These perks, a cultivated fear of communism and an understanding of Christianity shaped by priests like Padre Eduardo, provided many poor *campesinos* with a sense of security, mission and power. ORDEN was a valuable tool for the rich. It divided *campesinos* that, if united, would be dangerous. It also was an instrument of violence. It guaranteed poor people would kill poor people if the rich decided to escalate the repression.

Julio Díaz and other large landowners discovered a bitter-sweet and unexpected ally in their efforts to form ORDEN: the weather.

El Salvador was in the midst of its second consecutive year of drought. Poor weather impinged on the profits of the rich but it illustrated more dramatically the vulnerability of the communities. As the brutal sun withered the corn and bean crops, small landholders often lost their land, and landless people like Carmen and the others needed more cash to purchase food. When poor weather reduced both the quantity and quality of their coffee beans, and therefore profits, the wealthy coffee growers tightened their grip on *campesinos* trapped already in a vicious cycle of poverty. They lowered wages.

Desperate for cash, *campesinos* accepted employment under almost any conditions. It was an environment ripe for betrayal.

"You still don't get it, do you?" Raúl said. "The Bible has been our ally for so long that you can't comprehend that it is being turned against us and that it may be more powerful than our guns. You are underestimating our adversaries and overestimating ORDEN. Shit," Raúl continued. "We've got ORDEN, but so what? ORDEN is a vehicle that needs a driver. We are the driver. We've got to give it direction. I'm saying that ORDEN should deliver a long overdue message to the Church. That's all I'm saying."

"And I'm saying *not yet*," Julio said.

The discussion was over.

Raúl's suggestion to kill a priest seemed premature to the others. But they knew he was right. The creation of ORDEN and their other efforts had not stemmed the flow of remarkable changes in communities like Pueblo Duro. Although political power, land and the military remained firmly entrenched, little else was the same.

The people Padre Ricardo called together in Carmen's home along with hundreds of other *campesinos* formed Christian base communities throughout the region. Within them poor people studied the Bible, sang songs, worshiped, learned to read and write, analyzed their society and addressed pressing issues. There were more than a hundred such groups in the region around Somotillo.

The work of the base communities, like the spindly papaya tree, bore surprising fruit. They tapped incredible energy within the people.

With limited resources and help from strategic allies, progress was made in important areas such as education and health. The people themselves led adult literacy classes. Children attended makeshift schools staffed by students from the UCA and the National University who rotated in and out of the community. Medical students from San Salvador conducted workshops for midwives and trained basic health promoters, who in turn worked with others. The emphasis was on basic hygiene and preventive measures. This was a time when it was still possible to dig latrines rather than bomb shelters.

Padre Ricardo, through a branch of Literacy International in Somotillo and other contacts in the U.S. and Europe, acquired pencils, notebooks, blackboards, chalk and other supplies. He also received vaccines and other basic medicines for health-care efforts and even raised enough money to start a revolving loan fund that helped some of the *campesinos* break their dependency on Julio Díaz. These successes were limited but measurable.

As important as the external changes were those that occurred within. People in the base communities were not the same. They no longer saw their poverty and landlessness, their sickness and dependency as inevitable. They changed. Their understanding of

God changed. They forced the country to change. It was the rich who would decide ultimately between allowing these and other changes, and turning the country into a morgue.

Julio and the others who gathered that day were not ready to murder a priest but they knew Raúl Ortega was right. Things were slipping away. They needed to steer a new direction but too many drivers had hands upon the wheel. The result was a zigzag course that headed nowhere.

At the present moment they still weren't clear either where they or the country were going or just what they should do about it.

Seventeen

The Machete

The atmosphere in Isabel's family home was that of a truce about to be broken. Her father rarely spoke to her. Mario treated her with contempt. A formal rupture was a matter of time and timing.

What was true inside Julio's mansion reflected the society as a whole. A dark cloud was enveloping Pueblo Duro and similar communities throughout El Salvador.

Elena's nerves were fraying like an old rope. "Have you seen Sancho?" she asked. Her voice registered panic. Rafael shook his head. He had seen him an hour before at Carmen's. He tried to reassure her and failed. Elena ran out the door, looked around and returned. "Have you seen Margarita?"

"No. What's wrong? Let me help you," Rafael said.

"It's Margarita," she said, desperately. "I saw her with Mario. She was crying. I think he threatened her." Mario had ignored Elena since the afternoon of the rape. His attention and her concern shifted to Margarita, now fifteen.

Elena feared that Mario had threatened to fire them if Margarita refused his sexual advances. She overheard Mario tell Margarita to meet him at eight o'clock. The meeting place was the edge of the property at the boulder overlooking the pond, where Mario often met women. Elena was in a full panic, unaware of what she was saying. "He hurt me," she blurted out. "I won't let him hurt Margarita."

"No one will hurt Margarita," Rafael said, reassuringly.

Elena remained inconsolable. She heard a sound and whirled to face Sancho. She fell into his arms and wept. Sancho held her as Rafael repeated Elena's story. It was already dark. As they left, Sancho grabbed his machete and turned to Rafael who was ready to accompany them.

"Thanks, friend," he said. "But this trouble is ours."

Elena and Sancho ran as fast as the penetrating darkness allowed. As they approached Elena's house, their desperate voices cracked the silence.

"Margarita! Margarita!"

"Elena? Sancho?"

"Yes, Mamá," she said. Elena's voice was ripe with disappointment. "We're looking for Margarita."

"Oh that girl," her mother said. "Came in crying and wouldn't eat a thing. Didn't say a word. Left about twenty minutes ago. Maybe she and Carlos had a spat."

Elena walked inside, past her father, drunk, asleep and snoring in an old chair. She reached over, took Margarita's shawl and exited into the darkness toward El Patrón's estate. The pathways were more perilous at night. About half a mile from the entrance they heard footsteps. They stopped and listened. The sounds became more distinct. Someone approached on the pathway invisible in the darkness. Elena and Sancho waited until the footsteps were very close before Elena broke the silence. "Who's there?" she asked as Sancho tightened his grip on the machete.

"Elena?"

"Margarita," Elena said.

Margarita's voice was garbled with tears. "What are you doing here?" she asked.

"We came to find you," Elena said. They stood face to face

barely visible to each other beneath the emerging light of the stars. "Did he hurt you?" Elena asked. Tears streaked down her cheeks as she remembered her own pain.

"I never saw him. Rafael stopped me. He told me not to worry and to leave."

"Go home," Sancho said.

Before Margarita could protest, Sancho and Elena disappeared into the darkness. When they reached Julio's property Elena led them to a place where they could step over the fence.

On the left stood the pond, a deep black pool, nearly invisible except for an occasional flicker of starlight dancing on the water like muted candles. A pathway to the right circled the pond. It was surrounded on both sides by thick brush. The path sloped upward leading to a slight opening where Mario waited.

The rock was invisible to them. In their haste to find Margarita and now Rafael, Elena and Sancho had made no plans for when they arrived. "Sancho," Elena whispered. "Stay a few feet behind me." She stopped and placed Margarita's shawl over her shoulders. "When Mario comes I'll tell him to leave Margarita alone." Before Sancho could respond, Elena started up the path. He walked a few steps behind, invisible in the darkness.

Elena stood in the pathway, thick brush on either side, just a few feet from the rock.

"So you came," Mario said as he scrambled down. "A wise decision," he added. "Take off your clothes," he ordered. "Let's swim." As he took a step forward he made his discovery. "Bitch," he said. "And you?" His voice rose with anger as he reached for a pistol. "A reunion of la..."

At that moment, Elena crashed into Sancho and they sprawled into the brush. As they fell they heard a horrible thud. Then footsteps followed by silence. They waited a few minutes before Elena spoke.

"What happened?" she whispered.

"I don't know," Sancho responded. "Mario must have seen me after he recognized you. I took a step forward but I was knocked off the path."

"Someone pushed me," Elena explained. "Mario was reaching for something. Before I could react I was flying through the air and hit you."

Sancho and Elena made their way out of the brush cautiously onto the path. Mario's body lay still, a gun by his side. The thud they heard was a crushing blow to the side of Mario's neck. Someone killed Mario with the dull side of a machete. Had the murderer used the sharp edge, Mario might have been decapitated.

Elena and Sancho fled quickly.

They arrived at Padre Ricardo's out of breath, desperation rising within them. They pounded on the door and shouted but were greeted by silence. They tried to collect their thoughts, an impossible task given the circumstances and their exhaustion. Mario was dead. His body would be discovered in the morning.

Their minds swam in the backwaters of unanswered questions. What would Julio do? Did anyone else know Mario was meeting Margarita? Where was Rafael? What would happen to him? Should Elena and Margarita return to work? Could they act as if nothing happened? Where was Padre Ricardo?

At that moment Padre Ricardo ran up the pathway. He looked distraught. "Padre," Elena said. "Julio's son, Mario, has been killed."

Padre Ricardo opened the door. "Come in," he said, wearily. He lit the lamp and sat down with Sancho and Elena.

He looked as if he had encountered the devil. His eyes red, his face contorted, his cheeks flushed with tears. It was as if a recent event and horrible premonition took hold of his soul, threatening to overwhelm him. Padre Ricardo took a deep breath as he twisted a paper in his hand unconsciously. Suddenly aware of the paper, he walked over to the table by his bed and placed it within the lone drawer. He returned to his chair.

"Tell me what happened," he said.

They recounted Mario's threat to Margarita, their scheduled reunion, how Rafael stopped her on the pathway, and the events by the rock.

"Did you see Rafael?" Padre Ricardo asked.

"Not since we left his house," Sancho responded.

With the help of the lantern the three made their way along the pathway. As they approached Rafael's house, he sat outside smoking a cigarette. He retrieved a bench and the four of them sat down.

"Is Margarita okay?" Rafael asked.

"She's fine," Elena responded. "She said you sent her home. Thank you," she added.

"Mario was a bad man," Rafael said blowing a puff of smoke. "He hurt a lot of people. A human life is precious and maybe God finds good where we can't see it," he added, thoughtfully. "But I'm not sad he's dead."

Tears flowed down Elena's cheeks. She felt, and perhaps they all realized, they were talking to a condemned man.

"What happened?" Sancho asked him.

"You tell me," he said.

Sancho looked on in disbelief as Rafael took a long puff on his cigarette. "Did you kill him?" Sancho asked. Rafael took off his hat and rubbed his fingers across his forehead. "Maybe yes. Maybe no," he said. "It doesn't much matter. Mario is dead. We'll have to wait and see what happens next." Sancho wanted to ask again but Rafael spoke first. "Look," he said. "All we can do is wait. The next move is Julio's. Whether or not I killed Mario depends."

"On what?" Sancho asked. "He's dead."

"On what's best for the community," Rafael answered. Before Sancho or Elena could probe further, Padre Ricardo spoke.

"Rafael is right," he said. "We must wait. Spread the word to the others. We're meeting before worship tomorrow at Carmen's."

Padre Ricardo walked Sancho and Elena home and then returned to his house. He blew out the lantern, walked over to the table by his bed, opened the drawer and removed the piece of paper he had placed there earlier. He put it in a plastic bag, stuffed the bag inside a jar and walked outside. He dug a hole next to the rose bushes he'd planted by the house, placed the jar within the hole and covered it. Padre Ricardo went inside, plopped himself on the bed.

He wondered if this would be the last night of peace in the community. Before finishing his thought he was overcome by exhaustion and fell asleep.

———

A guard found Mario's body the following morning. Isabel, upon hearing the news, went to her father's study. She sat on her father's desk as her father refilled a drink at the liquor cabinet. It was the second to the last time she saw him. She expressed regrets, reached around, and turned the intercom button to its ON position. She left the room, went immediately to the laundry and waited. Within an hour Julio Díaz was surrounded by his son, Miguel, Raúl Ortega, Antonio Méndez, and General Calderón. They were there to express condolences and to avenge Mario's death.

Although tragic, his death provided a welcome pretext for the repression to begin.

"His neck was broken by a hard blow with a machete," Raúl reported. "Any idea who he was meeting?" he asked. He seemed disinterested in the response.

"He met girls up there," Julio said. "I doubt one of them killed him with a machete."

"Not likely," Raúl agreed.

"Perhaps a jealous boyfriend," Miguel offered.

"I think I know who murdered Mario," Raúl said. "I don't know why but I think I know who." The others looked at him in disbelief. Raúl Ortega paused for effect. "I don't have proof," he said. "If necessary we make our own proof."

"Get on with it," Julio said both interested and annoyed.

"Whoever delivered the blow probably stood behind Mario," Raúl said. "If his killer approached from the front Mario could have seen the blow coming and deflected it with his arms. There's only one mark on him, at the point on his neck where the machete struck."

"It's possible someone got close and hit him from the front," Miguel interjected. "Before he could react. After all it was dark."

"Possible but not likely," Raúl countered. "More likely he was hit from behind. Never saw it coming. If he was hit from behind then his murderer is left-handed." He took another shot of whiskey. Raúl Ortega was clearly impressed with himself.

"How do you figure?" Miguel asked.

"If he was killed from behind," Raúl said, turning Miguel away from him so as to illustrate his point, "and his murderer was right-handed then the machete would naturally land here." He swung his right arm down and stopped it where Mario's right shoulder connected to his neck. "A blow from someone left handed, delivered from behind, would naturally be on the left side." Miguel conceded the point.

"We know exactly one left-handed campesino," Raúl said, triumphantly. "He happens to be an expert with a machete."

Eighteen

Communion

Padre Ricardo and Carlos proceeded to the chapel following the meeting at Carmen's. They were joined by the others, minus Rafael who agreed reluctantly to hide out at Tomás and Ana's. Padre Ricardo stood nervously behind the altar of the newly constructed church.

The partially enclosed structure was simple and practical. Its roof was made of gray asbestos panels. Its lone wall, patched together with handmade bricks, mortar and community sweat, held a sturdy, wooden cross. Fewer walls meant less expense, more air to break the stifling heat and greater flexibility. People who would suffocate in an enclosed building gathered around the edges. Padre Ricardo liked the open chapel that he said invited participation by the people and God's spirit.

Padre Ricardo put on his robe as the people looked on. It was one of the many ways he communicated that a priest was a simple human being, as was Jesus, as were all the people of God. Carlos hooked up the battery powered sound system as parishioners from invisible houses and hamlets poured into the mass. Some carried children. Some chairs. Some Bibles. Some all three. Children played tag around the altar, dodging lethargic dogs who slept or collapsed wherever they pleased.

Padre Ricardo once suggested to researchers at the UCA that the best way to determine the economic well-being of a community would be to survey its dogs. Dogs offered an uncanny and accurate measure of social position. The dogs of the rich had names and enough flesh to cover their bones. The dogs in Pueblo Duro wandered aimlessly, their ribs protruding from their sides like the rocks in Juan's field.

As the people gathered, Carmen chased one dog from the baptismal font, where it was taking a long drink.

"Padre," Carlos said. "Company."

Padre Ricardo looked up. He followed Carlos' pointing finger to the edge of the field. "Looks more like trouble," Padre Ricardo said. The men in Julio's study had mobilized quickly.

This was not the first time soldiers from the garrison were visible at the community's mass. Padre Ricardo's sermons were recorded by members of ORDEN. Indistinguishable from the others, except for their motives for attending worship, they sometimes received a special welcome from Padre Ricardo. This added to their discomfort but seemed to ease the tension for the rest of the congregation like the removal of a mask from an unsuspecting villain.

In sharp contrast to Padre Eduardo, Ricardo's sermons were participatory. He invited parishioners to share insights into the gospel text. It took courage to speak. An hour after mass, those under the employ of General Calderón or Julio's son, Miguel, scrutinized every word. Today the soldiers were heavily armed and led by Calderón himself.

Padre Ricardo surveyed the poor and simple people before him. They sat in chairs carried from their homes. Or on the ground. Others stood. All held song sheets that Carmen and the others handed out. Many had learned to read through the literacy efforts of the community. The music was written by Carlos or borrowed from the Nicaraguan *Campesino Mass*. The words were powerful and courageous. To the government, they would seem threatening.

The soldiers inched forward, completely surrounding the gathering. The pit growing in Padre Ricardo's stomach threatened to explode until he noticed two gringos near the back of the chapel. Whatever Calderón had planned might be tempered by their presence.

"Before we begin," Padre Ricardo said, "I would like to thank our special guests for joining us." The people turned their necks to see. Foreigners were as rare in Pueblo Duro as a good meal. "Would you come forward and introduce yourselves," he asked. A young woman walked to the front and spoke.

"My friend and I are literacy trainers from the United States. We work here in El Salvador with Literacy International. My name is Cynthia and this is my co-worker Peter. We are here to learn about your country and to help communities with literacy programs. We are grateful for the opportunity to worship with you."

As the congregation applauded, Padre Ricardo breathed a sigh of relief. The presence of foreigners might handicap Calderón, who was unlikely to risk an international incident.

"These people are not strangers to us," Padre Ricardo said. "We have received pencils and paper used in our literacy training from Literacy International." This led to greater applause.

"I would like to invite our other guests to put down their guns and join us for worship," he continued.

There was an uneasy silence as the soldiers tightened their circle around the worshippers. They stood rigidly, guns by their sides.

The entrance hymn borrowed from the Nicaraguan *Campesino Mass* nourished Padre Ricardo's courage. "You are the God of the poor," the people bellowed with Carlos leading them. "The human and simple God. The God that sweats in the street. The God with a weathered face." Their deformed harmonies might have offended the deaf, yet the spirit of God seemed present in their voices. "For this reason," they sang more loudly still, "I speak to you as my people speak. You are the laborer God. The worker Christ."

Three years ago no one could have imagined a scene such as this in Pueblo Duro. But now, you could feel the confidence of the people. The music seemed to name and mysteriously change their reality.

After the song Carmen offered a prayer. It included thanks for the presence of their North American friends and a petition for the soldiers and their families.

Another song followed, a song whose words made it clear why its Nicaraguan writer was living in exile:

> Christ, Jesus Christ, identify with us.
> God, Lord God, identify with us.
> Not with the oppressor class
> that exploits and devours the community.
> But with the oppressed,
> with my people who thirst for peace.

Calderón stared ominously from the back of the chapel. He took a step forward and stopped as Doña María read the gospel:

> And Jesus lifted up his eyes on his disciples, and said: "Blessed are you poor, for yours is the kingdom of God. Blessed are you that hunger now, for you shall be satisfied. Blessed are you who weep now, for you shall laugh. Blessed are you when people hate you, and when they exclude you and revile you, and cast out your name as evil, on account of the Human One...
>
> But woe to you that are rich, for you have received your consolation. Woe to you that are full now, for you shall hunger. Woe to you that laugh now, for you shall mourn and weep. Woe to you when all speak well of

you, for so their parents did to the false prophets.

But I say to you that hear, 'Love your enemies, do good to those who hate you, bless those who curse you, pray for those who abuse you.' "

Padre Ricardo positioned himself in the midst of the people. "We have heard the gospel. It is a message of hope, a call to conversion and a plea for forgiveness. What does this gospel mean in our community?" he asked.

"It means we should not be surprised that the authorities are here with guns and tape recorders," Sancho said. "They treat us with contempt, exclude us from the common table where all Salvadorans have a right to eat. And," he said his voice cracking with emotion, "they call us communists and threaten us because we dare to speak, dare to take the words of Jesus seriously."

"And what are these words of Jesus?" Padre Ricardo asked.

A woman breast-feeding her child spoke: "We must hate injustice and work for change without hating those who are responsible."

"In the kingdom there is a reversal," someone else said. "Neither hunger nor unjust riches will last forever."

An old man stood up near the front of the chapel. "I would like to ask our friends from the United States a question," he said. "Look at the soldiers. Whose guns do they carry?"

He paused and then proceeded to answer his own question. "They are your guns, your government's gift to ours. Do you think these guns and these soldiers are here to protect us?"

A few of the people laughed. It was an uncomfortable laugh, a laugh of remorse and courage. The distribution of communion was tense as the soldiers grew restless in the brutal sun. Padre Ricardo, Elena, Margarita, Carlos, Doña María and Sancho stood with plates of communion wafers at various stations. As people made their way forward, Carmen walked to the alter and prepared an additional plate.

She made her way through the crowd and outside the church to where the soldiers stood. Without looking up, she stood in front of a soldier and spoke hesitantly, "The Body of Christ," she said.

There was no response.

The soldier raised the butt of his rifle slowly. A flick of his wrist would crush her jaw. Carmen looked directly into his eyes.

"The Body of Christ," she repeated, this time with more courage.

The soldier's arm relaxed. He set his gun down beside him and Carmen placed a wafer on his tongue. Carmen proceeded along the ring of soldiers offering communion. She looked at them and saw a mixture of fear and friendship. They too were poor. They were capable of killing her tomorrow but she knew Jesus was right. These were not enemies to be hated. For the moment at least, Carmen disarmed them with a wafer.

The final person in Padre Ricardo's line was Calderón. By the time he reached the front all eyes looked expectantly upon them. Padre Ricardo held out a communion wafer. "The Body of Christ," he said.

Calderón reached out as if to take the wafer and then clamped handcuffs on Padre Ricardo's wrists. The people stood up and surrounded them. At the same moment soldiers moved forward, their guns readied for violence.

"It's okay," Padre Ricardo said. The confidence with which he spoke calmed them. "They arrest me before a crowd of witnesses. Continue with the mass."

The stunned parishioners opened a path through which Padre Ricardo and Calderón passed. Murmurs gave way to an eerie silence. Carmen walked to the front of the chapel.

"The mass is not over," she said. "Let us sing the song Carlos taught us last week." Carlos picked up his guitar. The words they sang were prophetic.

> Just as our hope was defeated,
> Clear came the voice of the Spirit:
> See how your brothers have not given up
> in the struggle to better the world.
> See how your sisters have not given up
> in the struggle to better the world.

As Padre Ricardo was dragged away their voices, tentative at first, rose with courage.

> Just as our hope was defeated.
> Clear came the voice of the Spirit:
> I will be with you and I will uplift you
> and give you the strength to endure.
> I will be with you and I will uplift you
> and give you the strength to endure.

They joined arms and sang the chorus:

> God is uplifting the people.
> God is the power within us.
> Hope is our music and freedom our song
> And together our voices will ring.

On the dark day in which Allende was murdered and Chilean democracy undone, Peter had not heard Victor Jara's defiant music at the coliseum—the place where the military had locked up thousands of Chileans considered subversive by the U.S.-sponsored dictatorship. He heard it today, and it rekindled feelings and memories within him that he had safely deposited away from his heart.

Peter and Cynthia were starting on a risky journey. They did not know if they were traveling together, or where it would lead.

Nineteen

Betrayal

"Dwight Bench?"

"Yes. Who is this?"

"I can't say but there's a story unfolding that you might be interested in."

Dwight Bench, a reporter for the *Times* stationed in El Salvador received lots of dead-end phone calls that began like this. "Go ahead," he said skeptically.

"A priest in Pueblo Duro, Padre Ricardo, was taken into custody this morning during the worship service. General Calderón was the officer in charge."

"Calderón?" Dwight Bench's interest was piqued. He had evidence linking the general with a variety of human rights violations.

"Yes."

"Pueblo Duro is near Somotillo?" Bench asked.

"Yes."

"How do you know about Calderón's arrest of a priest?" Bench asked.

"I was there. Look, they took Padre Ricardo to the garrison outside of Somotillo. People from the communities are outside. The situation is volatile. Good-bye."

Cynthia Randolph hung up the phone.

"Padre Ellacuría?"

"Yes," he said.

"There's a young man here from Pueblo Duro who says Padre Ricardo has been arrested."

Padre Ellacuría looked up from his typewriter. His desk was neat, his shelves filled with books on educational theory and theology. He was a tall man, thin and balding with wire-rim glasses and a warm smile. "Send him in," he said.

Sancho entered the office and introduced himself. Padre Ellacuría poured water into two glasses from a pitcher on his desk. The two men drank as Sancho explained what had happened, including Mario's death and the arrest of Padre Ricardo at the community's morning mass. Padre Ellacuría stood up, and he and Sancho headed out the door on their way to the Bishops' Conference.

They were greeted by a nun whose mission seemed to be to drive visitors away. Bishop Rivera y Damas, she informed them, was away and would not return until the following Saturday. No. No one else was available to see them. Perhaps if they came back later in the week. It was Sunday after all. Yes. Another bishop was there but he was too busy to see them. Yes. She understood that it was urgent, but the new Archbishop had to prepare for his induction mass. She could not possibly disturb him. After much arguing back and forth, Oscar Romero opened the door to his office to see if he could quell the disturbance.

"Ignacio," he said. "Sister Loren. Thank you for your persistence but please let Ignacio and his friend in."

Padre Ellacuría knew Romero was a good man, but that he was a man of books with a conservative training. That's why the bishops considered him a safe choice for Archbishop. The oligarchy and military were pleased with his selection because Romero was unlikely to involve himself in the political controversies of the day.

"Thank you for seeing us," Padre Ellacuría said. "Sancho, tell the Archbishop what happened this morning during mass."

"I'm from Pueblo Duro. Padre Ricardo is our priest," Sancho began.

"I know his parents," Romero responded. "And I've heard more than a few complaints from Julio Díaz and other land owners in the area," he added. "I also know Ricardo is a good man and a good priest."

"General Calderón surrounded our church with soldiers during this morning's mass," Sancho said, "and arrested Padre Ricardo as he gave communion."

"But why?"

"Julio Díaz's son was killed last night. They are seeking revenge. They do not like the awakening of the people," he said.

Father Ellacuría reinforced Sancho's concern. "It's an emergency or we wouldn't be here. Padre Ricardo has received numerous death threats. If we let them arrest a priest during Mass without protest what will they do next? They are capable of worse."

"I agree that arresting a priest during communion is outrageous. Where are they holding him?" Romero asked.

"At the garrison outside Somotillo," Sancho responded.

Romero picked up the phone and motioned to the men to sit down. After a few minutes his call was put through. "This is Bishop, ah, Archbishop Romero," he said. "I want to speak to General Calderón."

After several minutes a voice at the other end responded.

"Archbishop Romero?"

"Yes," Romero said.

"This is Captain Canales. I'm sorry but General Calderón is very busy. He is unable to speak to you."

"Then I'll wait," Archbishop Romero said, firmly.

"But you may be waiting a long time," Captain Canales said.

"I'll wait," he repeated.

After several minutes Calderón spoke. "Archbishop. How good of you to call. Congratulations on your new position," he said.

Romero ignored the flattery. "I understand you arrested Padre Ricardo," he said.

"It became necessary to question him about a number of important matters," Calderón said.

"Such as?"

"The murder of Julio Díaz's son," Calderón said.

"You can't think Padre Ricardo was involved in a murder?" Romero responded.

"You misunderstand, Archbishop. But he may know a good deal about the murderer."

Romero's tone grew severe. "And so you found it necessary to surround his church and arrest him during Mass?"

"These are delicate matters. I'm sure you understand why I cannot tell you everything we know. Let us say we want to talk to Padre Ricardo about his connections to subversives in the area. It is for his own protection. We don't want him getting into trouble. He needs to understand that people don't like communists. Don't worry. He will not be harmed. He will be released soon."

"How soon?" Romero asked.

"Good day Archbishop." Calderón hung up the phone.

"What did he say?" Padre Ellacuría inquired.

"Padre Ricardo is not harmed. He will be released soon," Romero said.

Padre Ellacuría looked skeptical. "I would like to believe him but I think it would be a mistake," he said.

Romero stood up. "Keep me posted," he said.

"We are leaving for Somotillo. Could you join us?" Sancho asked.

"I'm afraid that's impossible," Romero said.

"Thank you for seeing us and for making the call. That is a

big help," Padre Ellacuría said, diplomatically.

They walked out of Romero's office and past the nun. Ellacuría checked his knuckles for bruises. The two men departed immediately for Somotillo, worried about Padre Ricardo, disappointed that Romero did not accompany them, but hopeful.

———

The charred remains of Rafael's house smoldered as Marcos, Elena and the López's returned from the mass. "My God," Elena gasped. "How could they know Rafael killed Mario?"

"Maybe they don't," Ana said. "If they suspect him in any way that is reason enough for them."

Tomás looked troubled. "Thank God he wasn't here," he said. "I hope he's okay."

When they arrived at the López house, Rafael was nowhere to be found. There was no sign of struggle. His machete stood leaning against the door. Apparently Rafael had gone willingly with his captors.

"I wonder..." Marcos began, then decided to leave his sentence unfinished. After the meeting at Carmen's, he realized, someone had alerted the authorities as to Rafael's whereabouts.

There was a traitor in the community.

Twenty

The Massacre

People sometimes "disappeared" while in the custody of General Calderón. The disappeared turned up dead if they turned up at all. The situation outside the garrison was tense. Hundreds of people from base communities carried signs: "FREE PADRE RICARDO." "STOP THE REPRESSION." By the time news of Rafael's arrest reached the crowd, the encroaching nightfall lost out to candles as the darkness called forth light from every flame. Within minutes "FREE RAFAEL" signs were visible.

"You're Carmen?"

"Yes," Carmen responded.

"I'm Cynthia and this is Peter. We were at the worship this morning."

"Oh yes," Carmen smiled, reached out instinctively and hugged them.

"We're concerned about what's happened," Cynthia said. "If it's okay we'd like to stay," she added.

"Of course," Carmen said, warmly. "We're grateful for your presence."

When Sancho and Ignacio arrived at the garrison, they saw Elena and Carlos feeding the people's spirits with music. Sancho embraced Elena.

Their reunion was interrupted by a stern warning from a soldier standing atop a guard tower that overlooked the entrance. "Disperse," he yelled through a megaphone. He was flanked by other heavily armed soldiers. "You have five minutes. Clear the entrance."

Doña María looked at Carmen. "What shall we do?"

The soldier repeated his warning. "You have five minutes. Disperse. Now."

The community gathered to make a decision.

"We should stay," Sancho said. "If we leave they will do what they want to Rafael and Padre Ricardo."

"I think we should go," Tomás countered. "What good is it to let them shoot us down?"

———

Carmen seemed calm. "I think we should move away from the entrance. We can stand over there." Carmen pointed to a grassy area less than thirty yards away. "Once things settle down we can demand to meet General Calderón. I am willing to request such a meeting," she said.

Sancho, retreating from his own suggestion, accepted Carmen's idea. The others agreed.

"This is your final warning," the soldier yelled. The megaphone magnified his evil intent. "Clear the entrance or we will open fire."

The crowd moved away from the gate as the soldier spoke. An uneasy calm prevailed. Carmen and Sancho walked to the entrance. They carried a candle and a white handkerchief. Soldiers, fingers poised nervously on the triggers of their rifles, tracked each of their steps. The thirty-yard journey seemed to last forever, like a childhood dream in which the flight from danger is obstructed by feet stuck in cement or quicksand. They reached the door, knocked and waited. After several minutes, an officer made his way to the door. It was Captain Canales. "What do you want?" he asked.

"We want to see General Calderón," Carmen said.

"That's impossible," Canales responded.

Carmen persisted. "We want to see General Calderón," she said again. "We want assurance that Rafael and Padre Ricardo are unharmed."

"Wait here," Canales said as he turned and walked away. He returned a few minutes later. "General Calderón has agreed to see you," he said. He led them into an office and left the room. A few minutes later Calderón entered. "What is it you want?" he said.

"We want to see Padre Ricardo and Rafael," Carmen said. "Why have they been detained?"

Calderón's desk was covered with papers and pencils. He reached into a drawer and removed a piece of paper. He handed it to Sancho. "As you can see," he said, "Rafael confessed to the murder of Mario Díaz. As for Padre Ricardo, we are questioning him about a variety of matters. He is unharmed."

"We are not leaving until we see them," Sancho said boldly.

Calderón glared at Sancho.

"You should not be so eager to remain. You may not like our hospitality," he said. "Captain Canales!" he shouted. Canales stood outside Calderón's office. He entered immediately. "Take our friends to see the prisoners. Then show them the door." He spoke angrily, but his decision to let them see their friends was calculated, its impact premeditated.

Canales led Sancho and Carmen down two flights of stairs into a dingy basement. The halls, dark and damp, were lined with cells on either side. They passed a room marked INTERROGA-TION and continued on to a cell at the end of the hall. Canales ordered the guard to open the door.

Before them, hanging from wall chains was Rafael, unconscious and barely recognizable. Rafael's torturers had eaten into his flesh like unfettered piranha in a human sea of tears. Cigarette burns left welts on his back and chest. His testicles were obscenely swollen, the aftereffect of repeated electric shock. His lips, puffy

131

and disfigured from constant beatings, merged with his fractured nose. The fingers on his left hand were broken. Before they reached Rafael the guard thrust a rifle in their faces.

"Unfortunately," Canales said, his voice without emotion, "Rafael resisted arrest. We hope he'll recover sufficiently for his trial. So we can hang him," he added. The guard laughed.

"Where's Padre Ricardo?" Carmen demanded. The guard's grim expression made Carmen shudder as they continued down the corridor to where Padre Ricardo was held.

His cell was a tiny cubicle, three feet high, three feet wide and four feet long. It reminded Carmen of a smaller, more cynical version of the housing Julio Díaz provided seasonal coffee pickers: eight foot by eight foot rooms stacked on top of each other in unventilated warehouses where entire families crowded during the coffee harvest. The door to Padre Ricardo's cell was about the size of a cardboard box. It provided sufficient space for a mid-sized man to crawl through. Canales, now flanked by three guards, opened the door.

Padre Ricardo lay crumpled within.

"Come out communist fool," Canales screamed. "We regret that you have received unequal treatment. Equality is one of your demands, no?" The soldiers smiled.

"Are you okay?" Carmen asked.

Padre Ricardo climbed out of his cell. He wobbled precariously like a three-legged table. It took a minute for his eyes to focus. "I'm fine," he said. "They seem reluctant to leave marks on a priest and so they torture me with Rafael's screams."

"He is barely alive," Sancho responded.

"That's enough," Canales snapped. He grabbed Padre Ricardo by the hair and slammed him to the floor. As the guards bent over Padre Ricardo, Canales placed a small, folded paper, about the size of a quarter, into Sancho's hand. Overcoming his initial surprise Sancho shoved it discreetly into his pocket.

"There are hundreds of people from the communities outside," Carmen said, reassuringly. "We won't leave without you."

"Tell the others I'm okay," Padre Ricardo said as Canales kicked him in the back. "Include a doctor for Rafael in your demands." Padre Ricardo crawled into the cell. As the door slammed he lay in total darkness.

Canales, accompanied by a guard, took Carmen and Sancho to the front door. They exited and walked over to the crowd. Sancho removed the paper from his pocket. He placed it near a candle, avoiding its flame but seeking to read its message in the dancing light. He strained to make out two words hastily scribbled:

OPERATION CAIN

Sancho knew something significant had happened but he had no idea what it meant. Canales, despite apparent hostility, had communicated with them. What he said was a mystery. Sancho placed the paper in his pocket. At that moment his thoughts were interrupted by Carmen's voice and the expectations of the crowd.

"Padre Ricardo is okay," Carmen said. The people strained to hear and moved closer. "He is held in a cell too small for him to sit, stand or lie down comfortably. Otherwise he is fine. His spirits are good. He is grateful for our concern."

"Unfortunately, we can not say the same for Rafael," Sancho said. "He has been badly tortured."

"They say he confessed to Mario's murder," Carmen added. "They showed us a confession with his signature."

In El Salvador prisoners could be detained for days without charge, and the courts accepted confessions even if obtained under torture. As the people listened in stunned silence, Dwight Bench stood off to the side taking careful notes. Carmen looked at the people.

"Those of you who can, return to your homes," Carmen said.

"Get a good rest and return tomorrow. Some of us will maintain a vigil throughout the night," she continued. "We will stay..." and then she paused. It was a long pause, unconscious and uncomfortable. Carmen was only half present. "We will stay," she repeated, "until Padre Ricardo is released and Rafael has seen a doctor."

Carmen's thoughts were short-circuited by a face visible in the candlelight. Cynthia, noticing the distraction, tracked the field of Carmen's vision to see the source of Carmen's anxiety. It was a face of a stranger and yet the face of someone strangely familiar.

When Cynthia realized who it was, it was already too late.

She was helpless, like a driver fated for an accident, immobilized by a deer visible in a car's headlights on a dark night. The familiar stranger was the first soldier Carmen had given communion to at Mass. He was dressed in civilian clothes. He, who had raised his rifle as if to crush Carmen's skull and instead received a communion wafer, once again raised a gun.

He fired a shot in the direction of the garrison and sprinted away. Cynthia knew this was not a shot intended to kill but a pretext to justify killing.

As the sound of the bullet drifted into the night, she screamed and hurled her body into the crowd knocking Carmen and Carlos to the ground.

Simultaneously, soldiers from the garrison fired into the crowd. People tripped over bullet-ridden bodies as they ran. Peter dragged Sancho, who took a bullet in the back of his left thigh, to safety. In doing so he himself was hit. He felt a mixture of warmth and pain as blood trickled down his arm.

By the time the shooting stopped, eighteen people were dead and dozens of others wounded. The soldiers made no attempt to pursue the unarmed protesters.

This was not yet a war. It was a message, a lesson in violence from El Salvador's powerful minority. Ignacio and most of the twelve had been fortunate. They were standing beside Carmen when the incident began. As Cynthia tackled Carmen and Carlos they became human dominos knocking others to the ground. The initial burst of gunfire passed above, enabling them to scramble to safety. Others, including Rosa, weren't so lucky. She took a bullet in the chest and died instantly.

Cynthia nearly panicked when she realized she had lost track of Peter during the chaotic moments following the massacre. She didn't know how serious his wounds were, and the uncertainty left her feeling dizzy, almost sick. Finally, she found him sitting next to Carmen two blocks from the garrison. Carmen had ripped a piece of cloth from her shirt and covered what turned out to be a superficial but painful wound. She walked over and thanked Carmen, who set off for Pueblo Duro. Cynthia knelt beside him.

Neither could find words for what had just happened.

She put her head on his shoulder and wept. Peter was thinking of the lives she had saved through her quick response to the soldier's provocation. Cynthia was thinking much the same about him. Peter had risked his life on behalf of people their report counted as enemies.

After several moments she lifted her head, looked at him shrouded in the mystery of the evening's grief and kissed him.

—

Dwight Bench captured part of the horror with his camera. He returned to his car to find it surrounded by soldiers. Foreign journalists would be killed in El Salvador but not tonight. They merely took his camera bag and film. Bench filed a story with the *Times* when he returned to San Salvador:

PRIEST ARRESTED,
SUPPORTERS MASSACRED
IN EL SALVADOR
18 die, dozens wounded including one U.S. citizen
by Dwight Bench

The conflict in El Salvador took another ugly turn when a priest was arrested Sunday morning during Mass and his followers gunned down later that evening during a peaceful vigil demanding his release.

Padre Ricardo Silva, the detained priest, is credited by some and blamed by others for awakening *campesinos* in this impoverished community.

In an area where hunger and landlessness exist side by side with the estates of some of El Salvador's wealthiest and most influential landholders, Padre Ricardo has formed Christian base communities, or BCCs.

The BCCs consist of small groups who gather for Bible study, analysis of problems, and action. In a country where education is a constitutional right yet unavailable to the majority, BCCs carry out literacy training and run schools. In areas where medicines and doctors are scarce and expensive, BCCs train health workers and operate clinics. The BCCs also form cooperatives and agitate for land reform. They are considered a vital expression of Christian faith by some and fronts for communist subversion by their detractors.

"They arrested Padre Ricardo in an effort to intimidate us," one member of the community said.

A local politician who requested anonymity saw it differently. "Our country is under attack. Regrettably, communists have infiltrated the churches. Padre Ricardo is a subversive." Referring to Padre Ricardo's supporters he added: "They are all subversives."

According to eyewitnesses, the church in Pueblo Duro was surrounded by soldiers under the command of General Aldolfo Calderón, a regional garrison commander with close ties to U.S. officials and a reputation for human rights abuses.

A U.S. embassy spokesman decried Padre Ricardo's arrest and indicated that his release appeared imminent. Padre Ricardo was detained at the garrison prison outside Somotillo along with another community member, Rafael Moises. Mr. Moises was picked up shortly after Padre Ricardo's arrest. He has been charged with the murder of Mario Díaz, the son of a wealthy landowner.

According to witnesses who were given permission to see the prisoners, Mr. Moises was severely tortured. Padre Ricardo is being held in a solitary cell barely big enough to hold his crumpled body.

The conflict turned bloody when supporters of Padre Ricardo gathered peacefully outside the garrison walls. In the presence of this reporter, a shot was fired from the crowd in the direction of the garrison. The gunman then fled. Soldiers from the garrison opened fire immediately into the crowd, killing eighteen people and wounding dozens more. One of the injured was a U.S. citizen, hit as he helped drag others to safety.

"The initial shot was fired by a soldier dressed in civilian clothes," Carmen Juárez said. "I gave communion to the same soldier this morning. His shot was an invitation to murder."

The embassy spokesman, in response to this account of events, said further investigation was needed but that preliminary reports indicated the soldiers' return of fire was justified.

HARVEST OF CAIN

Dwight Bench knew that Salvadoran soldiers were not his only censors. He faced editors who seemed reluctant to report negatively about actions taken by U.S.-backed forces. He wondered if and how long they would let him speak.

Twenty-one

Doubt

General Calderón, Julio Díaz and the others felt satisfied. They had delivered an intimidating message and had sent a chill throughout the community without murdering a priest.

Raúl Ortega smiled at the thought of arresting Padre Ricardo during communion. His arrest, punctuated by Rafael's torture and the brutal slayings outside the garrison, let the *campesinos* know that no one was safe. They could read and sing and even hope for a different future, but the present still belonged to landowners like Julio and to the generals.

In less than twenty-four hours of calculated violence, the community leadership had been decimated. Rosa was dead. Rafael imprisoned. There was also the specter of Rafael's betrayer. Someone from the community had told the authorities where to find Rafael. Reestablishing trust within the community would hinge on discovering who had betrayed him.

The authorities were so pleased with themselves that they were blind to the negative consequences of their actions. Julio's fears that direct confrontation with the Church might trigger an unpredictable response from the hierarchy proved accurate. Romero never again took the word of the generals. The guerrillas also benefited from the massacre. The bloodbath offered vivid testimony to the ruthlessness of El Salvador's elite and it demonstrated to many the limitations of unarmed resistance. Largely invisible in the area around Somotillo, armed groups began to operate.

Another consequence of recent events was that Peter and Cynthia were positioned to infiltrate the Church movements. Their presence at mass and massacre, Literacy International's contributions to community education efforts and the bullet taken by Peter, reinforced the community's trust.

And so Peter and Cynthia temporarily left the comforts of their elegant apartments (courtesy of the Agency) in a wealthy neighborhood of San Salvador, in favor of humble accommodations in Pueblo Duro. Cynthia arranged to help with literacy classes; Peter to accompany Padre Ricardo. In the aftermath of his arrest and the events that followed, Padre Ricardo agreed to be shadowed by a North American. The reasoning was logical enough. Salvadoran authorities might pay a political price for killing a priest but killing a U.S. citizen risked tripling the cost to themselves in terms of international scrutiny.

The community had no way of knowing their insurance policy in the person of Peter Jones could be a double edged sword. On the one, hand Padre Ricardo seemed safer because of Peter's accompaniment. On the other hand, Peter was a CIA agent. The U.S. embassy and key Salvadoran officials would presumably have instant access to the thoughts and actions of the Church movements.

Following the massacre, Cynthia and Peter's first encounter with Robert Barnes was tense.

"What were you doing?" Robert said through clenched teeth as they made their way around the track. The coliseum in downtown San Salvador was open to joggers. The crowd at the track provided a cover for their secret meetings. Robert's body contorted as he sought to keep his volume down while communicating the agitation he felt.

"We were doing our jobs," Peter replied.

"You damn near got yourselves killed," Robert responded, indignantly.

"Talk to Calderón about that," Cynthia said.

"I may have, had I known you were outside the garrison. From now on you plan on doing something like that, you talk to me first."

Cynthia pointed out the obvious flaw in Robert's thinking. "We can't do our jobs if we have to clear everything we do," she said. "The problem..." and then she stopped.

Cynthia was stunned by a revelation so startling that it left almost no space between thought process and spoken word, like the time she stopped mid-sentence after realizing she was asking a nonpregnant woman her due date. She wanted to tell Robert that he had it all mixed up. He should let *them* know what was going on so that they didn't walk into another massacre that Robert obviously knew about.

"You were saying?" Robert said.

Cynthia had entered a black hole in her mind where Robert's voice was as garbled as a speaker at the outdoor A & W stand she frequented as a teenager. She couldn't say whether it was the revelation itself, or that she was uncomfortable sharing it with Peter, that left her feeling more alone than at any time in her life.

"You okay?" Peter asked.

"I'm fine," she said as the three of them stood at the edge of the track. "The problem is tricky." It was such an understated finish to her sentence that it caught Robert off guard. She attempted to recover. "We'll keep you posted," she said, "but we can't always let you know exactly where we are or what we're doing. Look," she added, "we've stumbled onto the best cover imaginable."

"I'm not sure I'm ready to approve that," Robert said.

"You can't be serious?" Peter was incredulous.

141

"I'm not saying it won't be approved. I'm saying it hasn't been approved and before you do anything check with me."

"You're crazy to let an opportunity like this slip by," Peter said, but he realized there was no point in arguing.

That night Cynthia lay alone in bed, her mind swimming. She sobbed uncontrollably.

Her feelings were so mixed up she had a hard time tracing the tears through the multiple streams of her life. She was a CIA agent, increasingly uncomfortable in her role. She was in love with Peter, something against all written and unwritten Agency rules. What's more, she did not know if she loved Peter Jones the CIA agent or the Peter Jones who stood with the people during a massacre. Nor could she be sure he had crossed the threshold that she had crossed of standing with the people outside the garrison as a human being and not as an agent.

And what about her revelation? Did the Agency have prior knowledge of the massacre and Ricardo's arrest? If so, why weren't she and Peter included on policy decisions in an area where they were involved directly? And why would Robert consider passing on the opportunity to have two agents positioned within the community unless he suspected that she or Peter or both could no longer be trusted? How much did Peter know? And how was she to talk to him about any of this?

———

A flood of calls to Washington prompted cables to the embassy and to El Salvador's President. Calderón had little choice but to take notice. Padre Ricardo was released Monday afternoon, and Rafael was seen by a doctor.

If the massacre illustrated the vulnerability of the communities it also demonstrated their resiliency. In the aftermath, they organized with greater fervor. It was as if the hands of their murdered friends became extensions of their own. The community seemed to be a regenerating body that was impossible to kill even if individual members were murdered. Robert Barnes, whatever his reservations, found the benefits of having two agents rooted in the community too tempting to reject.

Twenty-two

༄

The Trial

After his release, Padre Ricardo visited Rafael. He was ushered into a dreary room. Its lone window provided a view of a brick wall from an adjacent building. When Rafael stumbled in, Padre Ricardo fought the temptation to turn away from his battered face. They waited for the guard to shut the door.

"At least I've confounded them," Rafael said. "I don't think they expected an old man to survive."

"Perhaps *guaro* has unknown medicinal qualities," Padre Ricardo said. His fleeting smile diverted attention from his anguish at seeing Rafael's pain. Rafael laughed, only to discover that it too was painful. "What happened?" Padre Ricardo asked.

They assumed the room was bugged. They would discuss what their captors already knew and ad-lib themselves into a code each hoped the other would decipher.

"Judas," Rafael said. "Where to begin?" Padre Ricardo nodded indicating he understood Rafael's inference of betrayal. "The soldiers came for me at Tomás and Ana's. Almost immediately. I accepted their invitation," he said. His speech was slurred. With each word, pain surged through his body.

"General Calderón showed Sancho and Carmen a confession. Did you sign it?" Padre Ricardo asked.

"Yes. Immediately," Rafael said. "I knew they would still

torture me but I hoped a confession might give them reason to leave the rest of you alone. I'm sorry," he added.

Padre Ricardo looked intently at Rafael. He wanted to communicate his knowledge that Rafael hadn't killed Mario. "You and I both know *you* have nothing to be sorry for," Padre Ricardo said. Rafael didn't respond, and Padre Ricardo found it impossible to read anything on his disfigured face. "They were not only avenging a murder," Padre Ricardo continued. "They were punishing the communities. If Mario hadn't been killed, they would have found another pretext for repression."

Rafael nodded. "How many people are dead?" he asked. Padre Ricardo was silent. He didn't want to heap greater pain on his friend. "Look," Rafael said, "if I am going to find courage to live, I need to know. I need to hold the memories of the dead in my heart in order to keep it beating."

"Rosa was the only one of the twelve killed," Padre Ricardo said. "There were seventeen others. Judas," he said with intonation of the profanity "shit." His intent was to bring Rafael back to the issue of betrayal. "Is there anyone in the community you would like me to send a special greeting to?" Rafael sat in silence for a long time. "I hope," Padre Ricardo continued, "that nothing this tragic happens again."

Padre Ricardo had an idea who the betrayer was. He hoped Rafael would provide a name. He wanted Rafael to understand that having an unknown traitor in their midst put others in danger. Rafael didn't answer. Perhaps he missed Ricardo's code. Perhaps he was unwilling, at least for now, to name his betrayer. A guard pounded on the door indicating their time was up.

"I'll see you at the trial on Thursday," Padre Ricardo said. "Pray for us tomorrow. We are having a memorial service for the dead. You're a good man, Rafael," he added.

"You know Padre," Rafael sighed, "I wonder if prayer is a waste of time. So many of my prayers go unanswered. Perhaps

145

God cannot be both powerful and compassionate. Maybe we are like Jesus. He was God's compassion in the world, and he was crucified. Maybe that is why we are crucified too. I will pray for you. At least it is a way of passing time."

"Even when we don't understand, God finds a way," Padre Ricardo said. His voice was reassuring.

Rafael looked troubled. "I'm sorry we have to go through the ritual of a trial," he said.

"Don't place yourself in the grave yet," Padre Ricardo said as he reached the door. "You never know what might happen. You just never know."

———

The service commemorating the lives of the massacred offered a mixture of remembrance, sadness, anger and determination. Padre Ricardo asked Archbishop Romero to give the homily. He refused. Romero was still cautious, afraid his presence would send a political message of solidarity to the communities and unaware that his absence might send an accommodating message to those behind the murders.

One by one, members of the communities stood up to praise the courage of their murdered friends and to recommit themselves to the ongoing work of building justice in El Salvador.

Peter and Cynthia listened. As their minds flashed to the report and to General Warren, they realized they had underestimated the power of this movement. They could not then know what they could only now feel: the depth of inspiration, the determination, the resiliency, the commitment and hope of the people. A liberating Gospel was a mystery that they did not fully understand.

———

The criminal justice system in El Salvador was itself criminal. Its twisted sense of justice presumed the accused guilty rather than innocent. Rafael had no chance of acquittal. Proving his innocence under any circumstance would be difficult, and given his confession, it seemed impossible. His legal prospects were dimmed further by the fact that the prosecution didn't have to convince a jury. The decision of guilt or innocence resided with the judge, in this case Julio's friend, Antonio Méndez. Yet his trial was a spectacle that no one could have imagined.

The tiny courtroom stood on the northern edge of Somotillo. It was half a mile from the garrison where the soldiers—now immune from prosecution—had gunned down the eighteen unarmed *campesinos*. About three dozen people crowded into the courtroom, including the judge, defendant and lawyers. Padre Ricardo and Carmen sat near the back. Julio was joined in front by his son Miguel, Raúl Ortega, and General Calderón. Julio's daughter, Isabel, sat with Padre Ricardo distancing herself physically and symbolically from her family. Julio and his friends, certain of a guilty verdict, were eager for the proceedings to begin.

"Is the prosecution ready to present its evidence for a guilty verdict against the accused in the matter of the murder of Mario Díaz?" Judge Méndez asked.

"We are. We ask you to note the written testimony of Captain Canales. He indicates that the defendant signed a confession in his presence two Sundays prior at 4:23 p.m. You also have a copy of the actual confession with the defendant's signature. With this evidence," the prosecuting attorney noted, "we see no need for witnesses. A guilty verdict is obvious and the prosecution rests."

Judge Méndez smiled. He appreciated the simplicity of the case. "Thank you," he said. "Is the defense ready to present evidence for an acquittal of the defendant in the matter of the murder of Mario Díaz?"

"We are," the defense attorney said. Uriel Baró was a professor of law at the UCA. "The defendant is innocent. We have proof of this in the form of a prior confession to the killing of Mario Díaz by another party. We will submit it into evidence momentarily." There was a gasp from the observers. It was followed by murmurs and then stunned silence.

"That's absurd," Julio protested.

Judge Méndez held out his hand encouraging his friend to remain calm while Rafael was led to the stand. Rafael walked slowly to the front, sat down and took the prescribed oath.

"I hold in my hand a written confession to the killing of Mario Díaz. Have you seen it before?" asked Uriel.

"No," Rafael said.

"Did you have prior knowledge I would admit it as evidence in this trial?" Uriel asked.

"No."

Uriel looked at the judge. "This confession is dated two Saturdays ago, 11:00 p.m, a day before Rafael's confession cited by the prosecution." He returned his gaze to Rafael. "Look at the signature at the bottom. Is it your signature?" he asked.

Rafael looked carefully at the paper, although he already knew the identity of Mario's killer. "No. I signed a confession the following Sunday afternoon while in the presence of Captain Canales."

"Did you kill Mario Díaz?" Uriel asked him.

"No."

"Why did you sign a confession indicating you did?"

"I thought the authorities might satisfy their thirst for blood by torturing and killing me. I didn't want anyone else to get hurt," he said.

"Were you tortured at the garrison?" Uriel asked.

"Yes."

"Before you signed the confession?"

"No. After."

"Do you know who killed Mario Díaz?"

"Yes."

"Do you know why he was killed?"

"Yes."

"I will recall this witness shortly. I now call Isabel Díaz," Uriel said. Julio looked up in disbelief as his daughter took the stand.

"Isabel," Uriel said, "look at this piece of paper and tell me if its contents were written by your hand?"

"I wrote it," she said.

"Would you read it to us please?" he asked.

"I, Isabel Díaz, killed my brother, Mario. I did so by the rock near the pond at my father's estate as he prepared to shoot me. I killed him with the machete that hangs as an ornament in my father's study. My finger prints and a trace of Mario's blood remain on the machete which I returned to the wall. I write this knowing my father is eager for a pretext to repress the people. I want to expose this pretext."

Uriel Baró was confident. He continued unraveling the case against his client. "You signed this statement two Saturdays ago at 11 p.m.," he said to Isabel. "Is that correct?"

"Yes. But I would like to read the rest of the statement," she said.

Uriel looked uncomfortable. "That's not necessary," he said.

"I want to read it," she repeated.

Sensing discord, the prosecuting attorney jumped in. "Judge," he said hoping that something in the final words of her statement might rescue his case against Rafael, "I request that you instruct the witness to read the remainder of her confession."

"So ordered," Judge Méndez said, hopefully.

"I am leaving to join the guerrillas." A collective gasp shook the courtroom. "My father and his friends have repressed every civil option. Armed struggle is regrettably the only recourse available to the people."

Judge Méndez ordered Isabel to take a seat near the front of the courtroom. He examined her confession as Rafael returned to the stand.

"Rafael. Did you see Mario Díaz threaten Isabel with a gun?" Uriel asked.

"Yes."

"Did you see her kill her brother in self-defense?"

"Yes."

Uriel turned to address the judge. "Given the evidence, you have no alternative but to release the defendant and absolve him of all charges."

"Don't tell me what I have to do," Judge Méndez snapped.

"We have a prior confession and an eye witness," Uriel said returning to the evidence.

"Unfortunately, you do. I'm sorry Julio. There's nothing I can do. The defendant is found innocent of all charges. He is free to go," Judge Méndez said.

"Then arrest my daughter," Julio screamed.

At that moment six people armed with rifles and a few grenades stormed into the room. "That won't be necessary," one of them said.

"Father," Isabel said. "We are arresting you. You call it kidnapping. I call it justice. We will see how valuable you are to your friends. It would take a lifetime to list all the charges against you," Isabel said. Her voice spilled over with emotion. "Murder with bullets and hunger, usury, torture, chauvinism, arrogance, child-neglect, adultery. These and much more. May God have mercy on your soul."

The guerrillas exited with Isabel and her father. They chained the doors shut and departed in an aging van. Within minutes they dumped the stolen vehicle in favor of another. They disappeared into the countryside before the stunned members of El Salvador's elite left the courthouse. Padre Ricardo was right. You never knew what might happen. Rafael was free.

During his time in the tiny cell at the garrison, Padre Ricardo had been afraid. His own death would have doomed Rafael as Isabel's confession would have been hidden forever next to the rose bush where he buried it.

Padre Ricardo sat in silence as the chains to the door resisted the blades of the hack saws. A single tear slipped out. He remembered that night, an eternity ago or so it seemed, in which Isabel confessed to the killing of her brother. That night they spoke honestly about many things, including their love for each other. It was a love they knew was impossible. He was a priest. She was about to join the armed opposition.

Padre Ricardo understood pain. He had buried too many children, listened to Rafael's tortured screams, cried because beloved friends were gunned down while seeking his release. But of the many holes in his heart, Isabel's departure was the biggest. She had died to her father years ago. Now for different reasons she walked away from his life. Once again he felt alone. Profoundly alone.

Twenty-three

Bubonic Plague

The capture of Julio Díaz left General Calderón and the others in a quandary. Their first impulse was to launch a wave of terror. But doing so might lead to Julio's execution, so they waited.

The day following the trial, Calderón received a call detailing the straightforward if unrealistic demands of the guerrillas. The caller said they were not vengeful people. Julio Díaz was fine but if they wanted him returned they would need to pay a million dollars cash, release political prisoners and distribute idle lands to local *campesinos*.

"We can't possibly do any of this," Calderón said.

"You will find a way or we will have a trial of our own," the caller warned. "Díaz may not like his captors, but he has no advocates among us, not even his daughter."

The demand for distribution of idle lands both reflected and solidified the guerrillas' base among *campesinos*. It also called attention to the greed of landowners who let people starve while placing only a fraction of their land under cultivation.

Julio's friends could easily comply with the first two demands. Money wasn't a problem. New prisoners could be taken. But they considered the third demand out of the question. Land was the basis of their power, both real and symbolic. Any land redistribution, no matter how insignificant, would fuel the fires of those seeking deeper reform. Linking Julio's release to land redistribution was both ingenious and dangerous. It rallied the poor but became a magnet for repression.

Calderón and the others weren't about to allow *campesinos* to invade lands and plant corn and beans. But that's exactly what the *campesinos* did. For a time they got away with it. As long as Julio was captive, the landowners were forced to choose between keeping him alive or reclaiming their lands. For the moment they decided to keep Julio alive but patience was wearing thin.

"Look," Calderón said, "Julio knows there's a line we cannot cross."

Julio's son, Miguel, looked anxious. "Even if it means his death?" he asked.

"Even if it means that one or more of us must die. None of us can afford to abandon our broader purpose," said Calderón. "If the day comes when you must choose between my life and sacrificing our country to communists, then I am prepared to die. It is your duty to let me die or at least risk my death."

"The General is right," Raúl Ortega said. "If we let them get away with invading our land we are finished. I say we release the prisoners and deliver the money. But that's the end. No more."

After pondering what others said, Antonio Méndez spoke. "They are in a difficult position also. They have created expectations," he said. "They are clever, but they have made a tactical blunder."

"How so?" Raúl asked. Antonio explained that in the short term the rebels were making life difficult for them and gaining support among the *campesinos*. But they could not protect the people. Faced with persecution, the rebels would either drop this demand or the people would pay severely for their foolishness. In either case, he assured his friends, it was they and not the rebels who came out ahead.

Miguel couldn't think beyond his father's life which hung in the balance. "If we get them to abandon the demand for land and get my father back alive then we are ahead," Miguel said.

"They are not foolish enough to kill Julio," Calderón noted. "The people have sampled a small dose of repression. It should be enough to deter them."

"It didn't deter them from taking Julio," Raúl countered.

"Taking and killing are different things," Calderón said confidently. "They will release Julio if we meet their first two demands."

The men who gathered that day knew they needed a strategy for before and after Julio's release. Some wanted to step up the repression. Others wanted a cooling off period. In the end both perspectives won out.

Calderón indicated that he and Roberto D'Aubuisson had discussed the matter and believed it was time to do both. D'Aubuisson was the founder of the Maximiliano Hernández Death Squad and charismatic leader of Salvador's extreme right. The plan was to allow for a cooling off period in Pueblo Duro and the whole area around Somotillo while escalating terror elsewhere. Somotillo was not the only community polluted with communists. A message anywhere would be important because it would be heard here as well.

———

Julio could only imagine what transpired away from his captors' hideout. He traveled on pathways largely invisible except to local residents and found himself fifteen miles up the Guazapa volcano, in an area so inaccessible he might as well have been in a different country.

For fifteen days he slept on straw mats in a one room house with a dirt floor. He ate beans and tortillas twice a day and an occasional mango. People came and went hardly noticing his presence. He was neither the object of envy nor contempt.

Julio's unsolicited immersion into the realities of *campesino* life had little impact on his demeanor. He spoke with the intonation of a master and became indignant when people ignored his commands. He had one conversation of note, a one-sided exchange with a rebel leader who made no effort to conceal his identity.

"How do you like your life as a *campesino*?" Rubén Torres asked.

Julio refused to look at him. "Go away," he said.

"Perhaps you haven't noticed, your orders mean nothing here," Rubén said. "I feel like talking."

"And I don't feel like listening," Julio grumbled.

"We are not so different. My parents too are large landowners," Rubén said. "You knew them, I'm sure. They fled to Miami. I am a doctor." Without realizing it Julio tracked the conversation. "Have you read *The Plague*?" Rubén asked. "It's by Camus."

"No."

"It's about a rat-infested city. The bubonic plague. Rats spread disease. People die. Dozens, then hundreds, then thousands and thousands of innocent people die. A doctor tries to treat the people. He cannot save them. He cannot arrest the needless death. He goes through a crisis. A moral crisis. A religious crisis. He no longer believes in a God who tolerates such suffering. His is the crisis of humanity in the aftermath of the holocaust."

Rubén looked at Julio, who sat dazed before him. "In many ways I am that doctor, and El Salvador is that plague-infested city." After a long pause he continued. "You know, I cannot remember the end of the story, whether the doctor lives or dies. I only remember his decision. He could not trust God or be certain of God's existence. The plague determined his destiny. He had to help the people as best he could." He paused again before continuing. "Do you know why I joined the guerrillas?"

Julio didn't respond and Rubén ignored his indifference. "I joined," he continued, "because you dragged my students out of the medical school and shot them. I have a confession. When you killed the politicians I remained indifferent. But when you killed my students who devoted their lives to healing, I could no longer be silent.

"Someone came to them in the middle of the night bleeding. They didn't ask how she got her wound or make their treatment contingent upon her answer. And so you and your friends murdered them. You killed other students too, detained them, disappeared them. Why? Because they volunteered in clinics started by the base communities," he said.

"The plague that threatens El Salvador is communism," Julio said. "Let me ask you a question," he said indignantly. "What do rats and communists have in common? They both are worthy of extermination. All of us are doctors in the fight to rid our country of this disease." Julio spoke with contempt. "Maybe Hitler was right."

"It's funny. You are one of the most wealthy people in El Salvador but I feel sorry for you," Rubén said. "You know nothing about the family in whose home you are captive and yet your life parallels theirs. Three of their six children died. One of diarrhea related dehydration, one of typhoid, one of dengue fever. In order for their children to live, El Salvador must change. You resist those changes and children die, including your own. Eduardo is gone, Mario killed and Isabel so distant she is for all practical purposes dead to you.

"Ironic, isn't it? The families of the rich and the families of the poor, their destinies linked more closely than we imagine. El Salvador. The Savior. It may be that by blocking social changes that our country needs so desperately, you choose against your own salvation. You choose a harvest of Cain."

Julio smirked. "You know nothing about me or El Salvador. Go to hell."

—

Three weeks after the guerrillas' original contact with General Calderón, a letter arrived at his office. It listed the names of political prisoners to be released and provided directions on how to deliver the million dollars. Two days later money changed hands, Julio gained his freedom, and political prisoners received asylum in Costa Rica. Meanwhile, corn and bean plants pushed through the rocky soil on illegally occupied lands.

Twenty-four

To Be A Patriot

In the following weeks the relative calm in Pueblo Duro and surrounding communities contrasted sharply with the violence escalating elsewhere. While Julio and the others waited for the opportune moment to displace *campesinos* from nearby occupied lands, they coordinated efforts with the death squads.

Raúl Ortega finally got his wish. Padre Ernesto, a priest working near the Guazapa volcano, was murdered. An eight-year-old boy who accompanied him was also killed. A note, attached next to the bullet hole in Padre Ernesto's chest, read: BE A PATRIOT. KILL A PRIEST. It was signed by the Maximiliano Hernández Anticommunist Crusade.

The following week the government deported several Spanish priests. The progressive churches were not the only targets of this most recent wave of repression. Leaders of unions, student movements and cooperatives were assassinated or disappeared by soldiers dressed in civilian clothes. Land takeovers in areas other than Somotillo were brutally suppressed.

The murder of Padre Ernesto, the expulsion of priests, and the escalating repression impacted Archbishop Romero profoundly. He was asked again to speak at a funeral of innocents gunned down by anonymous assassins. This time he accepted:

> The Church's task is to make each country's history a history of salvation. A Church that sets itself up

only to be well off, to have a lot of money and comfort, but that forgets to protest injustices, would not be the true Church of our divine Redeemer.

We confess that the Church shares responsibility for our country being far from salvation. Elsewhere, where the Church is timid the people are led astray. Here we can say that because the Church is timid the people die, *campesinos* die, priests die, little children die. No, it is not enough to say they die. They are murdered. And the ones murdered include living examples of what the Church must be.

And what do we say to the murderers of the people? To be a Christian now means to have the courage to preach the true teaching of Christ and not be afraid of it, not be silent out of fear and preach something easy that won't cause problems.

This is why the Church has great conflicts: It accuses society of sin. It says to the rich: do not sin by misusing your money, by feasting off the labor of the poor. Do not misuse your political influence. Do not misuse your weaponry. Do not misuse your power. Don't you see that is a sin? The Church says to sinful torturers: Do not torture. You are sinning. You are doing wrong. You are establishing the reign of hell on earth.

The Church, entrusted with the earth's glory, believes that in each person is the Creator's image. Everyone who tramples it offends God. Whoever tortures a human being, whoever abuses a human being, whoever outrages a human being abuses God's image, and the Church takes as its own that cross, that martyrdom.

My knowledge has come from books. In the area of books I have always been a fast learner. Now I am learning that life—your lives—and not only books, are my teachers. Forgive me for being a slow learner in life. It is the poor who force us to understand what is really taking place in our country. And I am learning as I stand over the bodies of Padre Ernesto and this innocent boy, this innocent Luisito, that the persecution of the Church is a result of defending the poor. Our persecution is nothing more nor less than sharing in the destiny of the poor.

Romero paused as the people sat in eager silence. They had never heard a bishop speak with such power and integrity. Romero reached deep, pulled out life stories from within their souls. Cynthia sat next to Padre Ricardo. She buried her face in her hands as Romero continued his homily:

We are living through difficult and uncertain days. We do not know if this very evening we will be prisoners or murder victims. We do not know what the forces of evil will do with us. But one thing I do know: even those who have disappeared after arrest, even those who are mourned in the mystery of an abduction, are known and loved by God.

If God allows these disappearances, it is not because God is helpless. God loves us, and God keeps on loving. God loves our history too, and God knows where the ways of our land's redemption will come out. Let us not lose hope in this great truth. As we bury our friends in the earth let us remember that our country's future hinges on what becomes of the land.

Many would like the poor to keep saying it is God's will for them to live in misery, without land. But it is not God's will for some to have everything and others to have nothing. That cannot be of God. God's will is that all God's children be happy.

Many would say the Church can not approve or justify bloody revolution and cries of hatred. But neither can it condemn them while it sees no attempt to remove the causes that produce that ailment in our society.

And so I say to those of you who murdered Padre Ernesto and this little boy, you who go on persecuting the people: you have hands stained with murder, with torture, with atrocity, with injustice. Be converted.

I love you deeply. I am sorry for you because you are on the way to ruin. What beautiful coffee groves, what fine cane and cotton fields, what farms, what lands God has given us! Nature is so beautiful. But we groan under oppression, under wickedness, under injustice, under abuse, and the Church feels its pain. Nature looks for a liberation that will not be mere material well-being but God's act of power. God will free nature from sinful human hands and, along with the redeemed, it will sing a hymn of joy to God, the Liberator.

That day, Archbishop Romero became the people's bishop, the people's voice. From then on, every Sunday—except on the occasions when the Catholic radio station was bombed—Romero's sermons were heard everywhere in the country by *campesinos* and workers gathered around transistor radios. Romero listened to the people and spoke for them. His message was enduring. His life in danger. His hope rooted in faith.

Twenty-five

Intellectual Authors

As the service ended, members of the community started out for Pueblo Duro only to be surrounded by soldiers near Somotillo. Cynthia, Peter, Padre Ricardo, Carmen, Juan, Sancho, Elena and Doña María were escorted to a waiting area outside General Calderón's office at the garrison.

As the others waited nervously, two soldiers grabbed Peter and ushered him in to where General Calderón waited. Calderón motioned Peter to sit down. He sat behind a large wooden desk. There was a cup filled with pencils and pens and several note pads in front of him. Calderón was an incessant doodler with nervous fingers. A half-dozen pencils with broken tips lay scattered on his desk, victims of his unconscious scribbling.

"I hope you will not be too inconvenienced," Calderón said. "I thought an interrogation might be good for your credibility."

Peter never knew who in the Salvadoran government and military understood his relationship to the Agency. By revealing knowledge of his CIA ties, Calderón made a statement of his own importance. This left Peter with competing emotions. He was relieved that his would be a mock interrogation. Yet he was troubled nonetheless. Calderón's reputation indicated he was capable of anything.

"It is good to finally meet you," Peter said, weakly. "What do you intend to do with the others?"

His question was of no consequence. Calderón wanted to communicate something to Peter Jones. "I understand you are troubled by the death of Padre Ernesto."

"Troubled may be the wrong word," Peter said, choosing his response carefully. "No. I wouldn't say troubled. I am interested."

"Why?" Calderón asked.

"I am interested in who ordered Padre Ernesto's murder," Peter said.

"Why does this concern you?" Calderón's voice was filling with anger.

"Let's say I have a curiosity about the truth," Peter responded.

Calderón reached into his desk and removed a document from the top drawer. He got up and walked towards Peter. "You Americans are such fine hypocrites." Peter seemed stung by the accusation.

"You are surprised," Calderón said with contempt. "Maybe you will find this interesting." Calderón opened the document, located the desired page, and began reading:

> Liberation theology, therefore, not Marxism, is the principal challenge confronting U.S. foreign policy as we seek to maintain long-standing interests in our back-yard. Stated another way, liberation theology and the subversive churches are the principal enemies of the United States and our traditional allies throughout Latin America. Waging war against these enemies will present U.S. policy makers with new moral as well as political challenges.

Peter was silent. In all likelihood Calderón read from a document that neither the President of the United States nor the present U.S. ambassador was allowed to see. "You are familiar with this fine document. Are you not?" Calderón asked, sarcastically. "Of course. It is very well done I might add. I assure you it is most useful to us," he added. Calderón's expression was grim.

"Where did you get it?" Peter asked.

Calderón ignored him. "You say you want to know the *truth*. But you do not want to know the truth about yourselves. You are not interested in who pulled the trigger that killed Ernesto. You want to know who gave the orders. Your search is for intellectual authors. Why is this important to you?"

"I have my reasons," Peter said.

"Your reasons," he responded, coldly. "Why do you care so much about Padre Ernesto? Is he so different than the thousands of others who have died? Who continue dying? Who will die? Yes, you Americans are fine hypocrites. You feed your self-righteousness with blindness. You want to find the intellectual authors of this crime as if a communist priest is precious to you. If you are looking for intellectual authors then look in the mirror, for you are the authors of the crime that is El Salvador."

Peter wanted to protest. He wanted to get up and leave the room. Before he could make a move, Calderón was on top of him, fiery contempt in his eyes. "You arrogant fools. You teach us your anticommunism. You declare this your battleground with the Soviets. You train our military and police and lecture our death squads on killing and human rights. You declare liberation theology an enemy and then express shock if a few religious die. And you want to know who's responsible for these murders."

Calderón's breath touched Peter's face. "You sicken me," he continued. "You come here to redeem yourselves from Vietnam, to purge yourselves of demons, to rescue your careers and to test your new theories of warfare. You teach us and then act concerned when we learn your lessons well. I don't know which disgusts me more, your unbearable arrogance or your feigned innocence."

Calderón pushed a finger into Peter's chest and smirked. "You wonderful Americans. You feel you have the right to control everything. And when our assessment of what is necessary diverges from yours, you feel betrayed. I wonder if you can imagine how much we hate you, our northern benefactors. At least we are honest with ourselves. We know what we do and why. I'm not sure if I should pity you as well as hate you."

"Pity us?" Peter said incredulously.

"We do what we have to because it is necessary. You can't stomach the truth and so you convince yourselves you are acting in the name of freedom and democracy. No matter how many people die, how many governments you overthrow, how many torturers you train, how many dictators you embrace, how much blood seeps onto our soil from your School of the Americas, you do it for freedom, for democracy. If this is tactical then I merely hate you for your arrogance. If you believe your own rhetoric, then I pity you for your ignorance and your diminished moral character. That is why we pity Carter and why, if he is elected, we will end up hating Reagan."

Peter could not escape the irony that he was receiving a lecture on morality from a man responsible for dozens of murders and massacres. It added to the weight of his condemnation.

"You look surprised," Calderón continued. "Do you think Carter is more moral because he means well? Reagan has no morality. His oratory is tactical. We will find a way of accommodating each other. But Carter? I feel sorry for him. His morality is stripped of all pretense by his actions." Calderón backed away. "I've grown weary of your presence," he said. He returned to his desk and pushed a button. Two soldiers entered the room.

Peter strained to hear their conversation but couldn't. Calderón and the others laughed. They cast glances in his direction that revealed nothing of their intentions.

Calderón's menacing presence caused fear to surface within Peter as suddenly as unwanted footsteps in a dark alley. Calderón was unpredictable enough and powerful enough to destroy him. But the fear gripping Peter was not that he would be killed. Even

Calderón was unlikely to kill a CIA agent with witnesses able to testify to his recent interrogation. Calderón could destroy him in another way. He could simply announce to the religious workers outside that Peter was an agent. Yes. That is what he intended. Peter was finished.

As he imagined his undoing, Peter's fear ebbed and flowed within him. At first the thought of disclosure filled his soul with terror. But just as quickly the terror fled, leaving relief in its wake. Peter had lived a lie for so long and deceived so many that his life was no longer his own. He was going to have his life destroyed and given back to him by General Calderón, an agent of repression and terror.

Peter's sense of relief was interrupted by soldiers who ordered him out of the chair. He approached the door leading to his friends, walking between honesty and hope with the dread of an execution and the anticipation of the Exodus competing for his soul.

Then, for just a moment, Peter felt the warmth of a bright light. He was crossing over to the other side, passing through the Red Sea, and ironically it was a soldier in Pharaoh's army who was giving him his freedom.

As he entered the room his friends stood up, their faces full of concern. "I return your friend to you," Calderón said. "He is unworthy of any friendship."

A soldier thrust a rifle into Peter's ribs. As he sagged to the floor, another blow landed solidly at the back of his head. Calderón spit on him as he shook with pain. He hated the Americans but he needed them. He would not free Peter whose pain went well beyond the agony of a broken rib. Peter was a broken man, a coward apparently unwilling to free himself.

Twenty-six

Dis-Ease

As Robert Barnes jogged slowly around the track, he was joined by Cynthia and Peter. He told them that Ambassador Nolte had requested a meeting. Nolte wanted an update on what was happening with the churches and he would share some concerns arising out of Nicaragua.

"Ever since Somoza's Guard executed that U.S. journalist last month in Nicaragua..." Robert said.

"Bill Stewart," Cynthia interrupted.

"Yeah. Stewart." Robert's tone was grim. "Can you imagine? He's covering a demonstration for one of the networks. A guard shoves a rifle in his face and orders him to kneel. After he complies, the guard shoots him in the head. His camera crew captures the whole damn thing in time for the nightly news. Carter had no choice but to cut the aid."

"I'd think we'd be glad to get rid of Somoza," Peter said. "Dictators are out of fashion."

Robert took Peter's flippant remark seriously. "They're not out of fashion," he responded. "But they don't always work. Dictators can be useful. But not if they create instability instead of stability. It's *awkward* with Somoza."

"How so?" Peter asked.

Robert searched for an analogy.

"You'd feel...well...awkward," he said, returning to the word, "if you complained about a car that worked well for fifty years. The Somoza family gave us many good miles, over many years and with only a few bumps in the road. It's hard telling him he's outlived his usefulness."

Robert explained that Carter had been trying to coax the stubborn Somoza out for months. Apart from the question of loyalty, even Robert wouldn't be sad to see him go. The bigger issue was his replacement. A revolutionary movement led by the Sandinistas was getting stronger each day that Somoza refused to leave. According to Robert, they were communists and even if they weren't, they couldn't be trusted. There was a nasty wind blowing, and if the Sandinistas came to power in Nicaragua it would put things in El Salvador on center stage.

Cynthia heard a mixture of gravity and exhilaration in Robert's voice. She knew the answer to the question she was about to ask but wanted to hear Robert's take on the situation. "Why are events in Nicaragua decisive here?" she said.

Robert took the bait. "Publicly the administration defends human rights. Privately, Nicaragua is a wake-up call," he said. "We've been walking a pretty fine line."

The casual nature of the conversation seduced him into a posture of unusual candor. "Our ties to President Ramírez were limited but friendly because nobody cared about El Salvador. They've been strained since Carter cut military aid after General Ochoa stole the latest election. Let's just say even now there are important ties, both official and unofficial. Of course we downplay them. But if Nicaragua falls, the human rights pretense will fall with it."

Robert was on a roll and neither Peter nor Cynthia wanted to interrupt him. "Carter's a victim of his own rhetoric. His flap over human rights encourages people to organize and gives the communists in and outside the churches an opportunity they can't refuse. The problem is that many of them foolishly believe his rhetoric. They think the U.S. is going to protect them. If Nicaragua falls into the hands of the Sandinistas, Carter will never allow another revolution in Central America. He'll jump into bed with Ochoa and the generals and they know it. They've got Carter by the balls. A revolutionary Nicaragua means military aid will flow again to El Salvador. Lots of it."

The silence that followed indicated that Robert's momentary lapse into honesty was over. Peter returned the conversation to the meeting with the ambassador. "What does Nolte want?" he asked.

"Your assessment of our efforts to contain the churches," Robert said. Peter hoped he wouldn't need to spend the rest of the night preparing for the meeting and was relieved that the meeting would be considered informal. "He's especially interested in your perceptions of Romero," Robert added. "So am I," he frowned. "Romero's a problem."

"When and where?" Cynthia inquired.

"The suite at the Sheraton. Eight o'clock."

As Robert departed, Cynthia's face appeared ghostlike. She took off around the track. It startled Peter, who sat preoccupied with thoughts of tonight's meeting. Cynthia made her way around once, then again and then a third time. As she completed the final lap she collapsed onto the grass next to him. Peter looked concerned. "We have to talk," he said.

"About what?" Cynthia asked, coldly.

Her question caught him off guard. They were about to talk past each other and he knew it. "About Nolte. What do you think?" Peter said.

"Excuse me." She spoke sarcastically. A mixture of tears and sweat poured down her face. "I thought maybe we should talk about us. About what we're doing. About what the hell is going on," she said.

"What do you mean?" he asked. His stupidity irritated Cynthia like a wool turtleneck on a hot day.

"Forget it." As Cynthia started to get up, he reached out, took her hand and restrained her gently.

"Okay," he said. "Let's talk." Peter hesitated. Neither one of them seemed to know how to start. They sat silently for a long time, oblivious to the joggers on the track. Peter sighed. "I've wanted to talk to you for months," he confessed. "But I was afraid to. We're becoming strangers. I hate it," he added.

"Me too," she said. "Let's get some coffee at my place."

On the way to her apartment, Peter and Cynthia said little. Each of them weighed the implications of honesty. Trusting a CIA agent under most circumstances was foolish. Falling in love with one bordered on insanity. They had avoided this conversation because it was risky. One or both of them could lose their job, perhaps more.

When they reached Cynthia's place, Peter broke the silence. "Do you remember what Robert told us when we were working on the report?" he asked.

"He said a lot of things," Cynthia said.

"He wanted complete honesty." Peter said. A mastermind of deception, Peter was having trouble deceiving himself. But he found honesty equally troublesome. He looked perplexed. "Robert didn't want us to tell him what we thought he wanted to hear. He asked for the truth about liberation theology as we saw it," he said.

Cynthia tried hard to track his words. She looked defensive. "I remember. I also wasn't allowed to see the report," she said. "What's the point?"

"The point is he wanted honesty. No matter the consequences," Peter said bringing the conversation back to them. "That's how I feel about tonight."

Cynthia's expression softened. "Okay," she said. As the aroma of coffee filled the room they struggled with how to continue the conversation.

Cynthia surprised herself. "I love you, Peter," she said. The directness of her remark startled him. She paused. "No, that's not entirely true."

"Now there's honesty," he said.

"What I mean," she continued, "is I love the Peter Jones who dragged Sancho away from the garrison, who accompanied Padre Ricardo, who was moved to tears as Romero spoke at the funeral."

She looked at him so intently it made him uneasy, perhaps because she was looking into his eyes struggling to see the man that lived somewhere behind years of deception. "If that person is Peter Jones then I love him." She paused for a long time. "The problem is I don't know if he's real."

"I think he's real," Peter said. "I came here from Chile convinced liberation theology was dangerous. I wanted to serve my country, and Robert allowed me to infiltrate the church movements. I didn't know the people would change me, would make me hate what we're doing here," he said. He paused. "I hope the Peter you love is real, because I find myself hating the other Peter Jones."

"Don't hate him," she said. "Let him go."

Peter looked into Cynthia's beautiful eyes. "I want you to promise me something," he said. "Whatever happens out of this, I want you to remember I love you." Peter managed a faint smile. "At least I love the Cynthia Randolph who introduced herself at the mass when Padre Ricardo was arrested, and whose quick reactions saved Carmen and the others."

Cynthia laughed. "It seems you love both Cynthia Randolphs," she said. "It was a calculating agent who spoke at the mass. I thought it was a good time to be noticed. Something happened during the mass. I don't know if it was the music, the sermon or Calderón's arrogance that got to me. Something did. I stood outside the garrison as a demonstrator, not an agent." She paused, placing herself in that setting once more. "It was the old man," she said.

"Which old man?" Peter asked.

"The one who asked where the guns came from and whether or not the soldiers used them to defend the people," she said.

"He made me think too," Peter acknowledged. "I listened but I was busy protecting myself from the weight of what he was saying."

Cynthia reached out and took his hand. "What were you unwilling to hear?" she asked.

He hesitated. "The events set in motion by my own damn report," he said.

"Our damn report," she corrected him. "I'm as responsible as you. At least one thing is clear." Cynthia seemed surprisingly cheerful.

"What's that?" he said.

"Cynthia Randolph and Peter Jones are in love. And they are in love with the right people." She pulled him closer. His fingers touched her face gently. As they kissed she tried to chase away unwelcome memories and lingering doubts.

———

The night's healing embrace sent deception fleeing and left Cynthia feeling free. But before she could fully embrace the emancipation, a tinge of doubt resurfaced. She wondered if it would ever go away. She decided to risk sharing the insight that held her captive since their meeting with Robert Barnes shortly after the massacre. "Do you think we know what's going on with the Agency?"

"What do you mean?"

"Do Robert and the others trust us?" she asked.

"I'm not sure." He paused for a long time. "It seems there may be different levels of policy being played out. We're involved on one level but not others." He spoke tentatively.

Cynthia was disappointed with his answer. "That's normal procedure," she said. "I'm talking about something else. Robert said if he had known we were going to be outside the garrison on the night of the massacre he might have talked to Calderón. That means he knew about the massacre." She paused to let the weight of her revelation sink in. "*Before* the massacre. There's something else I wonder about," she said.

"What's that?" he asked.

"U.S. soldiers were at the garrison that night. They were in the room during Rafael's torture."

Peter looked troubled. Cynthia told herself he was registering a perfectly appropriate response to her revelations. But the more she tried to convince herself the less secure she felt. Somehow, his discomfort re-triggered a battle within that raged out of control. It was a battle between trust and deception. Was he troubled due to the information she was revealing? Or was he upset because of what she knew?

Twenty-seven

Deception

Cynthia was so far in, and the alternative to trusting Peter so debilitating, she decided to continue.

"Rafael told Carmen he heard English spoken outside the interrogation room. And," she continued, "two U.S. soldiers entered the room when they assumed Rafael had passed out." Peter frowned.

"That's only part of it," she continued. "If Robert had prior knowledge of the massacre, then he must have known that Padre Ricardo was going to be arrested. It's hard to imagine Calderón acting on his own. And if Robert knew all this, and if he's taking steps to keep us in the dark, then he knows about us."

Peter seemed paralyzed by her words. "I see what you mean," he said, weakly.

"Do you remember the day you presented your report to General Warren?"

"Of course," he said.

"You looked like a ghost when you left the room," Cynthia reminded him. "Why?"

Peter struggled to remember his feelings that day. "I'm not sure," he said. "Maybe I was already afraid of the consequences of our report. That it would turn out badly. Maybe I knew intuitively then what I verbalized tonight. Maybe Peter Jones had already changed."

Cynthia looked at him sympathetically. "We were both changing," she said. "But you were afraid when you left the meeting with Warren. You knew he was dangerous."

"I can't remember what I said. But Warren seemed capable of anything. He didn't give a damn about liberation theology or any of the nuances of our analysis. He was eager for a war even before we spoke." Peter shivered. "Maybe I was too," he said.

Peter looked like he might collapse under the weight of the guilt he was carrying. "Warren gave me the creeps," he added.

Cynthia looked directly at Peter. She was searching his eyes and body language for clues, for reasons to doubt or trust. "What do you know about Operation Cain?" she asked.

Peter shrugged his shoulders. "What is it?" he said.

"The night of the massacre Carmen and Sancho went inside the garrison," Cynthia said. "Captain Canales took them to Padre Ricardo. He abused them verbally and he kicked Padre Ricardo in the back. When the guards were distracted, he handed Sancho a piece of paper. All it said was 'OPERATION CAIN,' " she said.

"That's all?"

"That's all." Cynthia repeated. She was exasperated by her lack of knowledge of what was really going on in El Salvador. "No one in the community knows what it means. What do you know about the School of the Americas?" she asked apparently changing the subject.

Peter was surprised by the question. "You know as much as I do," he responded.

"I'm beginning to realize how little I know about what my father or the School does," she said.

"How can you not know?" he said and then wished he hadn't. His remark hurt Cynthia like a bee sting on an open wound.

Peter felt foolish. "I shouldn't chastise you for not knowing," he said. "I went to Vietnam without a clue. When I heard that Robert and others with ties to the Agency were assassinating civilians suspected of collaborating with the Viet Cong, I didn't pay much attention. If our side were doing it then I figured there must be good reason. After a Vietnamese...a Vietnamese...friend of mine was murdered by the Viet Cong I hated communism to the point I couldn't see straight."

Peter thought about telling Cynthia about Bui Thi, but something prevented him. It was as if a cloud were hanging over the memory itself.

"I guess we're not supposed to see straight," she said. "Maybe that's the point. Noriega runs drugs through Panama but he works for us and provides useful information on Castro, and nothing else matters. I never questioned it." She paused. "I guess people who see straight wouldn't tolerate Marcos, the Shah, Stroesner, Somoza, Pinochet...God, the list seems endless! Then again maybe we just don't want to see." Cynthia returned to her question. "So what about the School?" she asked.

"It opened after World War II," Peter said. "Washington wanted to shore up ties to the militaries in the region. A couple thousand soldiers and officers are trained each year; basic counterinsurgency with a focus on internal enemies. It's known throughout Latin America as the School of Coups, Dictators and Assassins."

"I guess I don't need to ask why?" she said.

"Our clients aren't exactly guardians of democracy," he agreed. "President Ochoa and our own General Calderón were groomed there," Peter said.

Cynthia asked the question most troubling her. "Do we teach torture?" she said.

"Yes and no," Peter responded. "The School doesn't set out to feed sadistic impulses, if that's what you mean. Torture and repression actually come under the category of human rights training." Cynthia's expressive face registered abhorrence.

"As far as I know," Peter continued, "the focus of our training is on helping the military and police forces of a given country maintain or reestablish control in any given environment. The idea is to achieve this while employing the least amount of repressive force or violence. According to the theory, repression—including torturing political opponents—can be necessary in one setting and counterproductive in another. Human rights classes at the School help officers and soldiers learn the difference."

"Some difference," Cynthia said sarcastically. "Look what they did to Rafael. Call people communists and they cease to be human. You're no longer torturing human beings. You're torturing abstractions," she said.

"There are two purposes of torture," Peter said. "To get information and to sow terror. Whoever tortured Rafael wanted to send a message. It had to be calculated or they would have tortured him without leaving marks."

"So we're talking Psych Ops."

"Yes, I'd say so," Peter said.

Cynthia got up from the couch and walked over to the kitchen table. It was covered with papers and dirty coffee cups. She shuffled through the papers, retrieved a document and returned to the couch.

She handed Peter a stack of papers held together with a paper clip. It listed the names of Salvadorans trained at the School of the America's from 1946 to the present. "Ochoa and Calderón are not alone," she said.

"Where did you get this?" he asked.

"My father sent it along with this." She handed him a letter.

Dear Cynthia,

I received your note. Enclosed is the list you requested. With Nicaragua going to hell and El Salvador not far behind, the numbers of those coming for training will undoubtedly increase. Greet General Calderón for me. I'm sure you're aware he is very knowledgeable about the areas in which you are working. I consider him a great potential leader for the country and a personal friend.

Dad

p.s. Carter gave away the canal. If we can't undo this thing, it looks like the School will move to Fort Benning, Georgia. Pray for Reagan.

Peter put the letter on the coffee table. "There's more," Cynthia said. She handed Peter a report summarizing the human rights situation in El Salvador with the names of those considered most responsible for abuses highlighted with a yellow marker.

Peter glanced at the report. "Not many surprises," he said.

"The highlighted names indicate soldiers who were trained at the School," she noted.

"Looks like we're doing our job very well," he said. "Or very poorly."

"Either way it stinks." Cynthia looked exhausted. "So what do we tell Nolte?" she asked.

"I don't know. Let the ambassador take the lead. Besides," he said, "as long as we're on the same wave length I'm not worried."

"I'm more concerned with Robert," she responded.

"Me too," he said.

"You got any family pictures?" Peter asked.

Cynthia was surprised by his question. "There's a photo album on the bookshelf. Why?" she asked. "You want to see if I'm going to gain forty pounds in middle age?"

"I'd like to see some pictures of you when you were a kid," he said.

"I see," she said with a smile. Cynthia retrieved the album from the shelf and returned to the couch. "That's my father, Henry," she said. "That was taken a long time ago."

"Are you the cute one with the bandaged knee? How old were you?" he asked.

"Five." Cynthia turned the page quickly. "And my mom, June. I never really knew her," she said, sadly.

"When did she die?" he asked.

"Oh no. She's with my father in Panama. We aren't close," she said. "Here's a more recent shot of my father at the canal."

"Is that Warren?" he asked.

"Yeah. I told you before. They're friends," she said.

Peter looked preoccupied. "It's late," he said. "Thanks for showing me the pictures. I'd better go." After a long embrace he got up from the couch, took the album and placed it back on the shelf. "I'll see you tomorrow," he said. "I love you."

"I love you too," she said.

———

Peter arrived at his apartment looking dazed and determined. He took a picture off the wall and aimed an old projector in its direction. He walked over to a corner of the bookshelf, retrieved a small canister and removed what appeared to be a home movie. His hands worked quickly but awkwardly. His forehead bubbled with beads of sweat. He turned the projector on and watched intently.

Whoever had taken the film had moved the camera slowly so as to offer a panoramic view of a park in Saigon. There were cyclos and vendors on the edge and couples walking hand in hand along paths lined with trees and flowers. The footage then concentrated on Peter Jones walking in the direction of a young woman who sat on a bench and appeared to be praying. She arose and they embraced. As they began walking, a motor bike approached. The film clip ended as the woman crumpled to the ground.

"Damn fool," Peter said as angry tears drenched his face. He reached over in the direction of the projector reel, where the end of the film flipped wildly in circles. He pushed the off switch and then removed two photos and a small recorder from his pocket. He rewound the tape, and pushed play. It was Cynthia's voice:

I love you Peter. No. That's not entirely true.

He stopped the recorder and pushed fast forward. Stopped it again and pushed play. Cynthia's voice intermingled with his own.

Do you think we know what's going on with the Agency? What do you mean? Do Robert and the others trust us? I'm not sure. It seems there may be different levels of policy being played out. We're involved on one level, but not others. That's normal procedure. I'm talking about something else. Robert said if he had known we were going to be outside the garrison on the night of the massacre he might have talked to Calderón. That means he knew about the massacre. Before the massacre. There's something else I wonder about. What's that? U.S. soldiers were at the garrison that night. They were in the room during Rafael's torture. Rafael told Carmen he heard English spoken outside the interrogation room. And, two U.S. soldiers entered the room when they assumed Rafael had passed out. That's only part of it. If Robert had prior knowledge of the massacre, then he must have known that Padre Ricardo was going to be arrested. It's hard to imagine Calderón acting on his own. And if Robert knew all this, and if he's taking steps to keep us in the dark, then he knows about us. I see what you mean.

Peter shut off the recorder. He erased the tape, keeping only the section that betrayed Cynthia. He took out a faded picture of Bui Thi and wept.

The following morning Peter fixed himself a late morning breakfast of eggs and bacon. He washed the cholesterol down with juice and coffee and picked up the phone:

"Robert? It's Peter," he said.

"What's up?"

"I need to see you this afternoon. We've got trouble," Peter said.

"What kind of trouble?" Robert asked.

Peter was annoyed. "Meet me at the stadium at three o'clock," he said.

Robert protested. "I don't know if I can get there."

"Three o'clock, Robert. It can't wait."

Twenty-eight

Voices

Cynthia did not consider herself indecisive. But within the past hour she had picked up her phone three times, dialed and hesitated—only to hang up before completing the call. At this moment the source of her anxiety was Ambassador Nolte. He seemed to be a decent human being. How was it possible, she wondered, that so many bad policies could be determined and carried out by seemingly good people?

More troubling was her realization that putting better people in positions of power didn't seem to help much. Stansfield Turner, Cynthia thought, brought more integrity and better values to the CIA than previous directors William Colby or George Bush. And compared to Nixon, Carter appeared a moral giant. Why had Carter entered office pledging to rid the world of nuclear weapons only to oversee their escalation? And although she felt Carter was serious about promoting human rights in El Salvador, this commitment hadn't prevented the United States from being drawn more deeply into the violence against the people.

Cynthia wondered why better ambassadors, directors and presidents did so little to correct abusive U.S. policies and why the CIA, despite a purging at the top, remained out of control both here and elsewhere. And the purged agents? Cynthia suspected they had little trouble finding employment, often at the center of covert CIA actions.

It seemed to Cynthia that institutions like the Central Intelligence Agency, or corporations or the Presidency, had lives of their own. At their innermost core they had a... Cynthia groped hard for a word. When she finally settled on one it surprised her. But it seemed to fit. They had a *spirituality*.

Cynthia wasn't a deeply religious person. She grew up on army bases and in the context of the Church. But authentic community depended on a continuity of people, time and place that her father's frequent transfers precluded. Until her encounter with liberation theology and the community of Pueblo Duro, she believed that she served God by serving her country. Her faith journey was as flat and shallow as the "IN GOD WE TRUST" insignia on U.S. coins.

Cynthia perceived that institutions were not easily changed by well-meaning individuals. Her additional insight—that institutional resistance to change was rooted in a core spirituality—both pleased and disturbed her. It was a sign of her own spiritual growth.

On the other hand, the implications of her insight frightened her. Distorted spirituality enabled institutions to function largely independent of the people who supposedly ran them, subverting whatever legitimate intentions these institutions might claim. Cynthia shivered, as if her wisdom had awakened a demon. She chased it away by reminding herself that Ambassador Nolte was unlikely to openly sanction a war against the churches.

Cynthia picked up the phone, uncertain whether or not Nolte even knew about Operation Cain. She completed the call. As she did so, doubt, in the form of another "on the other hand," crept into her mind. Whether or not he knew about Operation Cain, Dennis Nolte might be unable or unwilling to stop it. Before she could hang up she was startled by a voice at the other end.

"Hello," Ambassador Nolte said. He waited, expectantly. "Who is this?" he asked.

Sensing he was about to hang up Cynthia spoke. "Ambassador Nolte?" she said. "This is Cynthia Randolph." She had never called him directly.

"Yes. What can I do for you?" he said. "I understand I'll see you tonight."

"I'd like to see you prior to our scheduled meeting," she said. After some hesitation she added: "Privately."

"May I ask what this is about?" he asked.

"I'd rather it wait," she said.

"Of course. Let's meet at the hotel at six." Nolte seemed concerned. "Is that enough time?" he asked.

"Yes. I think so. Thank you," she said.

"Are you all right?" he said.

"I'm...It's just..." Cynthia paused. She was searching for the proper words. "I think something may be terribly wrong."

"Can it wait until six?" he asked.

"Yes. I'll talk to you tonight," she said. "Don't say anything to Robert or anyone else," she added.

Cynthia hung up the phone. She looked expectantly at a note pad that lay before her with the eyes of a magician, hoping it might provide missing pieces to a puzzle which confounded her. What was Operation Cain? Who directed it? Who were its targets? She thought hard...about things she knew...about things she thought she knew...about anything that might be relevant in her quest to unravel the mystery. She wrote:

+ Canales leaked info.

+ U.S. personnel present during torture—advisor? agent? soldier? mercenary?

+ Robert Barnes: prior knowledge

+ Peter?

Captain Canales leaked information to the community about

the existence of Operation Cain. Why he did so wasn't clear. The presence of U.S. personnel during Rafael's torture implied policy approval at some level. But who was determining policy? Nolte? Barnes? Some one higher up still?

Cynthia considered Barnes a likely candidate. He was briefed by Peter on the dangers of liberation theology, had a reputation of questionable integrity, and he knew of Ricardo's arrest and the massacre before the Salvadoran authorities acted. Peter? The question mark spoke volumes. Last night they had broken new ground. Emotionally and politically. She loved him. She wanted to trust him...but she didn't.

Cynthia picked up her pen. She wrote, speculatively:

> OPERATION CAIN:
> operational=active=in motion.
> Operation Cain, underway.

She sipped her coffee, reread what she'd written and again thrust her pen to the paper:

> CAIN KILLED ABEL.

She struggled to remember the story. Cain killed Abel. But why? She got up, removed a Bible from her bookshelf and returned to the couch. "Cain and Abel were Adam and Eve's sons," she said to herself. "It must be somewhere towards the beginning." She was right. There it was in the fourth chapter of Genesis. She read:

> Cain said to Abel his brother, "Let us go out to the field." And when they were in the field, Cain rose up and killed his brother Abel. Then the Lord said to Cain, "Where is your brother Abel?" He responded, "I do not

know; am I my brother's keeper?" And the Lord said, "What have you done? The voice of your brother's blood cries to me from the ground."

Cain killed Abel in a jealous rage. He was envious because God accepted Abel's offering while rejecting his own. The result was violence. An innocent man was murdered.

Cynthia closed her eyes. "Am I my brother's keeper?" The question echoed through her mind like a shout in a canyon. Looking for clues to decipher Operation Cain, she was distracted by insights into herself. She was haunted by God's question to Cain...by Cain's answer...by her own indifference. All her life she had been insulated from the death of the innocents and thus from God's question to Cain. Her field of vision before Pueblo Duro was far from the killing fields where the rich denied the poor a place to plant their crops. And their lives.

Cynthia entered a space somewhere between sleep and wakefulness. In her dreamlike state she found herself being interrogated. By God.

"Where are your murdered brothers and sisters?" God's voice came from a distant place. She stepped forward, straining to hear.

"I can't hear you," she said. "What do you want?"

"Where are your murdered brothers and sisters?" God repeated. God's voice seemed somewhat closer.

"I do not know," she heard herself saying. "I am not responsible for them."

"What have you done?" God persisted.

The question, barely audible, triggered a defensive response: "I have done nothing," she said. "I told you: I am not responsible."

"You cannot hear the voices?" God shouted. It was not an angry question. It was as if God was struggling to be heard.

"I hear nothing," she said, defensively.

"Listen to their voices," God pleaded. "Listen *for* their voices. You can not hear them if they are far from you. Move closer," God implored. "Can you hear them now?"

"Yes. I hear them," she said. "But faintly."

"Then move closer," God said. As she moved forward she tripped over a body and fell, face down, into a pool of blood. It was Rosa's body. Her blood, mingled with the others, stained the rocky soil. As she struggled to her feet, Cynthia noticed for the first time that the voice of God and the cries of the people were one.

"Your murdered brothers and sisters speak to you," God said in a voice that was loud, clear and almost gentle. "They cry out. Their blood cries out from the ground."

"But it is you—not they—who speak," she said.

"We speak with one voice. We speak with many voices. They speak to you. Through me." There was a pause. "There is something more important," God said. "I speak to you and you to me through them."

She was desperate now. "I hear their cries. I hear your cry. God. Forgive me."

God's voice was reassuring. "Rejoice in your freedom."

Twenty-nine

Operation Cain

Cynthia awoke, startled by her dream. Her consciousness was once again rooted firmly in her apartment. She closed her Bible, picked up her pen and wrote:

> CAIN KILLED ABEL.
> BROTHER KILLS BROTHER:
> jealousy—offering—rejection—violence—
> death—denial—competing gods—
> innocent victims.

She pondered these words. Brother killing brother was an apt description of events in El Salvador. The murder of the poor was rooted in issues of land and hunger. But at the center of the violence was a theological dispute. Those who arrested Padre Ricardo and who murdered Padre Ernesto despised both their work among the poor and the God they worshiped. Cynthia again scribbled on her pad:

> CAPTAIN CANALES' WARNING, CONTEXT:
> 1. Padre Ricardo's arrest;
> 2. Rafael's torture.
> 3. Aftermath:
>   a. The Massacre.
>   b. Padre Ernesto's Murder.

Without knowing details of Operation Cain, Cynthia deduced its essence: Persecution of the churches was escalating. Or so it seemed. But who was directing it? The Agency? The embassy? Salvadorans? All three? Who was putting their report's recommendations into practice and who would be its next target?

Cynthia looked at her watch. It was several hours before her meeting with Nolte. She walked to the coffee table in her living room and removed the drawer. She reached underneath, took out a thick document stamped "top secret," opened it and read:

To the degree that liberation theology succeeds in withdrawing the veneer of legitimacy to an unequal society and in inspiring the hope of the poor majority, it guarantees that greater violence will be used against its proponents. We will need to work with our allies to manage terror effectively in relation to the political moment. The stronger the subversive movements become, the greater the terror which must be directed against them.

The Church cannot but be one of the principal targets of the violence. Justifying repression against the Church will require perception management unprecedented in our recent experience. If we define liberation theology as an enemy, and if we are committed to winning the war, then our hands will be stained with blood. The alternative is an unacceptable loss of control in a region considered vital to U.S. national security.

Cynthia sat in the midst of a dejected silence as deep and dark as an empty well. She wondered if the author of these words—words whose stench hung in the air like the smell of a decaying corpse in a garbage dump frequented by death squads, words that haunted, words that led to murder—could change. She wondered about Peter.

189

As her soul drifted towards despair, she remembered her own role in the report. She had changed. Peter could change. She hoped with all her might that he had changed. She hated the doubt. She hated herself for doubting.

Cynthia held the report in her hands and wept. Enemies were no longer abstractions. They had faces. And names. Carmen. Ricardo. Rafael. Romero. Sancho. Elena. If she had underestimated the humanity of her enemies, she was equally blind to the subtleties of evil. Evil veiled itself beneath layers of deception where it could remain invisible. It hid beneath the shadows of decency feeding on the morality of those whose sensibilities were atrophied by the chasm that separates the powerful from any unwilling subjects.

Cynthia learned her morality at the supermarket, money in pocket, surrounded by a thousand choices masquerading as freedom. Betrayed by the limitations of her experience, she realized only now that the majority of the people in the world awoke each day with survival on their minds.

Cynthia couldn't breathe. She forced herself to her feet. Changed clothes. Headed for the coliseum. Her growing field of resentment included the fact that even running had become a matter of deception. But not today. Today she would run in the midday heat, purge her body of impurities, renew her battered soul.

She entered the coliseum, knelt down and tightened the laces on her shoes. She glanced up and saw Peter and Robert walking around the track, conspicuous only because of her fears and the intensity of their conversation. She thought about approaching them casually but doubted her capacity to remain composed. She took one step forward and then retreated to the lonely silence of her apartment.

———

Robert was annoyed. "Look, Peter. You drag me over here under the pretense of crisis and don't tell me a damn thing. What the hell's going on?" he demanded.

Peter measured his words carefully. He was talking to his superior within the Agency, someone with power to break his career. Or perhaps worse.

"Why don't you trust me?" Peter said.

Robert pretended to be shocked. His denial was so overstated it confirmed Peter's suspicions. "Nothing could be further from the truth," he said. "I have complete confidence in you. Complete confidence."

"Cut the crap, Robert. We both know you've kept me at a distance ever since the report," Peter said.

"It's a masterful report, Peter. Brilliant. I'm sorry we haven't expressed sufficient gratitude for your efforts. I'm afraid that's life in the Agency. We get callous. We assume our work itself is reward enough. I'm sorry," Robert repeated himself.

Peter, his face flush with anger, grabbed Robert by the arm, turned him around and looked him dead in the face. "Look, Robert. The whole damn region is about to go up in smoke. As far as I can tell the Agency's not doing anything about it. I spent three years of my life assessing the danger and a few more years getting inside the movement. Hell, I'm inside their minds. I know what Ricardo and the communities think, what they say, what they do. Damn it. I know when they take a shit!"

Robert was frightened by the onslaught but had no choice but to listen as Peter vented anger so real and deep and hidden that it surprised even Peter himself. "I'll tell you what else I know," Peter continued. "These people are dangerous. And they're winning. Nolte has got his head so far up his rear end that he doesn't have a clue. It's up to you to stop it, Robert. It's up to us. For God's sake, stop twiddling your thumbs! You talk as though Carter is a wimp but you've got less balls than he does. I want to know why you're incapable of doing what has to be done. Are you afraid of Nolte? or Carter? or Turner? Well, I'm not," he screamed. "I'm not. They can all go to hell."

Robert was stunned, totally unprepared for the rage Peter vented.

"Do you think the Soviet Union is going to pass on El Salvador?" Peter continued. "They'll soon have Nicaragua as a base. For God's sake. Wake up before its too late."

Peter pushed Robert away, remembered his mission and regained his composure. "I'm sorry," he said. "I'm frustrated. What have I done, Robert? Why have you locked me out?" Not expecting an answer Peter continued. "I can help," he said. "Let me help. Before its too late."

Robert didn't know how to respond and he said so. "Look, Peter. I don't know what to tell you. I need to think about a few things. Then let's talk."

"You think about this," Peter said. "I know about Operation Cain." Robert's stone face revealed nothing. Peter laughed. "Don't worry, Robert. Right now all I know is that Operation Cain exists. But if I know it exists, then you know two things: I'm a good agent. And you've got a serious problem. You've got a mole somewhere in your operation. Sounds to me like we should work together. I'll find the mole but you've got to tell me what the hell is going on," Peter said.

Robert looked like a ghost. "I have to go," he said. And walked away.

———

Denied a chance to run, Cynthia polished off a bag of potato chips. She lay on her sofa and closed her eyes. Her mind carried her to Pueblo Duro where when helping with literacy she slept on a simple mat, ate beans and tortillas, and felt part of a community. The community welcomed her. Embraced her. Most ironic, they trusted her. Their trust converted her. She was bound to them now in ways that undermined all the other foundations of her life. And yet, even in Pueblo Duro, she was an outsider. And always would be.

Less than twenty-four hours earlier Cynthia felt free. She and Peter were on a dangerous path but it seemed as though they were walking together. Today she felt utterly alone.

The phone rang, startling Cynthia into consciousness. "I'm calling from Ambassador Nolte's office." The woman at the other end of the line spoke with a nasal tone. "He asked me to call you. Regrettably, he has to cancel your meetings scheduled for tonight, both the one at six and the one at eight."

"Did he say why?" Cynthia asked.

"All hell's broken loose in Nicaragua. Somoza's gone and so is his army. The Sandinistas are marching into the plaza."

July 19, 1979. The Nicaraguan revolution. It was the first of several foreign policy crises that would have aftershocks in El Salvador in the coming year. The people's destiny was being sealed by events both within and outside its borders.

Thirty

Mixed Signals

New doubts about Peter, an inability to penetrate Operation Cain and ineptitude in Washington combined to make Cynthia's head spin. She decided against confronting Peter directly about his meeting with Robert Barnes. Their conversation focused instead on the multiple volcanos that seemed ready to turn El Salvador into ash.

"The problem as Robert sees it," Cynthia said, "is you can't have a Pinochet if you don't have an army. He thinks we lost Nicaragua because we forgot Chile. He and Nolte agree on that much, but they couldn't differ more over the implications here," she added.

"Let me guess," Peter said. "Robert is advocating for General Ochoa." General Ochoa stole an election in 1977. He was the most recent in a long line of military leaders to become president with a wink from Washington and more tanks and guns than ballots. The present political climate in both El Salvador and the United States made him something of a marked man, but this hadn't dented Robert Barnes' allegiance.

"Robert supports Ochoa," Peter repeated, "and Ambassador Nolte wants Ochoa to go."

"You've got it," Cynthia said.

According to Robert Barnes, unless the United States backed Ochoa—really backed him—El Salvador would go the way of

Nicaragua, not only losing a known leader but in the aftermath losing the army as well.

Nolte and President Carter shared Robert's concern about preserving El Salvador's armed forces, but they differed over how to do so. Unlike Robert, they saw General Ochoa and some of his officers as the problem. If the U.S. clung to Ochoa, he might end up being another sinking ship that took the whole military structure down with him. The U.S. had coddled Somoza so long in Nicaragua that when Somoza finally left he had to take his disgraced and defeated army with him. Nolte and Carter were determined not to make the same mistake here.

"No wonder there's so much talk of a coup," Cynthia said.

Peter walked over to the coffee pot and refilled his cup. "It's not talk," he said.

"It's ironic," Cynthia said. "Nolte wants to reform the military. Robert wants to bolster it. But their bottom line is the same. Both want the Salvadoran military to be a key actor during and after whatever changes are coming. They disagree on who should lead the military and the role it should play."

Peter and others in the Agency monitored the actions of the main coup planners but he still wasn't sure how active a role the U.S. was playing. "Are we players? Or bystanders?" he asked.

"Nolte is ticked off," she responded. "He sends cables up to Washington and either hears nothing or some vague directive to get the sides together and set a date for new elections. Carter and the State Department are so obsessed with Nicaragua that they can't be bothered by stuff here," she said.

Cynthia realized she hadn't answered his question directly. "Mainly observers. Nolte wants us to be more active in the coup itself, but Carter doesn't want another Yankee-led disaster like Chile or Guatemala. I'm sorry," she said, quickly. "We've never talked about Chile. I don't know if it's a sensitive subject," she added.

"It was a long time ago," he said.

Cynthia felt better during these conversations. They made her feel more confident that she and Peter were on the same road. She wanted to shift their topic to Operation Cain but before she decided whether or not to do so, Peter spoke.

"I've been wondering," he said.

"About?"

"Operation Cain," Peter said. "I wonder what Ambassador Nolte knows."

Cynthia nodded.

"And what about Robert," he continued. "Both Nolte and Robert have concerns about the churches. They disagree about General Ochoa. The Ambassador thinks Ochoa has to go, whereas Robert supports him. Maybe Robert's support for Ochoa extends to Operation Cain. Operation Cain could be his way of shoring up Ochoa and circumventing a policy he disagrees with. If Ricardo's arrest, Padre Ernesto's murder and the assault on the base communities at the garrison are linked to Operation Cain, then it would seem that it clearly targets the progressive churches. Robert and Ochoa would clearly sanction that. Then again so might Nolte."

"It's all so confusing," Cynthia said, fighting a temptation to test a theory she had worked through in her mind. She was glad she waited when Peter verbalized what she was thinking.

"Let's suppose Operation Cain is a clandestine means to shore up Ochoa and his allies in the military and in the oligarchy by escalating repression against the churches," Peter said. "Ochoa is in trouble, even more so now that Carter thinks he's got to go. If Robert is defending Ochoa, then we can safely bet that individuals or groups on Operation Cain's target list are in grave danger." Peter hesitated.

"So Robert may hold the key to our understanding Operation Cain," Cynthia completed his thought, "and to our ability to warn those who are on our hypothetical hit list."

"So what now?" Peter asked.

"I don't know," she said. "Robert is dangerous. But...," she paused. "But we shouldn't lose track of another problem."

"What's that?" he asked.

"Carter and Nolte may have tactical disagreements with Robert, but they may pursue something nearly as bad," she said. "Do you remember what you told me the day before your briefing with Robert and General Warren?" she said.

"I have a good memory, ah, ah, Barbara," he said with a smile. "But not that good."

"You said you weren't concerned about Carter's election because no U.S. president, whether a Democrat or a Republican, would allow a communist government in Central America," she said. "They would do whatever was necessary."

"I remember," he said.

"The definition of what makes a country communist is as wide as a canyon," she continued. "Plans to isolate and destabilize the Sandinistas by directing economic aid to the business sector in Nicaragua are already underway," she noted. "And if they fail, members of Somoza's army are being trained in Honduras."

"In other words," Peter said. "Whatever their differences, Carter and Barnes may end up in the same place."

"Essentially, that's it," she said. "It was pretty easy for Washington to turn a blind eye to how the military and oligarchy ran things here until recently. Stevens was right. El Salvador has never had much of what the U.S. really needs. I think that's why Carter found El Salvador an attractive place to demonstrate his resolve to make human rights central to his foreign policy. It didn't cost him anything," she said.

"You think his commitment is more symbolic than real?" Peter asked.

Cynthia pondered his question carefully. "I'm afraid that's it," she said. "Nicaragua's revolution suddenly makes El Salvador important. Carter cares about human rights but his concern isn't deep enough to really change course. He cut military aid after the election was stolen but the military was still entrenched. As far as the military is concerned, Carter's action was more a nuisance than a nemesis. We're still training Salvadorans at the School of the Americas, and the U.S. recently approved loans and aid through the World Bank. I'd say Carter sent mixed signals to the generals but the bottom line is that they stayed in power," she added.

"Carter's commitment to human rights hasn't really been tested," Peter agreed. "Until now. With Nicaragua lost and trouble brewing here, El Salvador is practically and symbolically important."

"I'm afraid it's a test he's failing," Cynthia said. "He's under intense pressure in Washington and the revolutionary movement within El Salvador is strong and getting stronger. There's another problem," Cynthia added. "Carter isn't interested in a nuanced discussion of the popular sectors. The guerrilla leadership is sufficiently Marxist and the progressive churches are sufficiently radical so as to color the whole movement RED," Cynthia said.

"Especially given the cables Robert is sending," Peter agreed.

Cynthia looked discouraged. "The bottom line is Carter wants to preserve the military," she said. "He won't back deep reforms, let alone support a revolution he doesn't control. That leaves him vulnerable to some very unsavory alliances."

"It reminds me of Kennedy..." Peter began.

"I forgot you were a student of Kennedy," she said.

"Unfortunately, there are many Kennedys to choose from. Kennedy once said that blocking peaceful evolution makes violent revolution inevitable. I'm starting to recognize the wisdom of that Kennedy. Unfortunately, I was thinking of a different Kennedy."

"I'm sorry I interrupted," she said.

Peter smiled. "I've no train of thought to speak of," he smiled. "I was remembering something Kennedy said after he approved the assassination of Trujillo in the Dominican Republic. After Trujillo's death, Kennedy told Arthur Schlesinger that he hoped the U.S. could help develop and democratize the Dominican Republic.

But Kennedy was a pragmatist. He said there were three possibilities facing the D.R., in descending order of preference. A decent, democratic government. A continuation of a repressive, Trujillo-like regime. Or a Castro-type situation. Kennedy said we would aim for the first but couldn't renounce the second until it was clear we could avoid the third."

"And a few years later Johnson sent in the marines and installed a dictator," she responded. "I'm afraid that Carter, despite all the rhetoric about human rights, is equally pragmatic," Cynthia said. "He'll do anything to prevent El Salvador from becoming another Nicaragua. That makes our list of possible suspects concerning Operation Cain a long one."

Thirty-one

Goodwill Offering

The news of Somoza's ousting and the Sandinista triumph set off a mardi gras in Pueblo Duro and similar communities throughout El Salvador. There were celebrations everywhere. The gathering of Padre Ricardo and the others was joyous but more restrained. "I never thought I would live to see such a change," Rafael said. "Never." Rafael could not contain himself. "Never," he said again. "Who would have imagined it?"

Sancho savored the moment and a Pilsener. "I've imagined it my whole life," he said, taking a sip from a bottle of Salvador's best beer. "I'm not sure I believed it was possible. The octopus," he said, "has so many tentacles. You break free of one and it grabs hold with another. It has been that way always."

Rafael slapped him hard on the back. "Not today. Not today, my friend," he said.

Padre Ricardo couldn't decide if his glass was half empty or half full. One minute he joined in the celebration. The next he withdrew into himself. It was Elena who noticed his hesitancy, perhaps because it captured her own ambivalence. "Padre. You seem far away," Elena said.

"Not too far," he said, reassuringly.

"What are you thinking?" she asked.

"Tonight we celebrate. Tomorrow we think. Tomorrow is time enough to sort out what it means for us. For El Salvador," he said.

The others wouldn't leave the discussion until then. "We can celebrate and think at the same time," Rafael said. "My brain works better when I celebrate."

Padre Ricardo smiled. "I'm thinking Nicaragua experienced the Exodus. They confounded Pharaoh's army and passed through the Red Sea," he said. Padre Ricardo paused. It was a long pause. "But Nicaragua is far from the promised land. They have entered the wilderness. They will need many miracles to survive. Many, many miracles."

"They may be far from the promised land," Juan said. "But in my lifetime, few movements have won power. The Sandinistas will give land to people like us," he said. "It is a miracle they have gotten this far. It gives me hope that our struggle is not in vain."

Padre Ricardo nodded approval, but it was Sancho who spoke. "We will get there too," he said. "God-willing we will get there too. But at what cost? How many died in Nicaragua? Thirty thousand? Forty thousand? I wonder how many of us will live to see a new El Salvador?"

"I know people my age, even older," Rafael said. "They are breathing, but they died years ago. Their spirits dried up. They lived most of their lives without dreaming of something beyond another day of despair. Doesn't Jesus teach that the death we are to fear is a dying in the midst of life? Maybe it's easier for an old man," he said, "but I will gladly give my life if it contributes even a little to the dawning of a new El Salvador."

Tomás looked grim. "The victory in Nicaragua teaches many things," he said. "It gives us hope. It reinforces our will to struggle. But people like Julio Díaz and General Calderón are learning too. They will not sit idly by. They are wounded animals. They were desperate before. They are more desperate now. We must never forget that there is nothing more dangerous than a wounded animal.

"Tomás is right," Padre Ricardo said. "But wounded animals are also vulnerable."

———

Peter's outburst at the coliseum impressed Robert Barnes, who later initiated a conversation. Robert needed an ally. His disagreements with Ambassador Nolte led to a temporary demotion. When Robert arrived at the coliseum for their next meeting, he found Peter waiting.

Peter looked at the man who was his superior in the Agency. They had known each other a long time. Robert had investigated and helped Peter make sense out of Bui Thi's murder and arranged his transfer to Chile. He had followed Peter's work in Chile closely. It was Robert who approved Peter's transfer to El Salvador when Central America was ready to explode.

"If you don't mind my saying so, you look terrible," Peter said. "What's up?"

"Nolte replaced me this morning," Robert said.

Peter seemed shocked. "Why?"

"It's no secret we differ over what needs to be done," Robert said. "He says he respects my views and doesn't want to force me to carry out a policy I disagree with this strongly. The man's an idiot," he added, "but he's right about this one."

"I'm sorry," Peter said. "What's your status? Who's replacing you?" he asked.

Robert looked defeated. "Terrence Malcolm arrived last week. He's in charge of intelligence having to do with the coup. I stay on with unspecified duties, which means they'll try to bury me beneath an avalanche of papers," he said. His inflection rose, emphasizing the word "try."

Peter spoke supportively. "You'd think they'd jump out of

their shoes helping Ochoa. Instead they're determined to throw him out."

"I've been thinking about our conversation," Robert said. "There may be a way you can help." He turned to Peter. "Problem is, you were right. I didn't trust you. Problem is, I still don't know if I can," he said.

"Damn it, Robert, what do you want from me?" Peter asked.

"Earn my trust," Robert responded.

"How?" Peter said with anger. "You've got a mole or a leak or some problem with Operation Cain," he continued. "I want to help find it. But I can't do it without you," he pleaded. "You want me to earn your trust. How can I do that? And how the hell do I know I can trust you?" Peter added.

Robert interpreted Peter's remark as a challenge to his anti-communism. He laughed so uncontrollably that it offended Peter, who started to walk away. "Look, Peter. Meet me at my apartment tonight at eight. Bring something. Convince me. Believe me, I want you to convince me. But you've got to show me something. Eight o'clock," he repeated and walked away.

———

Robert's home was in an elite section of San Salvador, an area not unlike where Julio Díaz and others had their urban mansions.

"Come in, Peter," Robert said. "What are you drinking?"

"Coffee if you've got it," he said.

Robert walked into the kitchen and returned with a cup. "Anything else?" he asked.

"No, thanks," Peter said.

"I understand you've had the pleasure of General Calderón's company," Robert said.

"He said an interrogation would be good for my credibility. Apparently he felt the same about a broken rib and a cracked skull,"

Peter said rubbing his side. "He took offense to my interest in Padre Ernesto's murder."

"So I heard," Robert said.

"Understandable, I suppose. From his perspective," Peter added.

At that moment Calderón entered the room. He walked past Peter and took a seat on the couch across from him.

"Do you have something for me?" Robert asked. "Or should we finish our coffee and call it a night?"

Peter opened his briefcase and removed a cassette and a recorder. He exchanged uncomfortable glances with Calderón. "For your benefit, General, the male voice on the tape is mine. The female voice is that of another agent." He pushed play, allowing Robert to listen to the selectively edited tape of his conversation with Cynthia:

Do you think we know what's going on with the Agency? What do you mean? Do Robert and the others trust us? I'm not sure. It seems there may be different levels of policy being played out. We're involved on one level, but not others. That's normal procedure. I'm talking about something else. Robert said if he had known we were going to be outside the garrison on the night of the massacre he might have talked to Calderón. That means he knew about the massacre. Before the massacre. There's something else I wonder about. What's that? U.S. soldiers were at the garrison that night. They were in the room during Rafael's torture. Rafael told Carmen he heard English spoken outside the interrogation room. And, two U.S. soldiers entered the room when they assumed Rafael had passed out. That's only part of it. If Robert had prior knowledge of the massacre, then he must have known that Padre Ricardo was going to be arrested. It's hard to imagine Calderón acting on his own.

When Peter shut off the recorder, he noticed that Robert looked both disturbed and impressed. "A smart lady," he said.

"Perhaps too smart," Calderón added.

"How did you get this?" Robert asked.

"I've been suspicious of Randolph for a long time," Peter said with a frown. "The tape confirms my suspicions. The tape and this," he said. Peter reached into his briefcase and removed a large manila envelope. He handed it to Robert. "There were only three copies of this report," he said. "I left them with you and General Warren. I didn't see another one until our unfortunate meeting in your office," he said, looking in Calderón's direction.

"After taping this," he said, "I searched Randolph's apartment and found this. If you check the log you'll find a discrepancy of over three hundred copies just prior to our meeting. I don't know how she got access to the original but she did."

Peter looked at Robert. "I think you should talk to Malcolm and make sure he confines Randolph close to home," Peter said.

"Good idea," Robert agreed.

"Robert tells me you heard something about..." Calderón paused as if the name escaped him, "about an operation, yes, Operation Cain, I think it was."

"Yes," Peter said, calmly.

"Where did you hear of this so-called Operation Cain?" Calderón asked.

Peter ignored his question. "I think we'd do better working together," Peter said. "I hope you agree." Peter stood up, removed the tape and handed it to Robert. "Keep the tape and the report," he said. "Consider them goodwill offerings. Gentlemen, talk. But I'd say we're up to our eyeballs in shit. Don't talk too long. I'll wait to hear from you." Peter walked out the door.

———

General Ochoa looked grim. The handwriting was on the wall. Literally. Graffiti all over San Salvador called for his ousting. He was reluctant to read it.

"What do you think I should do?" he asked.

"I'd be lying if I said it was too early to panic," Robert Barnes responded. "It's no secret the embassy is open to a coup if it means a suitable replacement. Carter's so preoccupied with Nicaragua he's not saying much, but it's clear that Washington wants a civilian president and a strong military. They won't accept a strong military president. If I were you, I'd watch my back. Carefully," he said.

Ochoa walked over and refilled his glass of whiskey. "You got details?" he asked.

"Not yet," Robert said. "There is some good news." The prospect of good news lifted President Ochoa momentarily out of a deepening depression. Good news was a scarce commodity.

"Carter's in trouble," Robert said. "Interest rates in the U.S. have people screaming, and inflation is shooting through the roof. That's not all," he added. "Nicaragua and the flak over the canal make him vulnerable. Republicans are having a field day saying he's soft on communism. Another foreign policy disaster will dash any hopes for re-election."

Robert seemed buoyed by his own analysis. "Carter's determined not to repeat Nicaragua here," he added. "If you can demonstrate you're the only game in town, he'll eventually be a player. If not, you're in trouble. The other option is to outlast Carter. Hang in until after the election. Arnold Hacker will head the Agency under Reagan. He's an old friend. Hacker assures me that Reagan will give us everything we need."

Ochoa looked grim. The U.S. election was more than a year away. "A year is a long time," he said.

"Convince Carter you're the only game in town. Eliminate anyone who might be acceptable to Washington and let people in and outside of El Salvador know you're in charge."

Thirty-two

The Footsteps of Angels

Following the community's celebration Rafael returned to his house, a shell rebuilt from the ashes of the old. He was an old man. His walk, surprisingly brisk, was marred by a noticeable limp.

As he reached his door Rafael stooped down and tried unsuccessfully to gather up two mangos and a small bag of beans. His crushed fingers healed poorly. Like a child in pursuit of a slippery ball Rafael reached for a mango only to have it slip away, rolling further out of reach. His crippled body, like a used pesticide can holding precious drinking water, was an inappropriate vessel for his indomitable spirit.

Each week since the trial there were unsolicited gifts at Rafael's door: a few tortillas, mangos, a bunch of finger shaped bananas or a small bag of rice or beans. Occasionally, he found a pile of wood, neatly stacked like a house of cards. The items appeared at no particular time on no particular day. There was only the predictability of a weekly visit and much needed assistance. Rafael's benefactor preferred anonymity. It was a mystery Rafael knew would solve itself with the passage of time.

Rafael's eyes were as clouded as a May sky marking the beginning of El Salvador's rainy season. He opened the door, walked six steps to a wooden chair, reached to his left and retrieved a candle and a book of matches. With great effort he lit the candle and watched as the flame danced away the darkness.

His glasses, which he rested on the bridge of his nose, could have been retrieved from Buddy Holly's plane crash. They were a gift of sight from Padre Ricardo. Missing a handle, they dug into his nose. But they enabled him to read a few verses from the New Testament each night before sleep overtook him or before the candle extinguished itself in a pool of wax.

This steamy night Rafael sat shirtless, upright in his chair. A Bible lay open before him on an old bench, the same bench where Padre Ricardo, Sancho and Elena sat the night Mario was killed and Rafael decided whether he killed Mario depended on what was best for the community. His back bore the burden of numerous scars. They were the legacy of cynicism. The ugly remnants of torture where cigarettes fuse with madness. A few wounds remained open, ugly sores which embraced the night air in search of healing.

Rafael removed his glasses and listened. He heard them again, the footsteps of angels outside his door. This is how he thought of his benefactor. His betrayer. The footsteps of angels. The thought comforted him, healed him, sealed his forgiveness.

Rafael heard these footsteps often. Many times he wanted to call to the angel, invite it into his home. Somehow it never seemed the right time, the proper moment. He was afraid. Afraid the angel might flee, leaving two broken people to face each other. No. It never seemed the right time. Until now.

Rafael walked to the door and thrust it open. The angel retreated into the darkness. "Come in," Rafael said. "Please. Come in." There was only silence. Perhaps the angel is also afraid of this moment, afraid of this encounter, he thought. "Don't be afraid," Rafael said. "I want to speak to you."

There was more silence. Rafael sighed. It was a sigh longing for peace. He turned and walked in, leaving the door open. He sat, his back to the door, his face illumined by the faint light of a flickering candle. The angel's footsteps returned. He heard them come closer. "Do you know when I first forgave you?" Rafael asked.

"What I did is unforgivable," a voice responded.

"No sin is unforgivable," Rafael said. "Except a sin against the spirit. I forgave you even as they tortured me."

As Rafael spoke, the candle fought against the wind and the shadow of the angel danced against the wall.

"They had no reason to torture me," Rafael continued. "I confessed to the crime. I could tell them nothing they did not already know about the community. But still they tortured me. When I realized their reason, I was able to forgive."

"I don't understand," the voice said.

"Don't you see? By torturing me they thought they could destroy the spirit. The spirit of the community. You and I were co-conspirators with them," Rafael explained.

"But you conspired to nothing. It is I who conspired with them. Against you. Against the community," the voice protested.

"It is true. I did not choose to be a co-conspirator," he said. "I was chosen. But I also had to choose," Rafael said, "between hatred and forgiveness."

"My betrayal led to your torture," the voice insisted.

"Yes. But torturing me did not lead to their desired goal. Betrayal and torture. What better way to sow division and hatred. What better way to destroy our community. That is what they desired. When I remembered Jesus, I realized that if I hated you they would win at once."

"But how could you keep from hating?" the voice asked. It was a voice filled with doubt.

"They assumed no one could forgive a torturer. No one can. But Christ did. By forgiving you even as they tortured me, their spell was broken. Forgiveness saved the community."

The angel placed his fingers in Rafael's wounds. Rafael winced with pain that brought back all the battles within him. He remembered and felt each burn of the cigarette, each shock, each knuckle cracking. His soul was the object of a tug of war. After a few minutes the pain subsided.

Rafael turned to face his betrayer. "I counted," Rafael said. "I counted each burn from their cigarettes and each electric shock. I forgave them and you each one."

"Why?" his betrayer gasped. "How?"

"I never reached seventy times seven."

Thirty-three

Towards Guazapa

Tomás López worked quietly. Efficiently. His apparent competency masked the terror that threatened to overtake him. He reached over, retrieved a dozen tortillas and placed them on a clean diaper. The tortillas were edible but poorly shaped, he thought.

He folded the diaper over the tortillas and packed the bundle, along with a handful of other diapers, into a saddlebag that hung from a nearby chair. He added several cans of tuna to the pack, along with baby bottle and formula, matches, an opener and a canteen filled with water.

Tomás walked over to a shelf near a simple crib, pausing only to glance at Juancito who slept soundly, oblivious to the chaos that would soon befall him. He took a flash light and package of double C batteries off the shelf and packed them neatly alongside the other items. He walked outside and secured the saddlebags to his horse.

Tomás looked at his house and crossed himself. He returned to the crib, cradled Juancito in his calloused hands, and wrapped him tightly in a blanket. Juancito embraced the blanket and the darkness with womb-like innocence. He slept as his father carried him to the horse and placed him in a makeshift carrier rigged to one of the saddle bags.

Before untying the horse, Tomás reached into his pocket, withdrew six bullets, loaded his gun and crossed himself again.

He then proceeded quietly down the path that led to the edge of his property. He tied the horse to a tree alongside the path and walked slowly toward Padre Ricardo's house. A sense of doom filled the air like the stiff fog encircling the Guazapa volcano.

"Padre. Padre." Tomás said. His whisper became a quiet scream. Desperation overtook him as he pounded on the door. It was three o'clock in the morning. Finally, he heard movement within. Padre Ricardo opened the door.

"Tomás?" Padre Ricardo said. He was half asleep. "Are you okay? What is it?" he asked.

Tomás pushed his way past Padre Ricardo, turned on the flashlight, and went to a chest where Padre Ricardo kept his clothes. He threw a pair of pants and a shirt in his direction. "Get dressed," he ordered.

Padre Ricardo started to protest but slipped into his pants as Tomás stuffed a change of clothes and Ricardo's Bible hastily into a small canvas bag.

"What's this about?" Padre Ricardo said as he put his wallet into his front pocket. He noticed the pistol that Tomás had strapped to his side.

"You're going to be killed," he said. "Tonight. Look, there's no time to explain. You've got to go."

"Who?...How do you know?" Padre Ricardo stammered.

Tomás looked desperate. He picked up the canvas bag and walked toward the door. "I'll explain as we go," he said.

They left the house and ran a short distance down the path where horse and child were waiting. Tomás handed Padre Ricardo the flashlight and the pack with his clothes.

"Here's seventy colones," he said. "It's all I have. There's enough food for several days in the saddle bags," he added.

"Tell me what's going on," Padre Ricardo protested. Just then he heard the sound of a whimper, a whimper becoming a full-fledged cry that threatened to shatter the silent darkness.

Tomás walked over to Juancito strapped at the horse's side. "It's okay," he said fighting back tears. Tomás looked at Padre Ricardo. "We sent the other children away," he said. "There's no time to explain." Desperation filled his voice. "No time."

Tomás reached into his pocket and withdrew a photo. It was a picture of Juancito being held by Padre Ricardo over the baptismal font with Tomás and Ana standing by proudly. He kissed the photo and gave it to Padre Ricardo.

"Leave it with my son," he said.

"Look, Tomás. You tell me I've got to go because someone is going to murder me. You give me your money, your horse and your son. Tell me what's going on," Padre Ricardo pleaded.

Tomás looked up sadly. "I'll tell you," he said "and then you must go. Señor Díaz, General Calderón and the others met last night. There were two gringos also. They are determined to avoid another Nicaragua and agree it is time to send another signal to the communities. To sow fear. To murder you," Tomás said.

"How do you know?" Padre Ricardo asked.

"Octavio was sent to call me to El Patrón's...to Julio's," he said.

"Octavio?" Padre Ricardo interrupted him.

"He hates you and the Church," Tomás said. "He found out that his mother prostituted herself to pay for Padre Eduardo's blessing, and he blames you for Eusebio's death because you let him carry the Bible. There's no time to discuss this now," he continued. "Octavio delivered the news that I am to be your murderer."

Tomás knelt down at Padre Ricardo's feet. "Father, I am in need of confession," he said. "I made a pact with the devil. The last few years of drought threatened to ruin me. I was about to lose my land. And so..." Tomás could barely speak.

"I know," Padre Ricardo said.

"And so..." Tomás continued, "I made a deal with El Patrón. I betrayed Rafael and agreed to provide information to them about the community. God forgive me," he cried.

"Your sins are forgiven," Padre Ricardo said. "As a priest I absolve you of all your sins."

Tomás rose to his feet. His sense of relief was short-lived. "Thank you, Padre," he said. "Octavio says they are holding Ana as their insurance policy. I kill you and they release her," he explained. "You must go. Take Juancito with you."

Tomás took a piece of paper from his pocket and gave it to Padre Ricardo. "Here is a list of several communities and towns in every direction and the names of people with whom you can leave Juancito," he said.

Padre Ricardo looked troubled. "I cannot go," he said. "Not if my leaving means Ana will be killed."

"There is no other way," Tomás protested.

"There is," Padre Ricardo said, "another way...." His voice trailed off like the disappearance of a shooting star. "You made a pact with the devil. Keep it," he said. "You must kill me." Padre Ricardo paused. "I absolve you of the sin you must commit. Before you commit it," he said.

Tomás wanted to do the right thing. He was unprepared for Padre Ricardo's words. He looked at the gun strapped to his side, removed it and raised his arm. His finger on the trigger, he closed his eyes. He breathed deeply but could not do it.

"No," Tomás shouted. "No. I will not. I cannot. Don't you see, I am already a dead man," he said. "Even if I kill you, do you think they will let me live? Let Ana go? I sealed our fate the first time I sold myself to them. Go. Now. You must leave. If not for yourself then for the community. And for Juancito."

Padre Ricardo hesitated, took the paper and mounted the horse.

"Where will you go?" Tomás asked.

"Guazapa. I am a Salvadoran," he said. "If I have to leave Pueblo Duro, then I will go where I can still work with the people.

215

What will you do?" Padre Ricardo asked.

"Alert the others and return to Ana," Tomás said. "Take care of Juancito. The list will help you," he added.

Padre Ricardo nodded.

"I reconciled myself to Rafael," he said.

"That is good," Padre Ricardo said. "Very good."

"Is there a resurrection, Padre?" Tomás asked.

"Yes, Tomás. There is a resurrection because there is forgiveness."

Tomás turned and walked quickly down the path.

Padre Ricardo returned to his house one last time. He reached around the door, picked up something and waited. It grew smaller in his arms until it could fit in the pack along with his clothes and Bible.

He breathed a deep sigh, said a short prayer and mounted. Juancito stirred briefly and then quieted as the horse moved carefully up and down the paths. They began their journey towards Guazapa.

Thirty-four

Sharks

Neither Operation Cain nor General Ochoa's vigilance could impede the tide building against him. He was a perfect replica of the cartoon figure whose desperate eyes peer out from behind a desk beneath the caption: "Just because I'm paranoid doesn't mean they're not out to get me." Rumors of a coup swirled everywhere around him. He knew it. He didn't know how to stop it.

Lt. Col. Felipe Esperanza wasn't paranoid. But he was concerned. Coups were risky, dangerous, bloody and betrayed with ease. The truth about coups is that they usually failed. As the primary architect of the coup against Ochoa, Esperanza thought of every detail, considered every contingency, anticipated every possibility. Or so it seemed.

What concerned him was not his immediate task. As Ochoa's senior aide, he could arrest the president without difficulty. His preoccupation was with Rivas and Crudo, two colonels who were latecomers to the military coordinating council where the coup idea was hatched.

Esperanza knew Crudo was corrupt from the time they overlapped at the state-run phone company where Crudo enriched himself as general manager. He argued against Crudo's participation and lost the argument because others were convinced that Crudo knew about the coup. If they didn't include him, Crudo would betray the coup plotters.

It was much the same with Colonel Rivas, who Crudo brought into the coordinating council. Rivas, like his friend General Calderón, headed a garrison. Although Rivas' reputation was less sullied than Calderón's, Esperanza didn't trust him.

Esperanza and the other younger officers saw the coup as an opportunity to chart a new direction for El Salvador, a direction that included land reform and other structural changes important to Salvador's poor majority. He suspected Rivas, Crudo and other more conservative officers had other reasons for joining the coup. For one thing they shared the Carter administration's fear that a bloody revolution to topple Ochoa might threaten the existence of the army itself. They weren't prepared to die or risk their careers on behalf of a sinking ship.

It was Monday morning, October 15, less than three months since Somoza and much of his army fled neighboring Nicaragua. The preferred days for a coup, Friday and Saturday, had passed. Monday provided an element of surprise, but it denied successful coup plotters a prized weekend to establish control.

Esperanza looked at his watch. It was 7:45 a.m. President Ochoa sat at his desk, finishing his breakfast and his presidency. At this very hour rebel officers were seizing control of garrisons throughout El Salvador and arresting commanders, including General Calderón. Esperanza entered Ochoa's' office and walked over to the president's desk.

"Buenos días, Good morning," Ochoa said, his eyes buried in a document.

Esperanza sighed. "It's over," he said. Ochoa looked up. His face turned suddenly grim as he noticed the revolver hanging at Esperanza's side. Esperanza looked at the disbelieving General. "On behalf of the military coordinating council I am here to tell you that your tenure as president has ended," he said.

Ochoa had worried about this or some similar moment for the past several months. Its actuality left him groping for words.

After a long silence, he spoke.

"The goddamn Americans," he said. His voice filled with resignation. "Do you know why the United States has never had a coup?" he asked, amused by his own riddle. "Because it is the only country in the world without a U.S. embassy." The wrinkles around his face tightened. "Damn Carter."

"It's funny," Esperanza said, thinking beyond Ochoa's joke. "You assume we are incapable of acting without the Americans. You feared them so long you cannot think as a Salvadoran. We have much to hate the Americans for." He paused. "But they have no role in the coup."

Crudo and Rivas had close ties to the U.S. embassy and kept U.S. officials informed of the coup but Esperanza had worked effectively to prevent direct U.S. involvement. It was for Esperanza a matter of national pride. And a practical choice. He knew Carter would disapprove of the young officer's commitment to deep reforms. And while the Carter administration wanted General Ochoa out in order to preserve the military, it chose to remain on the sidelines. For now. The U.S. wouldn't continue a hands-off approach for long.

Ochoa looked defiant. "A coup is not so easy," he said. "Are you prepared for the consequences? For the bloodshed?" His question in a few short days might be recalled as prophetic. At the moment it was a sign he underestimated the skill of the coup planners. "We have always stuck together," he screamed. "Do you have any idea what you are doing?"

"Somoza had loyal followers too," Esperanza responded. "They are either dead or in exile. Even a sturdy house can not withstand the winds of a violent hurricane," he added. "Our house has a weak foundation. We are realists. The winds are blowing. We repair the foundation in order to save the house. You and your friends in the oligarchy can no longer withstand the winds. Your stupidity threatens all of us. Besides," he said, "the winds are unpredictable. That much we learned from Nicaragua."

"Is that what you want in El Salvador?" Ochoa said. "That we become another Nicaragua? You hand our country to the communists? I would rather burn the house down. You are a fool."

"You are the fool," Esperanza said. "You are an ostrich hiding his head in the sand. We replace you to defend our beloved El Salvador. To make it something other than a cesspool outside the country clubs of the rich."

"And what will you do with the sharks?" General Ochoa asked. He knew there were those within the military leadership who would join a coup without sharing Esperanza's passion for reforms. He had feared them, but now he regarded them as possible instruments for revenge.

Ochoa, clinging to false hope, picked up the phone and dialed the garrison in the province of Usulután. He was mobilizing for a fight. After several rings the phone was answered. He was informed that his friend Colonel Palmero had been arrested. His stunned expression turned quickly to panic. He hung up the phone and dialed another number.

"What's the matter?" Esperanza asked, relieved that the take over of the garrisons had gone smoothly. "I will tell you," Esperanza continued. "Palmero is no longer in charge of the garrison." Ochoa looked grim. "It is the same all over the country," Esperanza said.

"Calderón? I want to speak to General Calderón," Ochoa shouted into the phone.

Captain Canales, who earlier tried to warn the community about Operation Cain, responded: "General Calderón is under arrest. It's no use, General," Canales said. "The coup is final."

———

The ouster of Ochoa went smoothly enough so as to mask deep contradictions within the coup movement itself. Ochoa was right about the sharks. And Esperanza was right to mistrust Crudo and Rivas, who sacrificed Ochoa for their own purposes. They shared few of the young officer's goals and set out immediately to subvert them in an effort to consolidate their own power. Disagreements surfaced at once.

Esperanza arrested Ochoa, intent on trying him for corruption and a long list of crimes against the people. But within a few hours Crudo and Rivas intervened on behalf of their old friend. Without consultation and in clear violation of Esperanza's wishes, they allowed General Ochoa to escape to Guatemala in a plane provided by that country's dictator. It signaled troubling divisions within the coup movement, divisions that soon festered like an open sore.

Thirty-five

A Coup Within A Coup

The Carter administration still had trouble seeing El Salvador as anything other than Nicaragua's shadow. This frustrated Ambassador Nolte and other U.S. officials on the ground. The successful coup presented Washington and the embassy with problems and opportunities requiring decisions.

When rumors of the coup abounded, the CIA monitored the coup planners, their goals, ideology and relative power. With Ochoa gone it had a similar task. Who was named to the governing *junta*? What interests and sectors did they represent? Who if anyone emerged in a dominant position? Which individuals and groups within the post-coup government would best defend U.S. interests? It was a confusing puzzle.

Ambassador Nolte called a meeting. He was joined by Robert Barnes, brought back into the inner circle, Terrence Malcolm, who had taken over many of Robert's functions over the past months, and Peter and Cynthia who came from a meeting with Archbishop Romero.

Nolte turned to Terrence Malcolm who fumbled through a stack of notes that lay before him. Malcolm explained that the situation was still unstable but that there was a five-person governing *junta* in place with three civilians and two officers. The role of the civilians was unclear.

Even more puzzling, Malcolm said, were pronounced divisions within the group of military officers that supported the ouster of Ochoa. There were two competing factions among the coup organizers, he explained. A more conservative group led by Colonels Crudo and Rivas and a radical group of young officers who instigated the coup and who carried out the takeover of the barracks. The radicals were led by Lt. Col. Esperanza.

"What do you mean by radical?" Peter asked. Cynthia noticed how Peter asked informational questions only. He never made statements that painted a portrait of his own mind. It made her uncomfortable.

"They are committed to sweeping land reform, elections, civilian control of the military and replacement of certain officers," Terrence said. "They emphasize human rights, at least in their rhetoric," he added.

"All compatible with the State Department's public statements," Cynthia reminded him.

Terrence looked skeptical. "Perhaps," he said. "Land reform has different meanings. They also want to dismantle paramilitary groups like ORDEN and nationalize both the banks and the export-import trade."

"They want to force the oligarchy to do something they've never done," Cynthia interjected. "Pay taxes."

"The radicals are communists. Plain and simple," Robert said. "Let's cut through the diplomatic bullshit and be honest. We don't want to deal with people who nationalize things that belong in the private sector. We don't know the details of their land-reform. They may not know. But it sure as hell will go beyond anything we can support," he said.

Ambassador Nolte seemed impressed with Robert's perspective. "Is it fair to say that Esperanza and the other young officers acted not only to preserve the military, but also because they sympathize with many of the goals of the Sandinistas in Nicaragua?" he asked.

"I would say so. Yes," Terrence responded. "They are seeking to restructure the whole society," he added.

"Absolutely," Robert agreed.

"They are communists?" Nolte asked, seeking clarity in a cliche.

"They are certainly leftists and not reformists," Terrence responded.

Cynthia looked uneasy. She tried to explain that leftist labels were no more helpful than communist ones. The left, she said, was divided. They couldn't even agree on the coup. Several of the guerrilla groups didn't trust the young officers. Others were willing to give the new government a chance but were concerned that it couldn't control the military.

She recounted her and Peter's meeting with the Archbishop noting that Romero had appealed this morning to the new government to act boldly. He asked the military to stop the repression and to accept civilian control. And he asked the revolutionary movements to refrain from provocative actions over the next several weeks. He wanted to give Esperanza and the new government a chance.

"I'd like to go on record as saying that Archbishop Romero is the most dangerous man in the country," Robert said.

"The most dangerous? Or the most endangered?" Cynthia snapped back. She was in a tag team wrestling match without a partner.

"Your concerns are noted," Nolte said. "It sounds like Esperanza and the other young officers will need to be watched carefully," he continued. "Who represents them in the *junta*?" he asked.

Terrence smiled. "That's what's confusing," he said. "By all accounts it's Esperanza and the young officers who led the coup. But they are the least represented in the post-coup *junta*."

"Romero expressed the same concern this morning," Cynthia interjected.

"I don't think it's a concern," Robert said.

"Me either," Terrence agreed. "But it's unmistakable. Colonel Montes was a unanimous choice by the military coordinating council to serve on the governing *junta*," Malcolm explained. "He's considered a moderate and was acceptable to both military factions. He's honest, which pleases Esperanza, but he's a military man through and through. The Rivas and Crudo faction knew he'd defend the institution of the military against radical reformers. They also knew he's acceptable to us. It's the other military member of the *junta* that was baffling."

"It's not Esperanza?" Ambassador Nolte interrupted.

"No, it's Colonel Crudo," Terrence responded.

"The way I hear it," Peter jumped in, "is that Montes was selected first. The progressive officers who voted for Montes assumed he would be flanked by Esperanza. The military would therefore be represented in the *junta* by a moderate and a revolutionary committed to deep reforms. It didn't turn out that way. When the ballots were cast for the second military representative to the *junta*, Esperanza was well ahead of Rivas but one vote shy of the required number. Rivas pulled strings and Crudo was accepted as a so-called compromise candidate."

"Essentially, there was a coup within a coup," Cynthia said. "The result is that the *junta* has two military representatives, one moderate, the other reactionary. And the reactionary is in control. I don't think that's reason to celebrate."

Nolte smiled. "I'm not so sure," he said. "It seems the military coordinating council saved us a lot of work. What about the civilians?" he said.

"It's pretty much the same story. There's a professor of engineering with no history of political involvement and no ties to political parties who's considered a moderate; and a right wing businessman who opposes land reform and the nationalization of banks or the export trade. He represents the Chamber of Commerce that Esperanza considers an extension of General Ochoa. The third civilian member is a progressive politician and Esperanza's only ally on the *junta*."

"And he has no power," Cynthia added.

Nolte seemed buoyed by the discussion. "Thanks, Terrence," he said. "So where are we?"

Robert was ready for the question. "You know I opposed efforts to isolate General Ochoa," he said. "I still think it was a mistake. The most important thing now is to prevent the communists from filling the vacuum created by the coup. We should continue isolating Esperanza and his allies."

Nolte looked to Cynthia. "You seem to be the dissenting voice," he said.

Cynthia started diplomatically. "I appreciate your analysis, Terrence. It confirms much of what we heard from the Archbishop this morning. But you and Robert are proposing policy options that will lead to a civil war. Isolating the Esperanza faction and reinforcing Crudo can only lead to bloody violence. You also left out one important detail," she said.

"What's that?" Peter asked.

Cynthia looked annoyed. She wanted an ally, not a straight man. Looking directly at Terrence she continued. "Esperanza told Romero that immediately after the coup you put at least fifty thousand dollars into an account for Crudo, money Crudo used to buy off other officers, to isolate Esperanza and to solidify his own position in the *junta*."

"I resent your accusation," Terrence responded.

"Resentment is more honest than denial," she snapped back. "Let me finish. After passing out bribes, the first thing Crudo did was appoint his friend Colonel Rivas as Defense Minister. And take a wild guess as to Rivas's first action as Minister." Cynthia paused for effect and proceeded. "He freed General Calderón and all the other garrison leaders locked up during the coup. He also ordered D'Aubuisson released."

Cynthia struggle to contain the rage welling up within her. "What would you call a *junta* where one of its members bribes other officers to solidify his power, appoints a right-wing defense minister unilaterally, sets free most of the officers the coup supposedly set out to pasture, and then releases the most feared death squad leader in the country?" she asked.

"Rivas stripped D'Aubuisson of his military credentials," Robert interjected.

"Death squads don't need credentials," Cynthia responded curtly. She looked at Ambassador Nolte. "I'd call it a military dictatorship," she said, returning to her own question. "You want to know where we are? General Ochoa is gone along with a few other officers. But, the military's housecleaning missed most of the dirt. We've got civilians on the *junta* who can't possibly govern because their voices cancel each other out. So what we're left with is more of the same. The military is in charge and it's pretty much the same military."

Thirty-six

The Party List

In order to justify U.S. aid to the new government, the Carter administration cited the young officers' coup like a mantra. It did so even as progressive elements within the coup's leadership were purged. After the meeting in his home, Ambassador Nolte sent a secret cable to Washington warning that the governing *junta* offered the last chance of staving off a takeover of the extreme left.

Cynthia's anger extended to Robert Barnes for his pathological anticommunism, Nolte and Carter for their interpretation of events and subsequent policies which guaranteed a bloody civil war, and to Peter for…. She was upset with Peter for so many reasons she had a hard time focusing her anger.

"For God's sake, Peter. Why don't you ever say anything?" Cynthia said. "We might as well turn the embassy over to Robert."

Peter hated being the object of her wrath. He felt that nothing he could say would appease her, but he had to say something. "Do you think anything I would have added would have made a difference?" he asked. "Terrence and Robert controlled the meeting. Nolte wanted it that way. He was waiting to hear that the coup justifies U.S. aid because that's what Carter wants to hear. Nolte knew we wouldn't say it."

"You didn't say anything," she reminded him.

Now it was Peter who seemed annoyed. "Look, if I join you in that meeting I reinforce your argument in a situation where we can't win. We gain nothing and lose a lot more than you think. I lose Robert. If I lose Robert our chances of getting inside Operation Cain are a lot worse than they are now," he said, convincingly. "Do you think I didn't want to speak up? The whole thing makes me sick."

Cynthia understood his point, but she hated riding an emotional roller coaster in an effort to trust him. Maybe Peter was right. But a chance for real change in El Salvador was slipping away. Peter looked troubled. "We did learn something," he said. "Robert's assessment of Romero, you know, 'the most dangerous man in El Salvador.'"

A lot of things about the meeting made Cynthia uneasy, none more so than Robert's comment about Archbishop Romero. If they were right about Operation Cain, then Romero was in grave danger. She looked grim. She hoped his office as Archbishop or his international reputation might make him untouchable. Romero was the most popular bishop in Latin America. He was also the most hated.

She took a deep breath. "Until yesterday I thought Carter's threat to tie aid to human rights might help keep Romero safe," Cynthia said. "I feel like I'm hoping against hope."

"We've got to find a way to get inside Operation Cain," Peter said. "I'm leaving for Somotillo in five minutes." Peter was immediately furious with himself. The last thing he wanted was for Cynthia to accompany him to Somotillo. But the damage was already done.

"What for?" Cynthia asked.

"To talk to Captain Canales," he said. "I've wanted to ever since you told me about his actions on the night of the massacre. Canales is our only real link to Operation Cain," he said. "It was too dangerous to approach him before but the coup gives me an opportunity. I'd feel better if Calderón were out of the picture completely," he added. "Unfortunately, Rivas transferred him to the Treasury Police. Calderón's dangerous but at least he's no longer in charge of the garrison."

"I'm going," she said.

Peter looked uncomfortable. "I don't know if that's a good idea," he said.

Cynthia looked directly at him like an owl sweeping down on its prey. "Why?" she asked. "Why don't you want me to go?"

Peter had a hundred reasons, but none he could share with her. He weakly argued that she should keep an eye on Robert, but she knew Robert avoided her like the plague. She was worried about Carmen and the others in Pueblo Duro, and Peter offered to drop her there but she wasn't buying it. They could stop on their way back from Somotillo, after meeting Canales.

"I'm coming, Peter," Cynthia said. It was foolish to argue further and Peter knew it. Cynthia was at least as stubborn as he.

The trip to Somotillo was tense for reasons beyond their icy standoff. There were military road blocks every few miles. Fortunately, they had authorization to move freely from officials in both the deposed and the new government.

When they reached Somotillo, Canales explained that the situation there and all over the country was so unstable he would have to keep their meeting brief. Cynthia and Peter were alarmed by news about Pueblo Duro. They could not travel there, Canales said, because of ongoing violence. As far as he knew Padre Ricardo was still alive.

This attempt to reassure them had the opposite effect. He explained that Raúl Ortega and Julio Díaz had mobilized their friends in ORDEN. They'd terrorized the whole area but especially where the communities were strong. General Calderón and troops from the Treasury Police were also involved. The communities in and around Pueblo Duro had been decimated. Tomás and

Ana López were dead. The rest, including Padre Ricardo, had apparently fled.

"Can't you stop them?" Cynthia asked.

"I've sent troops to try to maintain order but it's difficult to say the least. Quite frankly," Canales said, "our forces are no match for the Treasury Police and ORDEN..." Canales stopped in midsentence, "...particularly when the loyalty of our own troops is in question. The situation is so unstable we are nearly paralyzed."

"We understand," Peter responded.

The phone rang on Canales' desk and he answered it. "Eight o'clock. I'll leave here at quarter of and meet you. Yes. Eight o'clock. Adios." Canales looked preoccupied. "I'm sorry," he said, "I have only a few minutes. How can I help?" he asked.

"Tell us about Operation Cain," Cynthia said. "You gave a note to Sancho on the night of the massacre."

Canales knew that passing the note was like placing a message in a bottle and casting it into the ocean. "Two words," he said. "I hope you can help me decipher them."

"Help you?" Peter said. "We thought you could help us."

"I wish I could," Canales said. Seeing disappointment overtaking Cynthia's face he continued. "Let me tell you what I know." Canales opened a file on his desk. "You can have these," he said. "I found them in Calderón's file cabinet the day of the coup. Maybe they can lead you to Operation Cain."

Canales handed Cynthia a copy of the top-secret report that she and Peter had written. "The report is not new to you," he said. Cynthia cast a glance at Peter. "It's Calderón's notes that might be useful. Most of it is initials and shorthand. Quite frankly, I'm in the dark about some of it," he said. "Hopefully, you can do better."

Cynthia and Peter paged quickly through the report. There were initials on various pages. The words "Operation Cain" appeared at least twice. Most interesting was what appeared to be a guest list for a dinner party that Calderón wrote on the final page of the report. There were two columns. The left side was labeled "Hosts." The right side "Guests." The only actual name on the guest list was that of Ambassador Nolte. The rest consisted of initials.

"I see Calderón's party list has your attention," Canales said. "There's one other item. I found this in the file." He handed a piece of paper to Peter. "I first saw it on the Thursday before Padre Ricardo's arrest when I brought Calderón some coffee. He was scribbling on a pad. That's how I learned of Operation Cain."

Peter and Cynthia looked eagerly at the paper containing the following words:

> Operation Cain.
> Ilopango
> Pick-up, 7:00 am., Friday.
> End.

"I can help you with this one," Canales said. "Two North Americans were here during Padre Ricardo's arrest and Rafael's torture. I first saw them at the garrison late Friday morning. They came with Calderón. I think they flew into Ilopango air base from outside the country. Calderón probably met them. And "End" in all likelihood refers to Colonel Crudo. End is his nickname and Ilopango is his territory."

"If you're right then Operation Cain, whatever it is, has a friend in the new government," Cynthia said.

"I'm afraid that's right," Canales responded. "I don't trust Crudo. We ousted Ochoa but we're losing control. I'm afraid," he said, soberly, "I'm afraid you may be talking to..." His sentence broke off.

Peter removed a picture from his pocket, a photo taken at an embassy picnic. "Recognize any of these faces?" he asked. As Canales scrutinized the photo Peter removed his glasses, placed them on the desk, and rubbed his eyes.

"I recognize the two of you," he said. "And him." Canales pointed to Robert Barnes. "He didn't come from Ilopango," he said. "But he's been here several times. I've seen him with Calderón, D'Aubuisson, Raúl Ortega and Julio Díaz. I suspect they are the nucleus behind Operation Cain, along with the other North Americans who don't appear in this photo. One other thing," he added. "Our mystery men flew into Ilopango the day after the coup. They stayed a couple of days. It may be a coincidence but before they left, Calderón was released and put in charge of Treasury."

"How do you know they were here?" Peter asked.

Canales didn't want to betray a trust. "Look," he said. "Everything's up for grabs. Everybody's vulnerable. Nobody wants to talk, to say anything because it doesn't take much to get someone angry and yourself killed. Let's just say someone at Ilopango knows. No names. Just a someone. I'll tell you something else. There's a lot of shit going down at Ilopango. Operation Cain's only part of it. Nicaraguans are all over the base, former officers in Somoza's guard. They've got money and guns. According to my source, lots of guns are being flown in at night from somewhere."

"You've helped us a lot," Peter said. "Is there anything else you can tell us. Anything at all?"

Canales thought for a long time. "Find out what's happening at Ilopango. It's important. But don't let it distract you from Operation Cain," he said.

Cynthia was frustrated because the meeting had to end. She had a thousand questions and the possibility to ask just one. "What do you think Operation Cain is?" she asked.

"We know more or less who is at the core. What is it?" Canales repeated her question. "Someone is implementing your recommendations," he said. Canales stood up. The meeting was over.

He walked them outside his office and said good-bye.

Peter took several steps and then stopped. He left Cynthia in the hallway and went to retrieve his glasses. My glasses," he said as he walked over and showed a photo to Canales. "Are these our mystery men?" Peter asked.

"Yes," he said.

"Permit me one final question," Peter said. "How do you explain Nolte's name on the guest list?"

Canales shivered. "Operation Cain targets the Church," he said. "But the same people who terrorize the Church are active elsewhere, independent of Operation Cain. They were worried about a coup, particularly worried about young officers like Esperanza and myself who want real change in El Salvador. My guess is they planned to assassinate Ambassador Nolte to undermine U.S. support for a new government."

"You're speaking in the past tense?" Peter asked.

"Yes. Their plan predated the coup. It was shelved because Crudo, not Esperanza, is in control. Nolte is safe because the coup ousted Ochoa, but it failed to change El Salvador. Nolte and Carter are eager to play ball with Crudo. Now, permit me a question. Who are the mystery men in your photo?" Canales asked.

"I'd rather not say," Peter said. "Not yet anyway." He put the picture into his pocket and walked out.

Thirty-seven

Bad Dreams

Cynthia left the meeting with Canales both excited and drained. She and Peter had considerably more information about Operation Cain. They knew its essence, and the nucleus of who carried it out. They also had Calderón's "party list" complete with initials and notes waiting to be deciphered, and leads pointing to Ilopango.

Peter knew more than that. But he had no intention of sharing what he knew with Cynthia. At least not now.

Operation Cain existed and it had friends in the new government. Cynthia wanted to warn Archbishop Romero. But what could she tell him? He knew about death squads and death threats. Besides, most of what they had was speculation.

Cynthia was also concerned about the community. It had been attacked. Decimated. Tomás and Ana were dead. The rest gone. Were they alive? Where had they gone? Canales made it clear they could not travel near Pueblo Duro. Being powerless to do much of anything for the community, Cynthia argued for pursuing new leads. Peter was determined to stay in Somotillo. Alone. "You take the car. I'll find a way back to San Salvador tomorrow," he said.

Cynthia thought about roadblocks and difficulties encountered on their trip to Somotillo and cringed. "I'd rather travel together," she said.

"I would too," he said. "But I need to be here. If time weren't so important I'd suggest we both stay," he added. "But it is. What do you see as next steps?" he asked.

Cynthia wasn't about to let him change the subject without resolving the other issue. She decided to answer but vowed to return to the earlier discussion. She said they needed to find out more about Ilopango, the Nicaraguans and the weapons. She'd love to get inside the base and see the flight log. It wouldn't say anything about the weapons, but it might tell them the origin of the flights of the mystery men.

Peter looked skeptical but said he had been thinking along the same lines. Cynthia couldn't be sure whether he was searching for a plan or a way out. His mind was like a computer in danger of overload.

Something seemed to click and he spoke. "How about alerting Dwight Bench? Tell him something's going on at Ilopango. He's a good reporter. It's a good story. Canales doesn't think Ilopango is critical to understanding Operation Cain. Bench can help sort that out," he said.

Cynthia liked the idea of getting Bench involved. Something told her, however, that Ilopango was more important than Peter or even Canales thought. Maybe the mystery men weren't connected to the Nicaraguans. In that case Ilopango was simply their entry point into El Salvador. But exposing Operation Cain still depended on knowing the identity of the mystery men and Cynthia wasn't sure Bench would uncover their names in the course of his investigation.

Peter seemed to sense her discomfort. "Tell Bench that two North Americans flew into Ilopango on several occasions," he said, "at least once prior to Padre Ricardo's arrest and immediately following the coup. Tell him they left after Calderón's release. Give him dates and tell him we don't know if there's a connection to Ricardo's arrest, the Nicaraguans or to Calderón's release. Let him dig around."

"Okay," she said.

"If he's skeptical then reveal our relationship to the Agency with the understanding that anything we give him is off the record," Peter said. "Not many reporters have sources like us knocking at their door."

Cynthia was excited. "Agreed," she said. For the first time they had concrete leads, actual clues into Operation Cain. "We also need to go over Calderón's notes and 'party list,'" she continued. "If Bench is interested in Ilopango, and I think he will be, then that frees us to examine Calderón's copy of the report."

Peter looked at his watch. It was only 11 o'clock. He estimated times, calculated roadblocks. If they left now he could drop Cynthia in San Salvador and return to Somotillo by dark. Cynthia was about to ask Peter why it was so important for him to stay in Somotillo. Before she could ask he announced their departure. He asked her to meet him with the car around the corner in five minutes and then disappeared into a crowded street.

Peter walked into a store, bought Chicklets and proceeded to a phone. He dropped in several coins, shuffled through his little red book and found the number he needed. After several rings General Calderón answered.

"This is Peter Jones. I need to talk to you. I'm in Somotillo," he added, "but I'm leaving for San Salvador in a few minutes. If you're interested in moles you'll want to hear what I have to say," he said. Peter paused. The silence at the other end was somehow reassuring. Peter read it as a sign of interest. He wasn't mistaken. "If everything goes well I'll be back later tonight. Can we meet around eight?" Peter asked.

"At my office," Calderón said. "Call first. If I don't answer then the meeting is changed to seven tomorrow morning. Understood?" he asked.

"Yes," Peter said. "Good-bye."

Peter walked to the corner where Cynthia waited with the car. He reached over, kissed her on the cheek and offered her a Chicklet. It was a rare sign of affection as tension had been building between them for days. "Let's go," he said.

On the return trip to San Salvador Cynthia tried to make sense of Calderón's "party list." The left column said "Hosts." The right column, "Guests." Initials were scribbled underneath, along with one name, Dennis Nolte.

HOSTS	GUESTS
grupo	c.ps & ns:
c.p.o.	sal/inter—mary
G.W.	bc
C.R.	R.
	subu
	Dennis Nolte

Cynthia knew Calderón's list had nothing to do with a party. Beyond that she found the whole affair confusing. Why were some initials capitalized and others not? Why did Nolte appear on the list? And why was his name on the "guest" side along with "bc?" This she assumed stood for base communities. It was the only clear reference in the bunch.

Did grupo refer to the initials of people below? Or was it the core group Canales named plus those initialed? Maybe G.W. and the other initials didn't even refer to people. If she were in the Dominican Republic then G.W. would seem an obvious reference to the Gulf & Western company which dominated that island's economy. But Gulf & Western had few or no interests in Salvador. Nothing made sense.

Peter, who seemed totally preoccupied, was of no help. He dropped her off, reminded her to call Dwight Bench, and announced he would be gone for a few days. Before she could protest, he drove away leaving her with Calderón's copy of the report and a thousand questions.

Cynthia's conversation with Bench went well. He appreciated the tip, accepted their condition of anonymity, and promised to keep them posted of his findings to the degree that seemed appropriate. Cynthia returned to her apartment. She was exhausted. Calderón's dinner party had to wait. She curled up under her sheet and went to sleep. It was another night of dreams, of painful revelations rooted in childhood memories and modern day torture.

The nightmare began, as always, on the playground. Cynthia is a young child. In the script of her dream, boys taunt her. Mercilessly. They are at least a head taller than she is. They feed off her pain as they race around, zigzagging in and out. The purpose of the game is to get close but not let Cindy touch you. To let her touch you is to get cooties and risk humiliation. Better to humiliate Cindy.

The boys scream as they run. Their voices are like a sadistic mantra. "You can't catch us. You can't catch us." She is five years old. The playground is a war zone. "Cindy can't catch us. Cindy can't catch us."

She looks to her father for comfort. He sits unconcerned on a nearby bench reading the paper. His boots shine, his uniform is pressed, always pressed to perfection. He is clean shaven. His hair, like the stubble of a young man's day-old beard, blankets his head uniformly. He peers over the top of his paper. His look, always the same, expresses disapproval. He smiles at the boys, turns to Cindy, and speaks harshly.

"You can take care of yourself," he says. "Don't expect me to solve your problems." Tears stream from her tortured eyes. Cindy covers her ears as the taunts continue. Finally, desperately, she gets to her feet. She runs. She runs as fast as she can. But the boys are bigger. Older. They run faster, pursue her, weave in and out of

239

her path. They are as persistent as a swarm of bees.

One of the boys darts in front of her. He gets close. Too close. As his foot clips her leg, he stumbles but keeps his balance. She goes down. Hard. The asphalt has no mercy. Her exposed knee rips open as sand and blood grind into her torn flesh. Her father walks slowly to her side, stands over her like a morbid statue. "You're not hurt," he says. It is a command and not a question.

Cindy rises to her feet, inconsolable because there is no one to console her. Two blocks to the base. It is a walk through an eternity of silence interrupted only by sobs that penetrate her trail of tears. Her father carries a paper folded neatly beneath his arm. She trails behind, dreading what is to come. It is a familiar ritual.

Pain breeds familiarity. Pain triggers long memories. Even in a five-year-old. As they enter the house she sits down on the red stool in the kitchen. It is her father's choice. Red vinyl. Red blood. Vinyl won't stain. He walks into the bathroom and opens the cabinet. As he returns, she braces for pain. He is armed with cotton and iodine. Even the tears that water her barren soul are dry now. They leave stains on her face like cracks in a parched river bottom during the dry season.

Her father proceeds methodically, oblivious to her pain. She closes her eyes and tries to flee to a place where pain can't reach her. Everything is in slow motion. He shakes the bottle, endlessly. When he removes the cap, it unleashes an odor that triggers nausea. Her father holds the open bottle in his hand like a sacred instrument, tips it carefully until it touches the cotton ball like a wet kiss. Absorbent cotton, saturated with pain, transfers its venom to her wound. "It's for your own good," he reminds her. The sting of the iodine rises to the level of a hundred bees as her father attacks the wound aggressively. Her winces become screams echoing in a canyon. But her father does not hear them. He is standing somewhere beyond their reach.

Cynthia woke in a bloodless sweat. She clung to her sheet

like a lifeline descending into hell. Her body convulsed against the air as she stumbled forward. Out of bed. To her feet. "No. My God, No," she screamed. The nightmare of her childhood receded into the darkness then regrouped like an angry storm. She could not bear to look but something pulled her from her bed, in the direction of Calderón's report.

She wanted to leap out the window and save herself the trauma of knowing but she could not *not* know. As her fingers touched the pages, she recoiled like a cobra. Finally, she forced herself to go forward. She read quickly, casting aside useless pages until her eyes zoomed in like a fine camera on the final page.

The party list was an invitation into hell. As her own voice was silenced, the initials screamed out from the page threatening to smother her. G.W. C.R. She slumped to the floor. G.W.—General Warren; C.R.—Colonel Randolph. The mystery men of Ilopango. Participants in Rafael's torture. Members of Operation Cain's deadly nucleus.

Her pulse racing, Cynthia struggled to her feet. Another memory was triggered. The embassy picnic photo that Peter showed Canales was hers. She walked to the book shelf and removed the photo album. There were two pictures missing, the embassy picnic photo and the one of her father and General Warren in the canal zone. Peter knew and had said nothing. She wondered what else he knew. What he might be concealing.

Thirty-eight

The Mole

Peter passed through roadblocks without incident. He arrived in Somotillo at 7:30 p.m. His head was spinning amidst the darkness of a cloudy, moonless night. He walked towards the garrison, glanced at his watch, and positioned himself carefully. Peter waited, invisible in the shadows.

After fifteen minutes the garrison door opened. Canales took two steps before five quick shots rang out, shattering the silence and his chest. Peter looked out of the shadows like a frightened cat. The eerie silence was broken by his footsteps against the sidewalk. As he ran around the corner his pace slowed, like a runner cooling down after a difficult sprint.

Peter entered the store where he purchased Chicklets that morning, thought about rum but drank a soda and waited. His hands were shaking.

Just before eight, he picked up the phone and dialed General Calderón. After several rings General Calderón answered. The meeting was tonight. Peter wondered how to convince Calderón of his loyalty. He knew his life depended on it.

The five blocks to the Treasury Police headquarters led him away from the garrison where soldiers surrounded Canales' lifeless body. Peter walked quickly. He entered Calderón's office relieved yet nervous. Calderón was businesslike but seemed pleased to see him. Peter looked toward the window and then back at Calderón. "What's the commotion?" Peter asked.

Calderón seemed unconcerned. "I don't know," he said. "Violence has escalated since the coup. Unfortunate. But unavoidable I suppose," he said.

Peter and Calderón surveyed each other like prize fighters wondering if they belonged in the same corner. "I have information you may find useful," Peter said.

"You indicated as much on the phone," he responded somewhat coldly.

Before Peter could speak, a group of men paraded into the room. Calderón preferred neither to kill a man nor bring him into his confidence based on his intuition alone. Calderón's eyes flashed towards Raúl Ortega who immediately walked over and searched Peter. "We are most interested in this mole of yours," Calderón said, "but one has to be careful. I'm sure you understand." Peter nodded. "It would be impolite to proceed without introductions," Calderón continued. "You know Robert Barnes, of course," he said. "And this is Roberto D'Aubuisson, Antonio Méndez, Raúl Ortega, Julio Díaz and Julio's son, Colonel Miguel Díaz." They shook hands. "Now, what is it you have to tell us?" Calderón asked.

"I presume General Warren and Colonel Randolph have left the country?" Peter began.

"You have a smart mole," D'Aubuisson said. "A very knowledgeable mole. Who is it?" His voice was cold but it was D'Aubuisson's smile that irritated Peter. It was a handsome smile, a smile that took pleasure in a good glass of rum, a joke or a timely death.

Peter's life hung in the balance. There was a noose hanging around his neck. A mispoken word would tighten it. For all he knew the hangmen's decision was already made. Against him.

He wanted to plead his case. To remind them that his report was the foundation of Operation Cain, that his own track record of anticommunism stretched back to Vietnam where it was sealed with Bui Thi's blood and to Chile, to Allende and Pinochet.

He wanted to replay his tape detailing Cynthia's suspicions, a tape which he shared willingly with Robert and Calderón. He wanted to trigger the fury that gripped him that day at the coliseum as he and Robert walked around the track. He wished Cynthia could testify against him, reveal her suspicions, all her reasons for not trusting him.

"Captain Canales is a mole," he said, calmly.

"How do you know?" D'Aubuisson asked. His voice revealed nothing.

"Canales betrayed you even before the coup," Peter said. "On the night of the incident outside the garrison he delivered a message to members of the community in Pueblo Duro about the existence of Operation Cain. Fortunately," he added, "Robert positioned us in the community and I followed the path back to Canales," he said.

Peter thought of telling them that the mole was eliminated but decided to speak of Canales in the present tense. "Canales is dangerous," he said.

"Tell us what you know about Operation Cain. What did Canales tell you?" Julio said.

Peter was fighting for his life. Despite all the reasons why they might, he knew they did not trust him. Peter insured they couldn't ignore him. "He told me there's another mole," he said. "I don't know who. Not yet, anyway. He also told me that Archbishop Romero is a target."

Peter's comments had the desired effect, especially his revelation of another mole in their organization. It left them anxious, and anxiety showed on their faces like juice around the lips of a thirsty child. The possibility of another mole could not be disproved and to dismiss it out of hand could be costly. And they knew it. The prospect of another betrayer made Peter potentially useful to them. He had uncovered Canales. Naming Romero as a target also added to his credibility.

Most of the oligarchy and much of the military hated Romero and wanted him dead. It was a virtual certainty that this group discussed and probably developed plans to kill Romero. Having gotten their attention, Peter shored up his position with a few details.

"Canales didn't know Warren and Randolph by name," he said. Peter looked at Calderón. "But he knew you picked them up at Ilopango, at least twice. Before and after the coup," he added. "General Warren's involvement didn't surprise me. I respected his readiness to do whatever is necessary from the very beginning," Peter said. He turned to Robert who weighed each word carefully. "Canales identified your photo, Robert. It ended his speculation that "c.p.o." referred to chief political officer."

D'Aubuisson seemed impressed by Peter and troubled by how much he knew. "What else?" he asked.

"Canales explained a party list at the end of your copy of my document," Peter said to Calderón. "I don't know whether he deciphered it on his own or whether the other mole deciphered it for him," he said. "He didn't say."

Raúl noticed that Peter spoke with authority about the party list without saying anything about the "Guests" side of the ledger. Still suspicious, he wasn't about to let it slide. "What did he tell you about the party list?" Ortega asked. "About the guests?"

Peter had realized in Canales' office that the guest list at the end of Calderón's copy of the report was Operation Cain's target list. He speculated that the core group agreed to have no written notes concerning Operation Cain. The party list and initials weren't a secret code. They were the product of Calderón's nervous pen. The fruits of a potentially costly indiscretion. From there Peter deciphered the initials. If Raúl wanted specifics he could have them.

"Communist priests and nuns, Romero, base communities, the Jesuit university or subversive U as you call it," he said. Peter suspected "Sal/inter" referred to Operation Cain's willingness to target Salvadoran priests like Padres Ernesto and Ricardo, as well as foreign church workers in El Salvador. In all likelihood "mary" referred to the New York based Maryknoll sisters who were working in base communities throughout the country. He would share these insights if they still doubted him.

Raúl, who had hoped to trip up Peter, looked disappointed. "What about Nolte?" he asked.

Peter knew hesitation would cast doubt. He was baffled initially by the inclusion of Nolte's name on the list but found Canales' explanation convincing. He regretted having to share it. It was possible Calderón wrote Nolte's name down without any discussion among the group. Possible but not likely.

Peter faced an immediate dilemma. If he claimed Canales knew nothing about Nolte's inclusion on the list and the core group behind Operation Cain had discussed it, then his claims of another mole might be called into question. Why would a mole know so much about Operation Cain and know nothing about Nolte? On the other hand, if he speculated wildly and inaccurately about Nolte's inclusion on the list he would also undo himself. Peter was caught in a trap. He decided that his best hope was to trust Canales' interpretation but focus less on Nolte and more on the possibility of another mole.

"Canales didn't say much about Nolte," Peter said. "He did say he was told, presumably by his mole, of a plan to assassinate Nolte that became meaningless when Colonel Crudo gained control of the new government."

"You've been most helpful," Calderón said. "Anyone else have a question for our friend?" he asked.

Raúl, who had chewed on a cigar so that tobacco drooled from his mouth like a teething child, looked uncomfortable. "I have a question," he said. "What about the other agent, the woman? How much does she know?"

"As you probably know, she is Colonel Randolph's daughter. She doesn't know much. Robert and I can take care of her," Peter said, confidently. "Now that Nolte is back in our camp, we can have her confined to paper work at the embassy. She's got nothing so far. If that doesn't work, there are other, less pleasant, steps we can take. I'm sure you gentlemen understand."

"Of course," General Calderón said.

Robert nodded. "We can handle Randolph."

"Two other things before I go," Peter said. "I want in. No one recognizes the dangers of what's happening here more than I do," he said. "Make a decision. Say yes. Or say no with a bullet. Either way I want an answer." Peter looked each man in the eyes and then spoke. "I'm staying at the hotel down the street. Room 242. If you have any doubts, then kill me. I would do the same.

"Finally, Canales' mole is high up. I've got some ideas, some leads that will take me to Panama. Tomorrow. If your answer is no then I wish you well in finding him. If yes, I will need your help. You can start by bringing me a letter addressed to General Warren, something that will let him know it's important that we talk. I'll be waiting for your answer." Peter turned and walked out the door.

Raúl set the stage for the discussion that followed by loading and polishing his gun. "I think we have too much to lose. To trust him would be a mistake," he said.

"He's a good agent. I think he can help us," Robert countered.

"I agree with Raúl," Miguel said.

D'Aubuisson looked in the direction of Julio. "What do you think?" he asked.

Julio hesitated. "I agree with Robert," he said. "And you?"

"Jones' report is the basis of Operation Cain," D'Aubuisson

247

began. "He has uncovered an important mole and betrayed that mole to us. I think he can be useful to us, especially in finding whoever leaked information to Canales."

Raúl was about to protest but D'Aubuisson's icy stare stopped him cold. He realized that D'Aubuisson and Julio were assessing the possibility of another mole high up in the organization, a traitor in their midst. If Raúl continued lobbying to murder Peter, against the wishes of the others, it might cast additional suspicion in his direction. He decided to let the others decide.

At the hotel Peter waited in silence, surrounded by the darkness of Room 242. He had confronted death many times. But never his own. The CIA was living up to its reputation for the bizarre. Peter had invited a group of cold blooded murderers to kill him.

The knock at his door was determined. He hoped it was Robert who was unlikely to pull the trigger himself. He feared Raúl Ortega who caressed his gun like a lover and whose noxious drool gave him the appearance of a rabid dog.

"It's open," Peter said.

Raúl walked in. Peter, visible in the shadows of the street light that penetrated his dirty window, fought off a temptation to run. Ortega walked forward, raised his gun and shoved it hard against Peter's chest. "Had my vote carried the day, our message would be that of a bullet," Raúl said. His breath reeked of old cigars and rotting teeth. "I will be watching. I don't know which would be more pleasing. To find out I am wrong about you and have you help save my country from the Jesuits and all their godless friends. Or to be right so I can have the pleasure of killing you myself."

He pulled the gun away and dropped a letter from Calderón in Peter's lap. "By the way," Raúl said. "There's a small initiation fee to our little club. Kill the Randolph woman by week's end. Enjoy Panama," he added. "They've got nice whores in Panama."

Peter's stay in Panama was productive if uneventful. He visited briefly with General Warren, lunched with Colonel Randolph and visited the records room at the air base where he copied two pages from the flight log. He returned to El Salvador exhausted and worried. Time was running out, and he would soon have to deal with Cynthia.

Thirty-nine

Free Press

Dwight Bench's story about Ilopango made the front page of the *Times*.

Ilopango air-base is the site of intense activity that could be a precursor to renewed warfare in neighboring Nicaragua. The base, located just south of San Salvador, is at the edge of Lake Ilopango. According to intelligence sources, local residents and eyewitness accounts, Ilopango is home to members of ousted dictator Anastasio Somoza's National Guard.

Somoza and his army were overrun less than three months ago in a revolution that ended nearly fifty years of dictatorial rule. Rumors that exiled Somoza guard members are organizing a counterrevolution have circulated since immediately after Somoza's fall. Most have focused on activities in Honduras.

According to a disgruntled European diplomat, the presence of Somoza's guard at Ilopango and indications of a significant movement of weapons onto the base are the first indications that the United States is using El Salvador to further pressure the Sandinista-dominated government in Nicaragua, a government regarded by many within the administration as unpredictable with ties to both Cuba and the Soviet Union.

Local residents report nightly flights into Ilopango. Sources speculate that weapons delivered to El Salvador are for transhipment to Nicaraguan forces in Honduras and Costa Rica if a war against the Sandinistas intensifies.

The country of origin of these weapons is unknown. However, according to one intelligence official the weapons are traceable to surplus U.S. stock evacuated from Vietnam and shipped to third countries prior to the fall of Saigon. CIA and military officials, according to the same source, removed and stockpiled weapons from Vietnam in an operation never approved formally in Washington.

Reliable sources also report that two high ranking U.S. military officials visited Ilopango several times during the past months. One source, who requested anonymity, says these officials intervened to secure the release of General Calderón and Roberto D'Aubuisson who were arrested during the October coup which ousted General Ochoa.

Calderón and D'Aubuisson, accused of numerous human rights abuses in El Salvador, were released just days after the coup. D'Aubuisson was forced out of the military but maintains numerous ties with military leaders and paramilitary organizations, known commonly as death squads. General Calderón was reassigned and now heads the Treasury Police in Somotillo.

When asked to provide access to flight records at Ilopango, records essential to tracing the identities of the U.S. military officials, Salvadoran officials claimed to have misplaced them for the requested time period.

A Carter administration spokesman denied allegations of U.S. support for Nicaraguan counterrevolutionaries as well as allegations of other activities at Ilopango. He also denied knowledge of the involvement of U.S. military officials in the release of Calderón and D'Aubuisson but expressed concern over the allegations. When asked if he would relay concerns to Salvadoran authorities and to the U.S. embassy in El Salvador, he indicated that he would first seek to confirm the allegations.

The Carter administration has cited the October coup as a reason to improve relations with the new government in El Salvador and has renewed military aid. Critics charge that the governing *junta* is dominated by Colonel Crudo and other hard-line military leaders who have systematically purged the coup of the younger officers who had hoped the coup would provide a last chance to reform El Salvador and prevent a bloody civil war.

Bench's article generated a flurry of activity. Neither he nor Cynthia, who had served as his unidentified source, anticipated its far reaching consequences. The Carter administration found the allegations sufficiently disturbing so as to raise doubts about information received from the embassy.

Carter dismissed Robert Barnes and replaced Ambassador Nolte. Robert Barnes, whose stock in the Agency went up and down like an elevator, wasn't the only one facing unemployment. With U.S. hostages in Iran, Carter's popularity plummeted and a Reagan electoral triumph and appointment of Arnold Hacker as CIA director seemed more certain.

Cynthia knew Robert wouldn't be unemployed long and that

he wouldn't wait for the Reagan administration to act. He could be fired from the Agency but not from Operation Cain. Saving El Salvador from communism corresponded nicely with Robert's intent to avenge those responsible for his ouster. Robert sent the following letter immediately after his dismissal to his old friend, Arnold Hacker.

Dear Arnold,

The situation is desperate. Unfortunately, problems won't wait for the advent of a new administration. The next few months are critical.

Despite my dismissal, I'll be staying on in El Salvador. I'll be in New York for a few days next week. Recent press coverage threatens more than you can imagine.

We need Bench's head and we need it now. Set up a meeting with Hornsbee on Thursday. He's a damn liberal but he hates communism and isn't stupid.

I'll confirm when I get to Miami. Calderón sends his greetings.

Read and destroy,
Robert

The following Thursday in a quiet restaurant overlooking Central Park, Robert Barnes, Arnold Hacker and Calvin Hornsbee shared good wine, fine food and conversation about kids, hostages and the long awaited spring. Hornsbee was chief editor of the *Times*. He was approachable but Hacker knew the topic he was about to broach was a sensitive one. As lunch wound down, the three men looked increasingly uncomfortable, like school kids talking about sex in front of their parents.

"Calvin," Hacker began, "as you may be aware, Robert has spent a good part of the last decade in El Salvador as chief political officer at the embassy. He is concerned about events in the whole region, but particularly about present circumstances in El Salvador." Robert nodded and looked on like an obedient puppy. "News coverage in such a sensitive area must be as accurate as possible," Hacker continued. "We are not trying to interfere with your job. But, in order to do ours we feel it's our responsibility to alert you when one of your reporters abandons any semblance of objectivity. I trust we know who we are talking about?"

Hornsbee nodded. "Yes," he said, simply.

"Recent articles are journalistically compromised," Hacker continued. "None more so than the piece on Ilopango."

Robert wanted to say that Bench's articles threatened sensitive missions in El Salvador, but that would bolster the accuracy of Bench's reporting. "Apart from the fact that he is oblivious to U.S. national security interests, his story is based entirely on unnamed sources," Robert said.

Hacker, smiling as he spoke, noted that the Ilopango article embarrassed the Carter administration. "I'm sure you realize this is not generally of great concern to us," he said. "But given the stakes in Central America, neither Carter nor a future Reagan administration can conduct foreign policy if the press gives us a biased hearing. We expect scrutiny. Not witch hunts."

Hornsbee stood up, shook hands and prepared to exit. "Gentlemen," he said. "Thank you for lunch."

Forty

Bloody Shins

Padre Ricardo made his way towards the Guazapa volcano. As he passed through the little village of Berlin, he located a family Tomás identified rightly as a home for Juancito. It was a poor family, burdened with their own difficulties but welcoming of a child they had never seen. As he departed Padre Ricardo left almost everything: Juancito, the money, even the horse. "Here is a picture of Tomás and Ana," he said. "It is for Juancito. Show it to him often."

"We will," Juancito's new mother said, simply.

Padre Ricardo sighed. "They are not coming back."

"We understand," she said. Her mouth curved upward in a gentle smile as tears filled her eyes like a rising pool during the rainy season. "Juancito is our son now," she said.

"Tell him..." Padre Ricardo paused. He was searching within his soul, reaching deep into a well where gratitude and forgiveness live precariously amidst the darkness. "Tell Juancito his parents were good people. They loved God and tried to do what was right. Tell him to be proud of his parents. If he lives in an El Salvador without misery, it is because of people like them. But if misery surrounds him it is his duty to continue their struggle. Teach him what his parents understood well: God desires justice and forgiveness," he said.

Ricardo spent the next days walking deeper into the womb of the mountain. The war against the people was expanding to all areas of El Salvador, including Guazapa. Padre Ricardo felt disoriented. Guazapa was an unfamiliar place and its unfamiliarity reflected a deeper spiritual uncertainty that threatened to engulf him. His internal compass was breaking. All he struggled for seemed to be lost.

On the third day he came to a community in which he felt surprisingly at home. Children studied in outdoor schools. There were literacy classes, Bible studies and cooperative efforts to farm the steep hillsides in order to provide corn for tortillas, corn for life. It was in this community that Ricardo met Dr. Rubén Torres, the doctor who had warned Julio Díaz about choosing a harvest of Cain.

Padre Ricardo felt at home in this community because in it, he tasted the fruits of Isabel's labor and the spirit that lived within her. This was her community. Her home.

"She was an amazing woman," Rubén said. "She fit in with the people. She heard them, understood them and at least in some small way, helped them find meaning in their daily lives. The only person she judged harshly was herself," he added. Rubén smiled and shook his head. "And her father. He is a thoroughly impossible man. I suspect people like Julio Díaz test not only our capacity to forgive but God's as well."

Padre Ricardo nodded. "Isabel was the only woman who made me regret being a priest. How did she die?"

Rubén rubbed his hand across his face as if to chase away an anticipated tear. He saw no reason to torture Padre Ricardo with gruesome details and he didn't. "About two weeks ago," he said, "shortly after the coup. They strafed the area from the air and came in with ground troops on three sides. It was possible for us to move everyone but the oldest and the sickest. Isabel stayed behind to care for them. We returned to find them dead. We buried her there," he added, pointing to an area of wildflowers.

Padre Ricardo walked over to her simple grave, knelt and prayed. After sitting in silence for a long time, he returned to where Rubén was standing. "If you need a priest, and if you accept someone unwilling to carry a gun, I would like to stay," Padre Ricardo said, "to be with the community. Whatever happens."

Rubén smiled. "You would be most welcome," he said. "We are a community on the run. When the authorities harass us we flee deeper into the mountain, or we live in underground shelters for days at a time. When it is quiet we come home. Sometimes for only a day. Sometimes for weeks. It's been a long time since we've seen a priest," he added.

Rubén reached out his hand and gave an envelope to Padre Ricardo. "She wrote it after the coup and two days before her death," he said. "She made me promise to keep it and share it with you. If the occasion presented itself," he said. "Only in the event of her death."

Padre Ricardo walked back to the grave site and sat down. He opened the letter and read:

> My dearest Ricardo,
>
> I write to you as flowers miraculously come to life. I wonder if they are a sign. With Ochoa gone our hopes for a new El Salvador may be blooming also.
>
> Yet as I focus on the glory of the flowers, I am distracted by death. Perhaps it is because these beautiful petals are watered with blood. So much needless blood. If you read this then chances are the repression has escalated.
>
> They wanted to kill you from the beginning but were afraid of the consequences. It seems they are afraid no longer. My father and the others blame you and the Church for the hope of the people.

They hate you as the powerful hated Jesus, and they hate the Jesus you introduced to the people.

They blame you. But you must never blame yourself for their decision to hate. The reasons to struggle are always close at hand. So much hunger and misery. And hope. Last week I helped an 80-year-old woman practice her letters. Even bullets cannot kill a spirit such as this.

Not long ago I met a U.S. doctor who works further up the mountain, a bomber pilot turned pacifist. He's a good man. You would like him.

The army swept through recently. The people prepared well and so there was only one casualty. That and dozens of chickens and cattle.

The soldiers kill us indirectly through hunger, with bullets when they can. Our medical supplies, always minimal, were exhausted. We amputated Gracia's leg with a Swiss army knife. It is a scene like many others I wish to forget. Two days later she was teaching the children to read.

If it makes you feel better, I fired a gun only once. I missed the iguana so badly it convinced them of my capacity to serve in other ways. Mainly I teach and assist the sick.

I hope thoughts of death are not a premonition. I am surrounded by death but my own death remains an abstraction. I think not of its ugly circumstance, for death here is always ugly, but of missing you. Of not seeing you again, of never having the opportunity to talk about Freire, to teach literacy, to see the spirits of the people blossom as they discover the Gospel and their own dignity.

I wonder if Jesus saw flowers in Gethsemane? Or only darkness? It's hard to see the flowers in El Salvador, but they are here.

You must always remember that you are one of the flowers and others are blooming because of you. Flowers grow wherever God's word takes root. And flowers die along the way. Those of us cut early and out of season, even we serve a purpose. We are the spiritual compost out of which stronger and more beautiful flowers will one day bloom in El Salvador.

I love you, Ricardo.

I am haunted by the question you asked by the soccer field, me in my Beatles shirt, you and your bloody shins. Do you remember? You asked what I would do if I were you. I told you to go on being a priest, to awaken the people, to learn from them and to trust God. Jesus shows us that life, not death, has the final word, if we witness with our lives to a different truth.

You taught me a new metaphor for the Kingdom. It is like a soccer game. The delight with which the children chased you and that dilapidated ball of yours is my image of the Kingdom. Their joy was possible because you bloodied your shins. Jesus, who was killed in his struggle for life, bruised by the powerful but not defeated, expects us to get our shins bloody too. We are people of the way. People of the bruised shins.

Good-bye, Ricardo. IT'S NOT YOUR FAULT.

Perhaps you will find a new home, a new community in Guazapa. Remember. Go on being a priest, awaken the people, learn from them and trust God. It is all you can do. It is all any of us could ask of you.

Padre Ricardo dried his tears, folded the letter and placed it in his pocket. He walked to his pack and removed the soccer ball he had retrieved from behind the door of his house. His head hurt as he blew life into it.

He approached the children who screamed with delight. "*Mire. Un sacerdote que juega fútbol*—Look. A priest who plays soccer," they yelled. He kicked the ball back and forth between them. Laughter, God's antidote to despair, filled the air.

During today's lull in the war, a war that would intensify, a war that would one day end, a piece of the Kingdom came to Guazapa. Padre Ricardo found a new home.

Forty-one

Romero

The situation in El Salvador deteriorated quickly. A second set of civilians resigned from the governing *junta* protesting the military's continued control and exercise of abusive power.

Despite the embassy shake-up, the Carter administration remained committed to the post coup *junta* that was almost indistinguishable from the repressive government that preceded it. The new U.S. ambassador, still captive to his predecessor's reasoning, insisted the U.S. was helping the new government in a struggle against a Pol-Pot style of communism.

Archbishop Romero saw things differently. His heart throbbed with the pulse of the people. Romero had advised the progressive coup plotters but now openly opposed the governing *junta*. His sermons reminded the powerful in El Salvador and Washington what the poor in El Salvador knew: the coup changed nothing.

The cathedral overflowed as Romero rose to give his weekly homily. Others listened to radios as Romero risked his life speaking their truth:

> The land in El Salvador contains much that is of God. That is why it groans when the unjust monopolize it and leave no land for others. Land reform is a theological necessity. A country's land cannot stay in a few hands. It must be given to all, and all must share in God's

blessings on the land. There will be no true reconciliation between our people and God as long as there is no just distribution, as long as the goods of the earth in El Salvador are not for the benefit and happiness of all Salvadorans.

What terror is being sown among our people that friends betray friends whom they see in trouble. If we could see that Christ is the needy one, the torture victim, the prisoner, the murder victim, then we would pick him up lovingly. We must see in each human figure thrown shamefully by the roadside Christ himself cast aside.

How far people are today from realizing that all the world's money is good for nothing, is worthless compared to a human being—especially those people who torture and kill others and who value their investments more than human beings.

I have no ambition for power and so with complete freedom I tell the powerful what is good and what is bad, and I tell any political group what is good and what is bad. That is my duty.

Last week I sent a letter to the President of the United States telling him not to send more military aid and advisors to our country. U.S. support for the governing *junta* does not favor the cause of justice and peace in El Salvador but instead it increases the injustice and sharpens the repression.

The congregation applauded, shouted their approval, and added their voices to Romero's appeal.

I told the President that the present *junta* government is incapable of resolving the country's problems, that political power is in the hands of the armed forces who use guns to repress the popular organizations who are fighting to defend their most fundamental human rights. The military, which controls the governing *junta,* always resorts to violence—violence made more lethal by the assistance of the United States.

President Carter, as a Salvadoran and as Archbishop of San Salvador, I have the obligation of seeing to it that faith and justice reign in my country. Therefore, I ask you to prohibit all military assistance to the Salvadoran government and to guarantee that your government will not intervene, directly or indirectly, by means of military, economic, diplomatic or other pressures, to influence the direction of the destiny of the Salvadoran people.

The people's organizations are the only social force capable of resolving the crisis. It would be totally wrong and deplorable if the Salvadoran people were to be frustrated, repressed or in any way impeded from deciding for ourselves the economic and political future of our country because of intervention by your country.

The people in the cathedral and Archbishop Romero were bound together in a symbiotic union, feeding off of each other's courage. Finally, after many minutes of applause, Romero finished his homily:

I also make a special appeal to Salvadorans in the armed forces: to soldiers, national guardsmen and police. Brothers, each one of you is one of us. We are the same people. The *campesinos* you kill are your own brothers and sisters. When you hear the words of a man telling you to kill, remember instead the words of God, "Thou shalt not kill."

No soldier is obliged to obey an order contrary to

the law of God. In the name of God, in the name of our tormented people who have suffered so much and whose laments cry out to heaven, I beseech you, I beg you, I order you in the name of God, *stop the repression.*

General Calderón, Julio Díaz, Raúl Ortega, Antonio Méndez, Roberto D'Aubuisson and Robert Barnes listened to Romero's homily in the comfort of Julio's study. And then plotted his murder.

Colonel Randolph and General Warren were in Panama. Most notable, however, was Peter's absence. Bench's article cast doubt in his direction like an inflated shadow under the harvest moon.

D'Aubuisson guided the discussion. "We are here," he said, "to decide if it is time to eliminate Romero. Your thoughts are welcome. We expect open debate but we will leave the room with one heart."

"The time has long since past," Raúl said. "If we had killed him years ago our problems would be greatly diminished."

Calderón was annoyed. "Beyond dredging up the past, what are you saying?" he asked. "The question is whether this is a good time to kill the Archbishop."

"Earlier would have been better," Raúl said, "but I say yes. Now is a good time. Anytime is a good time. I will do the deed myself. Gladly."

Julio looked concerned. "I'm not sure," he said. "Nobody wants Romero dead more than I. But to kill him now might be a tactical mistake. The coup has failed. We've outmaneuvered Esperanza and demonstrated our power, and the Americans, albeit with some reluctance, are supporting us. Killing Romero risks alienating the Americans whose support we have and need."

"Romero is a problem. Dead or alive," D'Aubuisson said. "The question is whether letting him live is more dangerous than the fallout from killing him." D'Aubuisson was not assessing these dangers for the first time.

"My view is this," he said with confidence. "Divided, the subversives are like gnats digging into our flesh. They are a nuisance. Nothing more. United, however, they are a real threat. Romero is a magician. He is capable of turning a gnat into a raging bull. He alone can unite the people. He must be killed."

D'Aubuisson was a skilled orator. He paused to survey the faces of his accomplices. "How will Carter respond?" he asked Robert.

Robert didn't hesitate. "He will not allow a revolution in El Salvador. He's in too much trouble elsewhere. Kill Romero and Carter will wring his hands in protest. Nothing more. He won't interrupt aid. He will choke on his commitment to human rights before allowing El Salvador to go the way of Nicaragua. Geopolitics will triumph," he added.

"Julio. You spoke against killing him. What do you say after hearing these arguments?" D'Aubuisson asked.

"I am convinced. It is a question of timing."

"Next Sunday during his homily," Raúl said.

D'Aubuisson shook his head. "No, it will be too crowded. It invites chaos," he said. "I suggest tomorrow morning, during mass at the hospital. He will be in a secluded place with a bunch of old nuns."

The Salvadorans drew lots for the honor of assassinating the Archbishop. Raúl Ortega considered himself a lucky man. Robert looked amused. It would be a hell of a welcome for the new ambassador.

Forty-two

Confession

Peter and Cynthia's relationship, icy before the Bench article, soured.

"You think I've conspired with them," he said.

"What am I supposed to think?" Cynthia responded. "One day you tell me you love me and hate the old Peter Jones. The next day I see you with Robert at the coliseum. And in what has become a rash of unlikely coincidences, a copy of our report is missing from my apartment along with several pictures from the photo album. I suspect that sometime thereafter you betrayed me further to Robert because all of a sudden I'm burdened with a load of shitwork that keeps me in the city."

Cynthia grew more agitated as she spoke. "At a meeting to decide the post coup line to Washington you back Robert with your silence. The following day you do everything but tie me to my desk in an effort to keep me from going with you to Somotillo. We meet Canales. You understand the party list, including my father's role in Operation Cain, but refuse to tell me what you know. You run into a crowded store to buy gum. That was a nice touch, Peter, never mind that at least twenty kids tried to sell us Chicklets between the garrison and our car."

Peter stood motionless as her justified tirade continued. "You earn an Emmy as a deaf mute on our return to San Salvador, drop me off and disappear for days. And a funny thing happens in your absence. Canales, our only real link to Operation Cain, is murdered. According to the paper he's gunned down at the precise time he told us he'd be leaving the garrison. Another coincidence, I'm sure. Then I do a little digging. I check the flights to Panama but your name doesn't appear anywhere. So I call my father. He tells me about a pleasant lunch with you. Yeah, Peter. This is great stuff. This is the stuff trust is made of. Do us a favor. Leave."

Peter looked dejected. "I can't," he said. "Romero's in too much danger. And so are we. I'm not leaving until you hear me out."

"Speak. Then leave," she said angrily.

"You've got a lot of it right," he said. "I suspected Robert and General Warren were involved in something ever since they heard our report. When you told me about Operation Cain it made sense that whatever it was, they were key actors. Problem was we didn't know anything about Operation Cain, we couldn't get to Canales, and Robert didn't trust us."

Peter paused briefly and then continued. "I had no idea your father was involved. Even after you showed me his letter praising Calderón I didn't suspect him. Then you showed me the picture of your father together with Warren. I didn't say anything because I hoped I was wrong. I took the pictures with the intention of showing them to Canales but approaching him was impossible before the coup. As it turned out it wasn't safe even after."

Cynthia listened skeptically. What Peter said made sense, but it had been Peter's job for many years to make lies seem reasonable. She found herself drawn into his words and wondering if she'd regret it. "You had nothing to do with Canales' death?" she asked.

Peter was indignant. "Of course not," he said. "There was only one way to get inside Operation Cain: through Robert. If I could get to Robert I could get to Calderón. I had to gain Robert's trust."

"So you betrayed me," Cynthia said.

"I stole the report from your apartment and gave it to Robert. That's not all," Peter said. He knew what he was about to say would not sit well. "Look, Cynthia, I meant every word I said that night in your apartment. You've got to believe that. But," he added, "I taped our conversation. I erased everything except a section that revealed your commitment to the community and your loathing of what the U.S. is doing here." Cynthia said nothing. "I played it to Robert and Calderón. And I suggested to Robert that he arrange to bog you down in San Salvador."

"Why?" she asked. "What use was I here?"

Peter looked frightened. "Robert is capable of far worse. You're more useful alive than dead."

Once again Peter had a point. "What happened in Somotillo?" she asked.

"I was eager to talk to Canales. I didn't want you along because by then I suspected your father's involvement in Operation Cain."

"But Canales never said anything about General Warren or my father," she protested.

"He knew faces not names. I recognized their initials on Calderón's party list. I left my glasses in Canales' office so I would have an excuse to go back and show him the photo of your father with Warren. He identified them immediately. When did you figure it out?" he asked. "About your father I mean."

Cynthia's thoughts drifted to a far away playground and back again. "When I was five," she said. She was both sad and strangely relieved. "It's a long story."

Cynthia no longer pushed away the painful memories. Knowing her father was a key actor in Operation Cain and that he participated in Rafael's torture both repulsed her and helped her make sense of a painful childhood. "When I recognized the initials were for General Warren and my father, then I knew c.p.o. referred to Robert," she said. "The other side of the list made sense too. Except for Nolte. Why was the ambassador on the target list?"

"Like everyone else, the group behind Operation Cain speculated about a coup to oust Ochoa. They considered a coup themselves. Their fear, of course, was of a progressive coup, exactly
the kind Esperanza orchestrated. Canales told me that if Esperanza
outmaneuvered Crudo, then Operation Cain planned to assassinate Nolte and blame it on Esperanza in the hopes of alienating
the U.S. from the new government. At a minimum, killing Nolte
would add to the chaos they were ready to exploit. When Esperanza
lost out to Crudo, the plan to assassinate Nolte was abandoned."

"You still haven't said what happened in Somotillo," she reminded him.

"Having established trust with Robert and Calderón at your
expense, I couldn't very well be seen with you. While you got the
car I called Calderón and arranged a meeting for eight o'clock
that night. I dropped you in San Salvador and headed back to
Somotillo. I arrived around 7:30."

"And?"

"I remembered Canales had said he was meeting someone at
eight o'clock. I was curious about who he was meeting, interested
in identifying another potential ally. I hid in a dark doorway and
waited. Canales comes out, takes a couple of steps, and is cut
down by shots coming from about twenty feet to my left. I waited
a few seconds, heard footsteps and took off in the opposite direction. Any number of Calderón's henchmen could have killed him."

Cynthia felt herself at the end of another roller coaster ride.
This one had moved her in the direction of trust. "Why see
Calderón?" she asked.

"The way to Calderón's heart is betrayal," Peter said. "He
seemed impressed the night at Robert's house when I proved my
loyalty at your expense." He looked up sheepishly. "I was going to
tell Calderón that I had a lead on the mole threatening Operation
Cain, a lead that necessitated my going to Panama. I wanted a

note from him to insure a warm reception from General Warren. I even thought of pointing in the direction of Colonel Crudo or one of his aides, you know, to sow divisions."

"Then Canales gets shot," Cynthia said.

"Exactly. I'm thinking how to tell Calderón something to convince him of my loyalty without putting Canales in danger. Then Canales gets killed and I get an idea. I can go to Calderón and betray Canales because he's already dead. They've done to him what they're going to do to me unless I'm very convincing. I tell them everything imaginable about Operation Cain, all deducible from the party list, which by the way was General Calderón's little indiscretion." Peter looked concerned. "You've got Calderón's copy of the report and his notes in a safe place?" he asked, suddenly.

"Of course," Cynthia said.

"Good. We're going to need them. If we're lucky they might save some lives. Anyway, I give details of Operation Cain and they seem impressed. But they know Canales is dead, and I'm thinking I'm a dead man too. Except one thing," he said, proudly.

"What?" she prodded.

"I tell them Canales gets his information from another mole. They can't disprove it and it puts them off balance. Then I tell them where I'm staying, and give them two choices: Kill me or bring me in," he said.

"They obviously didn't kill you," she said.

"Not yet. Raúl Ortega put a gun to my chest and told me, against his wishes, that I was in. Until Bench's article."

"I'm sorry," she said.

"The article only cost us a day," he explained, "because they gave me less than a week to bump you off. That was my initiation fee. After tomorrow my little charade wouldn't have been worth a penny. Nor my life for that matter."

"But why didn't you tell me all of this before?" she asked.

"I didn't know how to bring you in without tipping off Robert. It seemed safer to collaborate with him in getting you confined to San Salvador. As long as Robert didn't consider you a grave threat, I knew your life wasn't threatened," he said. "Of course that all changed with Bench's article."

Cynthia nodded. "Why did you go to Panama?" she asked.

Peter pulled out copies of the flight records from Panama. "To get these," he said. "They prove your father and General Warren traveled to Ilopango on the days in question."

"Everything we've got is still circumstantial," she said. "But with Calderón's scribbles, the CIA report and the actual repression, it's convincing testimony of a calculated policy."

"I agree, but will anyone else?" Peter asked.

"We've got to get a message to the Archbishop," she said. "His homily this morning! Telling soldiers to disobey orders and standing up to Carter. He's a brave man."

Peter approached Cynthia with the look of a dejected puppy, but she wasn't yet ready to forgive him.

She pointed to her couch. "You look exhausted," she said. "Get some rest."

Peter and Cynthia realized it was time to make plans for leaving the country and time to tell the world what they knew about Operation Cain. They hoped Dwight Bench and Archbishop Romero would help them. Since they knew Romero's phone would be bugged, they would visit him the following afternoon at the cancer hospital.

Peter positioned himself on the couch and then jumped up suddenly. Weariness had clouded his thinking. They were in grave danger if they remained in Cynthia's apartment. They grabbed Calderón's copy of the report and a few other essentials and left. An hour later armed men ransacked the apartment.

—

The Sheraton was the hotel of preference for most journalists, at least those with money. Cynthia registered under phony names and they retreated to the safety of their room. Peter placed a call to Dwight Bench and got no answer. Bench's phone was disconnected. Peter dialed the hotel bar and asked for another journalist. "Doug Spencer here," a voice said.

"Mr. Spencer, I'm a friend of Dwight Bench. I'm trying to locate him," Peter said.

"Bench is gone," he said. "The *Times* pulled him out last week. He was pretty ticked. Said they were assigning him to the Financial Page."

"Thanks," he said, weakly. He hung up the phone and turned to Cynthia. "Bench was transferred back to the States," he said. "We've got a story and no one to tell it to."

Forty-three

A Single Shot

Cynthia and Peter awoke as the morning sun invited itself in through their hotel window. It was the first opportunity for a good night's sleep either of them had gotten for weeks. The night before each had collapsed separately, Peter on the couch and Cynthia on the bed.

As she slept, Cynthia had felt the last remnants of distrust for Peter disintegrate like a marshmallow disappearing in a steaming cup of hot chocolate. She awoke feeling relaxed and refreshed. She walked over and stood close to him as he poured two cups of coffee. Before he could offer her one, she draped her arms over his shoulders, pulled him close and smiled.

"I'm sorry for all the deception," Peter said. "You know," he continued, "with all the stress we haven't had time to spend just with each other. Someday soon I'd really like to spend the night with you, but you know, do it right…eggs Benedict in the morning with a bottle of champagne."

Cynthia smiled. "Mmmm. Sounds like a honeymoon," she said playfully. "Now that we're ending our relationship with the Agency maybe we can have a normal relationship ourselves. And a normal conversation," she said. "Maybe we could even say something direct to each other."

"How's this for direct?" Peter said. "I spent the whole night on this poor excuse of a couch wishing I was with you."

"Bad mattress, huh," she said. "Remind me to tip the manager. I asked for the room with the lumpiest couch."

"Thanks," Peter said. He struggled to find the right words. "Last night...I needed you. I love you, Cynthia. I'm sorry I'm so bad at showing it." He kissed her gently on the forehead, on her eyes and then passionately on her lips.

"Whew! I'd say you're pretty good at it when you try," she said. "Maybe after thirty years of therapy I'll forget about my father and learn to trust men." She pushed herself away gently and retrieved her coffee cup. "Let's make it six months of therapy and a farewell to the Agency. That should do it."

Peter's smile gave way to concern, like a disappointed child who greets her parents at the door only to discover they're in the middle of an argument. "Last night I was thinking about what we should do if we get out of this alive. I'm not sure people like Robert and General Warren allow people like us to leave the Agency," he said.

Peter remembered hearing other agents talk about Phil Agee and John Stockwell, how they would never live to see their grandkids. He wished he'd paid more attention. Somehow such threats didn't seem idle anymore. Peter looked solemn. He fought and won another skirmish with despair. "I'm afraid after we tell what we know, we've got nowhere to go and nothing to do. Maybe the best we can hope is for the Agency to deny we ever existed," he said.

"I think you're wrong about one thing," Cynthia said. "Given what we know, there's plenty to do. Not only exposing Operation Cain but after." Cynthia remembered her dream in which God's voice and the cries of the people were one. "We can't leave here and walk away from what we've seen," she continued. "Father Ricardo says the Gospel has a claim on our lives. On what we do.

"After everything I've seen here—the courage of the people—I'm not the same anymore. I can't pretend that I don't know what

I know. I have to learn to live with what I know. That means exposing the Agency." Cynthia walked over, sat on his lap, and wrapped her arms around him.

"You know what's funny?" Peter said. "Last night I was lonely and miserable on that lousy couch. I worried about Romero. And about us. But it was peaceful listening to you breathe, watching the rhythm of your body. I thought it would be wonderful to wake up every morning next to you. Next to the person I love. I felt like I couldn't handle any more. Not alone. But now, with you, I could face almost anything the world could throw at us."

Peter paused and looked up. His eyes filled with tears. "You want direct? I'd like to get married," he said. "As soon as possible."

"Am I right to assume you want to marry *me*?" she asked playfully. "Or did you have other reasons for going to Panama? Because if you want to marry *me*..." Cynthia paused. It was a pause calculated to pay him back for all the doubting, all the deception. "I'm all for it. And now that we've settled that, there's work to do," she said. "We've got tough choices to make."

"I think we just made one," Peter said. He smiled and kissed her. "Okay," he said. "Where do we start?"

Peter and Cynthia struggled to find a way to expose Operation Cain. Should they release the information to one reporter and get out? Or hold a conference at the press club and hope somebody picked up the story? The problem with the second option was that it gave Robert and company a chance to kill them. If Bench was available it would argue for the former, but without Bench they weren't sure.

They decided to talk to Spencer and see if he'd help them. Peter searched his mind with the intensity of a parent looking for a lost child in a crowded park.

Then another option came to him. When they spoke with Romero, they could show him all their evidence. If he joined them at a press conference their charges couldn't be ignored and they'd all be safer.

For the next several hours Cynthia and Peter prepared press packets on Operation Cain. They made copies of the original report on liberation theology, including Calderón's notes and paper with its reference to Ilopango. They also copied Bench's articles detailing the massacre outside the garrison in Somotillo and the flights carrying weapons into El Salvador, as well as the flight records from Panama that proved that Colonel Randolph and General Warren made trips to Ilopango.

They explained their work and disillusionment with the CIA, their interpretation of the party list and Peter's brief infiltration of Operation Cain. They named the core participants including Robert Barnes, General Warren, Colonel Randolph, General Calderón, Roberto D'Aubuisson, Raúl Ortega and Julio Díaz and their suspected ties to Colonel Crudo. To them it seemed a convincing case.

———

The cancer hospital was home to Romero since his selection as Archbishop. It was located on quiet grounds at the edge of San Salvador where trees embrace wind and sky. It seemed far from the chaos unraveling the country. Romero's house, which consisted of two simple rooms, was his refuge from madness.

Outside, it was nearly overgrown with flower bearing trees that were home to all the birds in El Salvador—birds that mistook the Archbishop for St. Francis. Their incessant chatter would have annoyed the saints, but Romero preferred their music to the finest symphony. They reminded him of God's intentions for humanity, of a world full of wonder and surprises, beautiful songs and colors. Their testimony in some small way counterbalanced the horror that followed poor human choices like an accident on a curved highway.

As he entered the chapel, Romero greeted each of the nuns and patients that came for daily worship. The chapel was as simple and dignified as his home. Behind the altar was a large cross where a life-size statue of Jesus hung. The blood that oozed from Jesus' wounds was a stark reminder of the depth of human evil and of the boldness of the resurrection that defeated real pain, real greed, real and ugly death.

"Nothing is so important to the Church as human life," Romero began his homily. "Nothing is so important as the person, above all, the person of the poor and the oppressed, who, besides being human beings, are also divine beings, since Jesus said that whatever is done to them he takes as done to him."

As Romero spoke, Raúl Ortega walked up a pathway leading to the back of the church. He was a missionary to a cause that needed no converts, only guns. He positioned himself carefully.

"That bloodshed," Romero continued, "those deaths, are beyond all politics. They touch the heart of God."

Raúl Ortega, deaf to Romero's words, raised the scope on his rifle which centered an X over Romero's heart.

"We know that every effort to better society—especially when injustice and sin are so ingrained—is an effort that God blesses, that God wants, that God demands of us."

As Romero finished a sentence, a bullet finished his life. A single shot. Romero was dead.

Forty-four

The Coliseum

Peter and Cynthia entered the lobby, a scene of unimaginable chaos. It was as if they stumbled into a race in which the only common requirement was that each runner had to crash into at least one other participant and an item of furniture. Reporters shouted to camera crews and taxi drivers at the same time. Without asking, Cynthia and Peter heard from a half a dozen people that Archbishop Romero had been murdered by a gunman at the Cancer Hospital while saying mass.

Peter caught a glimpse of Doug Spencer desperately trying to flag down a cab. He raced out to the curb and handed Spencer a press packet. He told Spencer he was with the CIA and that the packet explained who killed Romero. Peter said he was in trouble and that if Spencer wanted more information he should meet him at 5:00 tomorrow morning at the coliseum. Spencer gave Peter a look of pathetic sympathy that he afforded any crazed idiot. But he took the materials and jumped into the cab as it pulled away.

Peter and Cynthia spent the afternoon in quiet panic. They booked tickets on three different flights under different names leaving El Salvador on the following day. Hopefully, Spencer would meet Peter at the coliseum and do a story that would enable them to leave the country. If not, they would hold a press conference at the club, hope for the best and return to the States to continue their efforts there. With Romero dead, and given what they knew, they could be the next targets.

The following morning Peter looked at his watch for the fiftieth time in the last hour. He started to get up but Cynthia wrapped herself around him like an octopus with no intention of letting go. Their long kiss was punctuated with tears.

After a few minutes of silence, Peter got up, put on sweat pants and running shoes, made his way to the sink and splashed cold water on his face. Cynthia sat in bed. She looked fearful.

Her worried eyes implored him to be careful but it was Peter who spoke. "Remember, if I'm not back by 7:00, take a cab to the press club. Pay the fare inside the cab and don't get out 'til you're right in front. Stay low and move fast," he told her.

They had reviewed it a hundred times. Peter turned to say that if he didn't get back to the hotel or to the press club she was on her own. But he knew there was no point. "I love you," he said instead.

She walked him to the door where they stood holding each other a long time. She had finally found Peter and didn't want to let him go. Kisses mixed with tears and fears gave way to the quiet assurance of togetherness amidst the necessary risks that awaited them. "I love you," he repeated and walked out the door.

It was 4:40 am when Peter left the hotel. The coliseum was fifteen minutes on foot, and walking was a necessity given the curfew imposed by Colonel Crudo at a press conference in which he accused a faction of the guerrillas of killing the Archbishop. Outside the hotel the tension of the city was as palpable as the smell of rotting garbage. The city that usually sprang to life about now was eerily silent. An empty bus chugged along the main avenue.

Peter walked quickly along deserted streets, his ears jolted by the sound of his own footsteps. A Salvadoran breaking curfew could be riddled with bullets. He hoped it was light enough for his light skin to provide him safety.

A block from the stadium a pickup truck approached, shattering the silence. It was filled with government soldiers. The shadows of their machine guns were visible in the faint light of dawn. For an uncomfortable moment Peter was seized by fear common to most Salvadorans.

It was fear that once led him to deny his humanity and that of others, fear that until recently had gripped his soul and held him captive. At the same time, Peter was vaguely aware of a feeling that went beyond fear. As the soldiers approached he realized he hated them. The flood of emotions that threatened to overtake him were as confusing as his life in the Agency.

At one in the same time he wanted to shout a defiant obscenity and a self-protecting plea. "Go to hell," an internal voice thundered. It was nearly silenced by another: "Don't shoot. My government is helping you." The soldiers turned their guns, followed him as an animal in the sights of a hunter. And then passed by without incident.

Peter arrived at a stadium, surprisingly bustling with activity. There were only a few joggers, but dozens of evangelical Christians were decorating the coliseum for the revival scheduled the following day. Huge banners hung throughout the stadium providing evidence that another of Peter's recommendations was taken seriously, and that the Agency's contact with the fundamentalist sects had borne fruit.

SOLAMENTE DIOS—ONLY GOD
JESUS LA LUZ—JESUS THE LIGHT
ESPERANZA EN EL CIELO—HOPE IN HEAVEN
JESUS SI! COMUNISMO NO!—JESUS YES!
    COMMUNISM NO
SOLO JESUS LIBERA—ONLY JESUS LIBERATES

The familiar slogans were written by groups with ties to Agency money. The contrast between such platitudes and the terror outside was part of a deeper contradiction that led Peter to this place. He looked for Spencer in the faces of any one near but saw only images of Romero lying in a pool of blood.

As he jogged slowly around the stadium track, the slogans appeared as demons reaching down and sucking the wind from Peter's chest. Strengthened with the still fresh blood of Romero, they refused to give him back his soul. Peter labored to the side of the track and vomited. He regained his breath and looked up. In his face stood Robert Barnes, a gun protruding from beneath his jacket like the bulge in a well-worn soccer ball.

"We've known each other a long time," Robert said. "There was a time I would have been sorry to kill you," he added.

"You can no longer seal my allegiance with Bui Thi's blood," Peter said.

"Hate is a good motivator. I thought you would always be with us. When did you figure it out?" Robert asked.

"One night Cynthia and I were speculating about Operation Cain. She started lamenting the past, what she didn't know. It got me thinking about Vietnam and when I first heard rumors about Plan Phoenix and your involvement in political assassinations. It finally occurred to me that you were the one who traced Bui Thi's death to the Viet Cong and some pieces fell into place.

"I had looked at the footage you gave me many times," Peter continued. "You said an agent filming a demonstration at the park had inadvertently captured her assassination. I finally noticed that there wasn't any sign of a demonstration in the park that day. All the protests were near the Embassy. I knew then that you were the responsible party."

"When I discovered you knew about Phoenix," Robert responded, "I couldn't take any chances with a Vietnamese girlfriend."

"Bui Thi wasn't active in politics. She hated the war, but her sympathies were with the Buddhists."

"I thought that was the case," Robert said. "Like I say, we couldn't take any chances."

"So you had her killed?"

"You know the best part. After I told you the VC did it, you were so filled with hate that you belonged to us."

"I'm sick of hate," Peter said.

"You don't know the half of it," Robert said. "Aren't you even a little curious how I knew to find you here?" If Robert's climactic pause was intended to make Peter squirm he was disappointed. "You can count Cynthia as a loyal friend, but torture did not suit her well. Her death should offer you a good test for your anti-hate campaign."

"You're a sad case," Peter said calmly.

Robert seemed agitated. "Dead men aren't good investigators of the truth," he said.

"Sadder still," Peter interrupted, "not long ago I would have believed you. Maybe, you should ask yourself why I'm here, and how you're going to kill me in front of a reporter."

Peter's demeanor was out of place, like Pacabel's music on death row, but it surprised Robert and disarmed him momentarily. It was then that Robert Barnes made the mistake so many others had made before. He got lost in Peter's eyes. More specifically, on this occasion, he followed the trajectory of Peter's eyes to the entrance of the coliseum. This gave Peter an opportunity to deliver a hard blow to Robert's groin and another to the back of his head.

As Robert's body slumped to the ground, Peter raced toward the coliseum's main entrance and exit. In the course of a few seconds, Peter's mind and body seemed in perfect harmony as he weighed various options without breaking stride. His first impulse was to go left towards Roosevelt Avenue, to seek safety on a main street that normally bustled with buses, cars and taxis from before dawn to midnight. His other option was to proceed to the right, deeper into a residential neighborhood on streets lined with private homes and occasional restaurants frequented by upscale patrons and foreigners staffing the embassies dotting the neighborhood.

Peter knew that being in a public place didn't necessarily mean greater safety. Death squads executed people in the presence of others in order to sow terror. He decided that Robert would have killed him at the coliseum if he had been willing to risk a public execution. On the surface, this made a decision to head left, towards the main drag, a logical one. Too logical. Robert might employ the same reasoning. Besides, the main advantage of proceeding left was increased traffic, something negated by the curfew.

Peter turned right as he exited the coliseum. At the end of the block he took a left turn onto another street hoping to move out of sight of the entrance. As he did so, he glanced quickly over his shoulder. It was a disconcerting glance. Peter's reasoning was undone by the speed with which Robert recovered and gave chase. As Robert emerged from the coliseum, he saw Peter and headed in his direction.

Peter realized his mistake immediately. The corner he had turned led onto a street that was long and straight. He was in better shape than Robert, but Peter could not possibly out distance the bullet he knew was coming.

Peter's heart pounded with an intensity he had experienced only twice before. The first was outside the garrison on the night of the massacre as the smell of death filled the air. The second in the hotel room where Raúl Ortega had shoved a gun into his chest with the regret of a killer denied.

As Robert turned the corner, about forty yards separated the two men. Robert fired three shots on the run, missing badly. Peter, looked behind him in time to see Robert stop and take aim. He waited half a second, dove to the sidewalk, and rolled as a bullet whizzed inches over his head. His momentum carried him into the street where he scrambled behind a car. He watched Robert walk slowly in his direction.

His arms clasping the bumper of the unknown car, Peter's mind flashed back to Allende, his body slumped over a desk, his head resting in a pool of blood. Just as quickly he returned to this quiet street in San Salvador, to Robert's obsession, to the scene of his own death.

Peter willed Cynthia into his mind, hoping she might stay with him in the unknown territory he would soon be crossing. It was then he looked across the street and saw his hope for survival. Peter's random pathway from the coliseum had taken him within a few yards of the Swedish embassy. An embassy guard, alerted by the shots, peered out from behind a steel door.

"Someone is going to kill me," Peter shouted in English first and then Spanish. "Help me. Open the door." As he heard the latch, Peter threw a stone in Robert's direction, a temporary distraction that facilitated his initial sprint towards the door. He did a somersault near the entrance as another bullet missed its target. Robert's final bullet clanked off the door as Peter crawled into the embassy compound. Peter was safe. For now.

Forty-five

Deniability

Cynthia waited nervously at the hotel. She left her room at exactly seven o'clock with half a dozen press packets and diminished hope. She walked through the lobby, stood beside the exit and looked outside. There were no cabs sitting in front.

As she turned to walk towards the front desk, she noticed a taxi approaching in the distance. It pulled in front and discharged a passenger. Cynthia jumped in. As the cab pulled away, she looked back and recognized several reporters standing outside. She ordered the cab back to the hotel and rolled down her window. "You going to the press club?" she asked.

"Trying to," one of the reporters said.

"Jump in," Cynthia said.

One of the reporters tied a white flag with "*PRENSA*" stamped in bold letters onto the radio antenna. She would be safer in route and less conspicuous leaving the cab. The reporters, grateful for the ride, paid cab driver and escorted her in. Safely inside, she told them she was holding a press conference in an hour detailing who killed Romero. They looked at her suspiciously as she handed them press packets.

Cynthia looked over and saw Doug Spencer seated at a table, drinking a cup of coffee. She approached him. "I'm Cynthia Randolph. My co-worker at the CIA, Peter Jones, gave you a packet of information that sheds some light on Romero's murder."

"Sit down," he said. "I went to the coliseum but he didn't show." Spencer said.

Cynthia looked concerned. "What time did you get there?" she asked.

"It wasn't easy," he said. "With the curfew and lack of cabs, I got there about half past five. I waited an hour and came here. I did see Robert Barnes," Spencer said. "He was coming in when I got there. He was covered with sweat and looked upset.

"Your report doesn't exactly flatter Barnes," he said. "When Barnes asked why I was there I told him I was doing a story on how fundamentalist Christians felt about Romero's murder. Actually, that might be a good story," he said. "The whole damn stadium is filled with banners. I actually saw one that said, 'ROMERO: THE WAGE OF SIN IS DEATH.' The whole thing gave me the creeps."

Peter might meet me here, Cynthia thought. Either way she would hold the briefing in less than an hour. Before she could finish her mind's plan, she saw Peter walk into the press club flanked by the head of the Swedish consulate and several other Swedish diplomats. Her heart jumped at seeing him safe and it was all she could do to keep from sprinting from the table to embrace him.

Sweden, it turned out, had sent an unusually stinging cable to Washington following Romero's murder. It reflected its growing frustration over U.S. policy in the whole region. Peter showed his escorts the coffee and walked over to where Spencer and Cynthia were seated.

"What happened?" she asked

"It's a long story," he said giving her hand a gentle squeeze and looking at Spencer.

"I got to the coliseum a few minutes late," Spencer said, "waited for an hour, and left. I'm glad you're okay."

Cynthia looked in Peter's direction and then at Spencer. "I

was just about to ask Mr. Spencer if he's interested in the story," she said. Spencer looked uncomfortable.

"A lot of it is circumstantial," Spencer said glancing at the press packet that sat next to his coffee. "I called Terrence Malcolm at the embassy and he says, off the record, that it's bullshit. On the record, he says you two no longer work for the Agency and that the original report was written by Peter. According to Malcolm it was so out of line that it was rejected immediately as the work of a fanatic. He says Operation Cain exists only in the imaginations of those addicted to wild fantasies."

Spencer paused, took a sip of coffee and continued. "On the record, neither Malcolm or Barnes have ever worked for the CIA; they are political officers with the State Department. Off the record, Malcolm says Barnes left the CIA for personal reasons and will likely return to the Agency sometime soon. He says that accusations against Colonel Randolph and General Warren are nonsense."

Looking at Cynthia, Spencer continued. "He also said, on the record, that this was not the first time unresolved issues with your father have clouded your judgment and led you to place personal vendettas above responsible work on behalf of the Agency."

Cynthia and Peter were stunned as they realized that all they had put together could be dismissed as the vengeful fantasies of a deranged daughter and the work of an untrustworthy agent who wrote a fanatical report that reasonable people in the CIA dismissed obviously and wisely out of hand.

"What do you think?" Cynthia asked Spencer.

"I find both you and your information convincing. I called the offices of Literacy International in three countries and no one answered or returned my calls. Unfortunately, what I think doesn't much matter," Spencer said.

"My editor would have a field day with this stuff," he continued. "He'd say you've got nothing conclusive, that a story like this never gets past an endless string of deceptions. Regrettably, 'plausible deniability' is the name of the game. No one can be held responsible for abuses of power like these.

"Besides," he added, "Carter's going ahead with the aid. The parameters of the debate are set." Spencer looked up as if to say that, like it or not, this is the way politics and journalism get played. "Look," he added, "when someone like Bench gets yanked, we all pay attention to how our editors look at the world."

"And how's that?" Cynthia asked.

"They see Carter as a lame duck and November's election as a formality. The name of the game is biding time with Carter while positioning our papers and reporters to be in the good graces of a Reagan administration. Your story would not only hurt Carter, it risks the ire of a future Reagan team that is even more determined to roll back what they see as communism in Nicaragua and prevent it from gaining ground here.

"I'm sorry," he said. "Do your press conference. You can warn the Maryknoll Sisters and the Jesuits working here. If they are targets, then the architects of Operation Cain know someone is watching. And even if you're discredited now, history has a way of revealing truth," he said.

Following the press conference, the Swedish diplomats' accompaniment extended to the airport where Peter and Cynthia boarded a plane for the United States. Spencer said a lot of troubling things, but Cynthia and Peter were haunted by his final words.

——

Times, March 26, 1980, Dateline, El Salvador, p. 16A:
Two former officials of the Central Intelligence Agency charged today that the murder of Archbishop Romero was part of a conspiracy involving leaders of right-wing death squads, including Roberto D'Aubuisson

and U.S. officials with close ties to the CIA and the Southern Command in Panama.

According to these sources, Romero's murder was part of a broader targeting of progressive religious workers and communities under a code name, Operation Cain. Operation Cain, according to these same sources, has a list of potential targets that includes progressive priests and nuns, including Sisters of the Maryknoll order and the Jesuit priests who run the Catholic University in San Salvador.

U.S. embassy, State Department and CIA officials dismiss the allegations that they say stem from former agents whose dismissals were linked to a history of emotional instability and poor performance. Sources also indicate that the United States is assisting Salvadoran authorities in their investigation into the murder of Archbishop Romero who was gunned down on Sunday while saying mass.

Times, December 2, 1980, Dateline, Washington, D.C., p. 1A:

A source associated with the transition team of President-elect Ronald Reagan confirmed rumors that Arnold Hacker will soon be named to head the Central Intelligence Agency. The same source indicated that Robert Barnes would serve as associate director under Hacker.

In another appointment signaling changes in U.S. foreign policy, the President-elect is expected to name General Michael Warren to head the U.S. Southern Command in Panama. Experts in Washington agree these appointments reflect a strong commitment from the incoming administration to take a hard line against communist aggression in Central America.

Forty-six

Endings and Beginnings

The refugees crossing the Lempa River to Honduras numbered in the hundreds. They would soon be many thousands. They were very old or very young, mainly women and children. All hungry, all terrorized, all disoriented by past history and present surroundings.

The United Nations High Commission on Refugees established a small, UN-approved camp. It could have remained a barren wasteland without hope, a season of endless days and needless death. It became instead a seedbed of new life.

Within days of their arrival, Juan planted seeds carried from Pueblo Duro, reclaiming foreign ground. Each day he and Marcos took children to the fields, planted new seeds or tended the old. The stories they told were filled with promises of jubilee and abundant harvests.

Carmen organized people into work groups that transformed plastic into temporary homes, corn into corn meal, corn meal into tortillas and beans and tortillas into sustenance. Within weeks, children attended outdoor classes using sticks and dirt in place of the pencils they'd left behind. All but the very young and the sick attended. Carmen watched carefully over the pregnant women who needed assurance that there was still reason to give birth, to hope for life.

Each night the community gathered for biblical reflection and story telling. The people listened to Rafael with the anticipation of a child waiting for a ripe mango to fall after a direct hit from a slingshot.

"The authorities would not let me live in El Salvador," Rafael said. "My friends would not let me die there. We must never forget," he said, "that Jeremiah bought land as he and his people were led out of Israel into captivity. Why?" Rafael answered his own question. "He bought land to show people in their hour of greatest despair that one day they would return to their homeland. Exile was not their destiny."

Rafael's voice was both serious and calming. "Let us not grumble now that we find ourselves in a new wilderness not of our own choosing," he continued. "Let us remember the promises of God, prepare ourselves now for our return to our promised land. And how do we prepare? By teaching the children to read and write. By organizing ourselves so that we not only survive here but gain skills to help transform El Salvador when we return."

Rafael's failing eyes did not obscure his vision of the future that was as clear as a cloudless sky after a rainy night.

"There are difficult days ahead," Rafael said. "But I tell you the wisdom of an old man. The days of violence and destruction in El Salvador will end. To believe, to hope: this, Romero taught us, is the Christian's grace in our time. When many give up hope, when it seems to them that the nation has nowhere to go, as though it were all over, the Christian says: No, we have not yet begun.

"We are awaiting still God's grace. With certainty, God's reign is just beginning to be built on this earth. A time will come when there will be no abductions, when we'll be happy and can walk our streets and our countryside without fear of being tortured or kidnapped. That time will come. This is God's promise, Jesus' promise, Romero's promise to us. Neither Roman crosses nor U.S. bullets can undo it."

Rafael knew death was coming for him. He felt his spirit spill out upon the community. Holding his Bible, he stood and faced in the direction of El Salvador.

"I can no longer go out and come in," he said. "I will never cross the Lempa again. Never set foot in El Salvador. So you must be my feet and my hands. You must carry me back to El Salvador, not in a casket, but in your hearts and with the labor of your hands."

Afterword

Harvest of Cain is a work of historical fiction. This means that the book does not set out to be a factual account of actual events. It deals with real issues, however, and lays out situations that are representative of actual events: liberation theology was and is a powerful religious, social and political force; elites in Latin America and powerful U.S. leaders did declare liberation theology to be an enemy; progressive religious people throughout Latin America experienced unfathomable repression; the U.S. Army School of the Americas is a real institution and its graduates are deeply implicated in human rights atrocities; and the CIA has played a disturbing and deadly role throughout much of Latin America.

The dynamics behind the coup (see especially chapters 34 and 35) also roughly parallel events in actual history. I encourage readers interested in a historical treatment of this key moment in El Salvador's history and in U.S.-Salvadoran relations to read Raymond Bonner's *Weakness and Deceit: U.S. Policy and El Salvador* (New York, NY: Times Books, 1984).

The novel uses or develops many characters. Some are real people. Ignacio Ellacuría was the rector of the Catholic University in San Salvador. He was brutally murdered along with others in November 1989 by soldiers trained at the School of the Americas. Nothing Ellacuría "said" in *Harvest of Cain* are his actual words. Everything that he "said" or "did" in the novel, however,

HARVEST OF CAIN

in my judgment (having met him in El Salvador and having read some of his writings), is consistent with the thrust of his actual life and work.

Archbishop Oscar Romero is another case in point. Romero's words in conversation are my invention to fit the scene. But most of his words spoken in the context of discourses and sermons peppered throughout the novel are from Romero himself (sometimes with slight adaptations) taken from some of his many profound speeches. I encourage readers to go to my source for many of these: James Brockman, *The Violence of Love* (San Francisco: Harper and Row, 1988; reprinted Farmington, PA: Plough Publishing House, 1998). Perhaps the best single book about Romero is *Oscar Romero: Memories in Mosaic* by María López Vigil (Washington, DC: EPICA, 2000).

Other characters are composite portraits drawn from real people. Padre Ricardo's character, for example, is shaped by the actual life of Rutilio Grande—who was assassinated by death squads in 1977—but it is also based on other priests I have met in Central America. Still other characters, including Cynthia Randolph and Peter Jones, are products of my imagination.

References to the *Times* do not reflect any particular newspaper, and the words contained in any articles are my own. The words to the songs sung by the community in Chapter 18 are either based on my memory of the Nicaraguan *Campesino Mass* that I sang many times while living in Nicaragua or they are from the song *Canto de Esperanza* (Song of Hope) by Ester Camac and Edwin Mora G. as translated by Bret Hesla.

OTHER BOOKS AVAILABLE FROM EPICA

Oscar Romero: Memories in Mosaic, by María López Vigil.

Oscar Romero: Reflections on His Life and Writings, by Marie Dennis, Renny Golden, Scott Wright.

Red Thread: A Spiritual Journal of Accompaniment, Trauma and Healing, by Jennifer Atlee-Loudon.

The Economic Way of the Cross, by The Religious Working Group on the World Bank and IMF, Witness for Peace and EPICA. Bilingual.

Voices and Images: Mayan Ixil Women of Chajul, by The Association of Mayan Ixil Women. Trilingual.

Odyssey to the North, by Mario Bencastro.

Call, write or e-mail us today for a catalog:

EPICA
1470 Irving St., NW
Washington, DC 20010
202-332-0292
epicabooks@igc.org
www.epica.org